By Shannon Yarbrough

The Answers You Seek

Published by DSP Publications
www.dsppublications.com

SHANNON YARBROUGH

THE ANSWERS
YOU SEEK

DSP PUBLICATIONS

Published by
DSP PUBLICATIONS

5032 Capital Circle SW, Suite 2, PMB# 279,
Tallahassee, FL 32305-7886 USA
www.dsppublications.com

This is a work of fiction. Names, characters, places, and incidents either are the product of author imagination or are used fictitiously, and any resemblance to actual persons, living or dead, business establishments, events, or locales is entirely coincidental.

The Answers You Seek
© 2022 Shannon Yarbrough

Cover Art
© 2022 Kris Norris
https://krisnorris.com
coverrequest@krisnorris.com
Cover content is for illustrative purposes only and any person depicted on the cover is a model.
Author Photo
© 2022 Jost Heun Photography
Photos4uido@gmail.com

Mass Market Paperback ISBN: 978-1-64108-348-5
Trade Paperback ISBN: 978-1-64108-347-8
Digital ISBN: 978-1-64108-346-1
Mass Market Paperback published October 2022
v. 1.0

Printed in the United States of America
∞
This paper meets the requirements of
ANSI/NISO Z39.48-1992 (Permanence of Paper).

For J.K. and Mistress Gloria,
and for all the big-city fun we had
back when we were small-town boys and girls

SHANNON YARBROUGH

THE ANSWERS
YOU SEEK

CHAPTER 1

IT HAD been weeks since I'd had a decent night's sleep. I knew why I had not been sleeping, which made it even worse than just lying there for hours, tossing and turning for no apparent reason. Like every night since I'd lost my job, nothing on TV could hold my interest. No book could keep my attention long enough to offer an escape. My roommate, Ash, went to bed early most weeknights, so I could never rely on him to help occupy my mind. I tried in vain to go to bed, but sleep wouldn't save me either.

No matter how long I lay there trying to think about something else, all I did was stare through the darkness above me and obsess over the mistakes I'd made. All I wanted to do was fall into a heavy, dreamless sleep and hope to wake up and find that everything had changed. But I knew that wasn't going to happen.

My life wasn't going to get better for a very long time.

This pattern of boredom and restlessness wasn't new to me. It had been the same every night since I'd lost my job. But tonight I wanted to stop feeling sorry for myself. I needed a change of scenery. Tonight was going to be different—somehow. I got out of bed, put my clothes back on, and grabbed my keys. Seeking a distraction, I decided to take a drive around the city.

The streets were empty. The tawny lights of downtown were always on, but the people who lived in the gray, dismal buildings were sleeping. Unlike me, they had jobs to wake up and go to in the morning. I spotted a homeless person limping down an alley and a late-shift employee at a hotel stepping out into a breezeway for a smoke. Otherwise the city was hollow. I felt lonely, but it also felt nice having it all to myself. Sometimes that feeling of loneliness reminds us that we're still here.

But I'd had enough of this Zen moment for now and felt like I needed a drink. So, I went to Backstreet, a favorite gay bar of mine.

I parked right in front and checked my mirror for oncoming cars, though the street was dead. It was a ghost town, and I was the cowboy rambling in looking for trouble. Backstreet was too empty at that hour and only reminded me of that solitary feeling I was romanticizing just ten minutes ago.

The bar was a girl caught without makeup or a skin-shy mom whose pesky kids just walked in on her while she was changing clothes. There was no chatter of bar patrons, no bass-thumping music, no dancers. It was missing all those things that made it feel inviting and safe on the weekends. Or maybe this was its typical weeknight face. I was the one who was out of place.

I went there because it was the only gay establishment open past midnight on a Thursday. I wanted to drink and be around people who were awake and like me, out wasting the night away because they had nothing better to do with their lives. I needed to find people who might have more significant regrets than mine. Instead, Backstreet felt like another planet.

It would have to do tonight.

"Hey, Toby," Jimmie, the bartender, called out with a grin.

I was glad to see a familiar face; I think Jimmie was too. Some labeled him a muscle cub: buzz cut, broad shoulders, big arms, scruffy face, hairy chest, a chain with a padlock for a necklace. I was accustomed to seeing him dressed in a flannel shirt with the sleeves ripped off, his weekend attire, which earned him lots of tips when he left the shirt unbuttoned. (It was always unbuttoned.)

Tonight Jimmie wore a tight black T-shirt tucked into even tighter boot-cut jeans. His shirt read DADDY AF. Jimmie reached for a bottle, popped its top, and sat it down in front of me as I took a seat at the bar. My usual *cervesa*. Jimmie knew his customers well. I realized I knew nothing about him beyond what I could see. It was tempting to start a conversation with him—maybe try to get to know him more in a casual sense—but I knew if the time came for me to share things about myself, it would get messy.

"Thanks, Jimmie," I said instead. I picked up the bottle, held it up to toast him, and then took a heavy drink.

"What are you doing here?"

"Thirsty, I guess," I said, setting the bottle down.

"Not much going on in here tonight." He looked around the empty room.

I turned on my barstool and did the same. A couple of guys were playing pool in the back, another in the corner at an arcade game. Janet Jackson was singing overhead about nasty boys. She was wasting her time; there were no nasty boys here tonight.

"Better than being bored at home, I guess."

"There's an app for that." Jimmie grinned.

I took another drink. The bottle was a third of the way empty by now. Jimmie pointed to it. I nodded. He reached into the cooler for another.

I pulled out my phone as if I was taking Jimmie's advice. There were indeed several "dating" apps on my phone to rely on, but I hadn't been interested in that either lately. Instead, I checked the usual social media sites like anyone else sitting by themselves in a public venue. That's when I noticed my sister, Melaine, had called several times earlier in the evening. I'd missed her calls because my phone was muted when I was trying—and failing—to sleep.

My sister was supposed to be "Melanie," which she would have hated. It was a misspelling on her birth certificate. Our parents liked it and kept it, leading to a lifetime of people looking at her name and either mispronouncing it or calling her Melanie by mistake anyway.

She never called. No one ever called me except Mom, and I enjoyed talking to her each week. It reminded me of that connection all of us once had with our friends via the landline rotary-dial phones hanging on the kitchen walls—the ones with the extra-long cords that could snake throughout the house but still kept us tied up inside our homes.

We were just voices traveling through the long-wire bird perches outside, biding the time until we could see each other face-to-face. Not ready to say goodbye or hang up. Listening to the radio together.

But those days were over, and anyone else would have rolled their eyes at my nostalgia.

Melaine usually just texted, like everyone else. Why was she calling me now? It was too late at night—or too early in the morning—for me to call or text her back. I'd wait and try to text her later, after the sun came up.

Ms. Jackson faded to a Madonna ballad, typical gay anthems that Ash and I would have cheered for and sang out loud to on any given weekend. I sang along in my head, drowning out the crack of the balls on the pool table and the machine-gun fire blasting asteroids or villains on the arcade game.

"Last call, Toby. Time to close up," Jimmie said.

I looked up as he cleared the three empty beer bottles in front of me. I looked around. The pool game had ended. The jukebox had gone quiet. I checked the time on my phone. I'd already been at the bar for several hours. I grabbed the last half-empty bottle and finished it off.

"You gotta work tomorrow?" he asked.

"Nah," I said, fishing some bills out of my pocket to clear my tab.

"You know there's a little room in the back if you—you know."

"I'm fine. I'm okay to drive. Honestly, if I weren't, I'd make Ash come and get me. But you've seen how much we drink on the weekends. It would take at least another two or three bottles before my inhibitions... umm... oh."

I shut up. Jimmie raised his eyebrows and just shook his head in disbelief and smiled. He picked up my last beer bottle, now empty, and turned around.

"Have a good night, Toby," he called out over his shoulder.

I was an idiot. I thought Jimmie was offering me a place to stay to sleep off the alcohol if I needed it, but what bartender offers a back room in a gay bar for that? He would have just called a cab for me and sent me on my way.

I stood there for a beat, contemplating. It felt great to be desired—in person. No app on my phone could ever replace that. Maybe I could backtrack. Jimmie stood at the sink and cleaned some glasses with his back to me. Was he embarrassed, or did he think I was ridiculous?

I wanted to speak up, to get his attention and let him know I'd take him up on his offer, but when the weight of every wrong decision you've ever made is spinning in your head, a few seconds can feel like an eternity. I was indeed ridiculous. I'd come here for a distraction. Jimmie had offered it, but I was too distracted even to notice.

"Hey, Jimmie," I said.

He turned and looked at me. He waited. I waited. Finally he spoke instead of making me say something else I might regret.

"Good night, Toby. It's okay. See ya around."

"Okay. Yeah. Thanks," I said. *Thanks? For what?*

Jimmie turned back to his chores, leaving me to the walk of shame all on my own, as it should be. I'd been shut down. Like all those other opportunities you miss out on in life, you don't always get a second chance. I didn't even really want this. Did I? It probably would have just made me feel worse. After all, it was sex that had led to all my problems lately. I knew an affair in a barroom closet with a hot bartender wouldn't fix it. Long-term, anyway.

Outside, I approached my car but stopped when a bright light spilled out of the bar's window. I stepped back to have a look through the glass. Jimmie had turned on the overhead lights. I wasn't surprised by how different the bar looked when it was brightly lit; I'd overstayed my welcome here past last call more than once on the weekends. Ash joked that they had to turn on the lights to drive the last of us vampires away.

The jukebox had gone quiet while I was inside, but Jimmie walked over to it and punched a few buttons. "Relax" by Frankie Goes to Hollywood filled the space at a deafening volume. From outside, I could feel it vibrating the walls as the song's gritty electronic beat came to life.

Jimmie peeled off his shirt and began to strut around the bar as he swept the floor with a broom. He lip-synced to the song, using the broom for his microphone. I stood next to the window just out of sight and watched for several minutes. Spying on him like this felt shameful, but part of it also felt exhilarating. I was somewhat aroused. I wondered if Jimmie secretly knew I was watching. Did he like being watched?

When the song finished, Jimmie was also done cleaning up. The bar fell silent. He unplugged the jukebox and flicked off the lights. I rushed to get into my car. I didn't want to startle him if he exited through the front door. I waited for him, intending to forget my inhibitions and call out to him if he walked by. I didn't know what I might say, but I'd work it out.

Jimmie never showed. He must have left through the back door.

I pulled onto the street, which was now slowly coming alive with cars headed to morning rush hour, water coolers, phones, emails, and cubicles. I didn't miss that part of my life one bit. I watched the bar fade in my rearview; it looked like a boarded-up, abandoned building during the day. I was that cowboy again, leaving the old saloon and riding off on my horse. Cue the tumbleweeds!

Ahead in the distance, the nightfall over the city began to fade from black to a faint, tawny orange. I couldn't remember the last time I'd stayed out all night and got to see the sun come up. Sure, I'd been one of those vampires who shut the place down plenty of times. On those nights—or mornings—I was too drunk and exhausted to pause and look up. It felt good right now to be able to see the sun on my way home.

I was just a few blocks from our apartment when my phone began to buzz. It was Ash.

"Toby, where are you?"

"Driving home."

"Where were you last night? Your sister has been trying to call you. Have you spoken to her?"

"No, I missed her calls. I was going to call her back today."

"Are you almost here?"

"Yeah. Why? Is everything okay?"

"Well, no. I'm sorry, Toby. It's your dad."

"My dad? Is he okay?"

"No, sweetie. He's dead."

CHAPTER 2

LATER, AS I tried to recall the events of that morning, I could not remember the drive back to the apartment. Everyone goes into autopilot from time to time and completely forgets how they got someplace, don't they? That's why people can't put down their phones when they are driving. They go into autopilot but still need a distraction. Unlike those people, I didn't mind zoning out. I'd much rather do that while keeping my eyes on the road.

Ash was waiting for me in the parking lot of our apartment. He took me in his arms as soon as I got out of the car. I cried on his shoulder as we went inside, but I could not remember that either. Specific cloudy details aren't necessary. It doesn't matter if we remember them, but those crumbs keep us awake at night. We obsess over what we can't remember. We ask ourselves, how did we get here?

Now I was back where I started with another burden to face. First it was my job. Now, my father. No one in my family even knew about my job yet. Ash was the only one who knew what had happened. He had acted like it was nothing and that I should just shrug it off, but like any advice your friends give you, it's always easier said than done.

It was all so stupid, but it was my fault for allowing myself to break a cardinal rule listed in every employee handbook: don't date coworkers! We weren't even dating. It was just sex—which is worse, I suppose. Jacob was such a flirt, winking at me in the men's room or placing his hand on my lower back to pardon himself when we got in each other's way at the copier.

Sure, I'd done a double-take more than once to check out his backside when he walked by my cubicle. I'd caught Jacob doing the same to me. Then there was the night we bumped into each other as Jacob was coming out of the men's room at Amnesia, a gay nightclub that was my usual go-to spot on the weekends because Ash was a regular drag performer there, and I could get in without paying a cover.

"Hey, Toby! What's up? Come dance with me," Jacob had said, grabbing my hands like a needy child. He was drunk.

"Oh, hey, Jacob! Sure, let me use the restroom first."

We never made it to the dance floor. Jacob followed me into one of the men's room stalls and pinned me against the wall. We groped and kissed for a bit before continuing outside in the back seat of my car.

On Monday I was thankful we worked in different departments. I knew Jacob's routine, so it was easy to avoid him. Jacob seemed to be playing along and looking the other way too. We managed to go the whole week without crossing paths once. That didn't stop me from panicking all week that I'd run into him and another coworker would see us and read the guilt on my face.

On Friday Jacob messaged me and asked if I had any plans for the weekend. I played it cool and typed back no; we were having a personal conversation on the company's computer-messaging service, after all. Jacob didn't reply, and I had forgotten about it by the end of the workday until I ran into him in the parking garage. He'd conveniently parked right next to me.

"See you at the club tonight?" Jacob asked with that cocky grin that drove all the girls in the office crazy.

"Yeah, I was planning on going."

It wasn't a lie. I went every Friday and Saturday night if Ash was performing. We started at Amnesia, followed by Backstreet if I didn't get too tired and decide to check out early. I thought about not going, but Ash talked me out of it. We were two consenting adults. Jacob had not made a big deal out of it while at work; he'd not even spoken to me all week. Why should I stop going out just because of what happened? It was just sex. It was just once.

I still fretted over what might happen again. I wanted it to happen, but that responsible angel-on-my-shoulder voice in my head told me it was a bad idea. Unlike Ash, I couldn't just live in the moment and not worry about the outcome.

I didn't see Jacob in the club right away. I managed to loosen up after a few drinks. Maybe too loose. Jacob pounced on me again in the restroom and ended up back at my place that night. I texted Ash and apologized for missing his show.

"Never apologize for getting some," he texted back.

For the next several weeks, this became a steady routine between the two of us. We ignored each other in the office by day. We hooked up on Friday night, sometimes on Saturday too. I didn't even have a chance to order a drink one night. I had just walked in the door, and we crossed paths in the lobby. All Jacob had to say was, "Wanna get out of here early tonight?"

Then Eric got hired in my department, and everything fell apart.

"I told you to be careful," Ash told me.

"No, you told me not to worry over having sex with a coworker," I corrected him.

"With *a* coworker! I didn't say anything about *two* coworkers!"

Eric was attractive. Not as good-looking or as built as Jacob, but still a nice piece of office eye candy. I wasn't even sure if Eric was gay. I hadn't been around him much while he was training the first week. It turned out he was an "acquaintance" of Jacob's. They went to the same gym. I didn't know much more about their friendship, but I'd soon find out one Friday night when Jacob texted me. He wasn't planning on going out that night and told me to come over and "hang out" with him.

When I got to Jacob's place, Eric was there, and it was pretty obvious the two of them knew each other better than I had expected. They'd been to the gym earlier in the evening. They'd showered, and both were shirtless and still wrapped in their towels. I felt overdressed. A few drinks later and that feeling went away—so did the towels and clothes. I had never done anything like that before. It was always Ash who came home with lurid stories about the evening's bed partners.

It happened again the following weekend.

After we were done, I'd asked if I could use Jacob's bathroom. He pointed me down the hall. I didn't know if I'd taken a wrong turn, but I wandered into the master bedroom, which had an oddly feminine touch: floral bedspread, scented candles, and lots of colorful throw pillows.

There was a jewelry box and some makeup on the dresser. I spotted a lacy nightie thrown over the back of a chair in the corner. Did these things belong to him? Did Jacob lead some kind of double-life I didn't know about? That's when I saw it, something that confirmed my suspicions.

There was a wedding photo setting on one of the nightstands.

I picked up the frame. It was a photo of Jacob in a tuxedo. He was embracing a lovely bride and looking into her eyes. At first I thought maybe he was divorced, but what divorced man keeps his wedding photo next to the bed?

I put the photo down and looked around the room. Maybe he'd gotten divorced recently and had not had time to redecorate? But the makeup? The jewelry box? Even the bed was made and covered in throw pillows!

"Are you married?" I asked Jacob after I'd gotten dressed and returned to the living room.

"Yeah. Sorry, man. I thought you knew," he said like it was nothing.

"Did you know?" I asked Eric.

"Of course. I was a groomsman in his wedding."

"Are you married too?"

"Dude, why does it matter?"

"Why does it matter? What the fuck!" I yelled, as I rushed out the door.

It had been easy to avoid Jacob in the office, but Eric sat two cubicles away from me. Eric also made me nervous. He flirted, even more than Jacob had, and sometimes in the presence of other people! He winked and licked his lips. He squeezed my buttocks at the urinal in the restroom. It was impossible to avoid him, and we constantly had to communicate with each other.

I didn't have to worry for very long. Three weeks later, Human Resources announced Eric wasn't working out in the office. He'd been fired.

I hated to see anyone get fired, but I was a bit relieved. Then the following day, my desk phone rang a few minutes before it was time for me to leave. It was the head of HR asking me to come by their office on my way out. Eric had not accepted his termination very well. He was pissed and decided to take Jacob and me down with him.

It had now been a month since all of that had gone down. I still felt ashamed. I felt dirty. My indiscretions punished me with a strong sense of guilt. I hadn't bothered searching for another job yet. I avoided going out to the club for fear of running into Jacob. Ash told me not to beat myself up over it, but it had all been so out of character for me.

I might have done something like that back in my twenties when I worked various retail jobs or as a waiter while in college but never with a married man. I'd always partied with coworkers back then, drinking and smoking pot. I'd never made out with any of them, but there were plenty of teenage jock busboys I would have gladly taken to my bedroom had the opportunity presented itself. I knew most of them had girlfriends. Most of them also shed their inhibitions—and their clothes—once you got them drunk and promised not to tell anyone. But this was different.

None of that mattered now. I had to go home and face my family, but at least the focus didn't have to be on me. I could lie. I could say work was fine. Ash constantly reminded me it wasn't the end of the world. I had good experience under my belt; I knew I could find another job. I just needed to beat my anxiety. Again— easier said than done!

This wasn't just about me sleeping with a coworker and losing my job. Finding out Jacob was married had only added fuel to the fire. He had not even tried to keep it on the downlow. He didn't try to hide at the club. We'd had a threesome with another man right there in his house—twice!

I guess I felt betrayed somehow even though I knew there would never be anything serious between Jacob and me. It was just sex. Nothing more. But now that all of this was over, I couldn't stop thinking about Jacob's wife. How would she feel about this? Angry? Betrayed? Did she already know about Jacob's infidelity? Did they have an open marriage?

If so, it certainly wasn't one that allowed him to go to gay bars and sleep with men. Was it? Would she show up at my apartment and key my car? Would she bang on my door in the middle of the night to confront me?

I didn't like being part of something like this. I wasn't this kind of person. I'm not sure I even knew who I was anymore. I was pissed at Jacob for making me a part of it. I was ticked off at myself for allowing it to happen, even though I didn't know the consequences at the time. I was also furious because this wasn't the first time I'd been in a situation like this one.

I'd never been an adulterer before—at least, not to my knowledge. But my dad had been. He'd cheated on my mom before. And that's why it hurt. I'd never considered myself to be like my dad in anyway.

Until now.

CHAPTER 3

I CAME from a small town. Kids like me who were gay or different were filled with angst of some kind, and it was no fault of their own. Their parents ruined their lives. Or bullies. The lucky ones skipped town as soon as they got a chance, and they never looked back.

I always considered myself one of the lucky ones.

Others remained glued there and never tried to escape. They were either really skilled at ignoring the ridicule, or they didn't believe it any time some teacher or therapist told them it got better. I remember not knowing who to believe. I remember being afraid to move away. Funny how I had never been afraid to go back. I think it was because unlike those who were stuck, I knew I'd never have to go back there forever.

But now that my life had been thrown off course, I felt as if the big city had finally had its way with me. It had chewed me up and spit me out. I imagined the faces of all of those kids just like me back home rolling their eyes and saying, "We told you so." I felt like I had no one to blame this time except myself.

Even though the guilt was eating me up, I wasn't worried about what my previous job might say about me. I'd worked in enough offices to know the song and dance. From an HR standpoint, the worst they could say to someone calling to verify my employment was that they wouldn't hire me again, and most jobs wouldn't even say that. They avoided uncomfortable situations by saying they'd only verify when an employee started and when they left.

My old boss secretly offered to be a reference for me if I needed it. She'd always respected me and hated to see me get let go, but it wasn't her decision. She also teased and said we should get together for drinks sometime, and I could tell her all about what Jacob looked like without clothes.

With my father's death, suddenly being unemployed didn't seem like the biggest of my problems. *You were fired for having a three-way with two of your coworkers*, that voice inside my head reminded me. In time, grief would replace my guilt. That wasn't going to make things easier.

"What happened?" I asked my sister. I called her back once I'd composed myself.

"The nurses think he had a stroke, possibly a heart attack. They found him at breakfast this morning. They said he was still warm, so he hadn't been gone long."

Our father had been suffering from dementia. He'd been in a senior living center for the past three years.

"Do you need me to come home and help?"

"Where were you? I'm sorry I had to call and wake Ash, but you weren't picking up."

"Are you and Samuel going to make arrangements today?" I ignored her question and rephrased mine.

"Yes, at noon. Do you want to go with us?"

"I'll be there. Have you told Mom?" I asked.

"Yeah, she knows. She said she'd be there for us."

"At the funeral?"

"Yeah."

While packing, I asked Ash to help me decide what to wear to the funeral. He offered to drive me if I needed him. I told him I'd be okay. Shadow Wood, my hometown, was only an hour and a half away, and while I would have liked the company, I didn't want Ash to have to be there. Ash had never met any of my family except for Melaine. I packed more than enough clothes, not sure how long I'd be gone. I told Ash I'd text to let him know when I got there.

"I can take off and drive up for the funeral if you want me there," Ash said.

"No, it's okay. I appreciate it, but there's no reason for you to miss work."

"You just don't want me to meet your mother," he teased.

"She'd be pissed if you wore a nicer dress than her to the funeral."

"I could dress her. I'd do her hair too if she wants. I've got a new set of black pumps I bet she'd love."

"This is her ex-husband's funeral, the father of her three children. Not the Met Gala."

"Funerals can be so cruisy."

"Ash! The funeral home is just a few blocks away from a pig farm."

"So? Farm boys are hot."

"They'd beat you up."

"I like it rough… sometimes."

"Stop it!"

"Okay, drive safe. Seriously. Take as long as you need. Be there for your family. Text me. But don't forget."

"Don't forget what?"

"When you get back, you still have to tell me who you were with last night."

"How do you know I was with someone?"

"How long have we lived together? Believe me; I can hear it in your voice."

"You cannot."

"So you *weren't* with someone last night?"

"I didn't say that."

Though I had not been with anyone last night and didn't have a juicy story to share with Ash, it was fun to string him along. Had I told him the truth about the situation with Jimmie, he would only have shunned me for not accepting Jimmie's offer. I didn't really know if Jimmie was even offering me anything, though I was pretty sure that was exactly what he was doing. I'd ruined that by *not* keeping my mouth shut.

I thought about how I had felt while watching Jimmie through the window. It made me smile. I would never tell Ash about that. Despite Ash being my best friend, a person still needs their own secrets.

Back in my car, I knew I was going to zone out again. I always did during this drive back home. I hated the drive to Shadow Wood. I hated seeing the city slowly disappear in my rearview mirror, replaced by cheap motels, truck stops, and adult bookstores beyond the shadows of the city's skyline. I couldn't name one single town that lay between here and Shadow Wood. That's how unimportant they were. They were just dots on an invisible map to me, and I drove straight through them.

As I passed the last cluster of seedy shops, I recalled the time Ash took me on a shopping spree to every porn shop outside the city. He had filled his arms with DVDs and toys from the clearance bins. He wanted to go into the movie booths in the back, but I refused to go with him.

"You are aware of the amount of porn that is completely free on the internet, aren't you?" I asked him in the car as I looked through his bag of purchases.

"What? These aren't for me. They make good hostess gifts."

The interstate slowly turned into a two-lane highway. Motels transformed into one-room Southern Baptist churches. Bookstores morphed into dollar stores. The concrete façade of the city was now miles away. Fields of livestock and trailer homes were the only thing left between me and my destination. I dodged tractor-trailers and roadkill, hating each mile as the distance grew between me and my refuge, now far behind me.

Shadow Wood would always be home, even though I had not lived there in almost fifteen years. My family was the only reason I ever went back, but it still made me uncomfortable. The conservative minds, the racist bumper stickers, the thick country drawl of every person I encountered, everything made me feel like such an outsider. I'd escaped that small town and the backwoods, homespun values way of life. It was home, but I still felt like a stranger.

No one there knew what I had done. No one knew I was unemployed or why. Besides my family, I didn't even know if anyone in town knew who I was anymore. I hadn't kept in touch with anyone from high school nor seen anyone I went to school with since the night of graduation.

The miles ticked away, and I soon pulled into the driveway of our old family home, where Mom still lived. Like always, I'd blotted out the drive and just focused on the road and what lay ahead. And like always when I was in the car alone and headed back to that town, my mind cycled through every piece of gossip I'd heard about someone, every horrible decision someone had made that someone else had exploited. Every newspaper headline that caused some neighbor to keep their curtains drawn scrolled through my mind. Every small town is full of those. Shadow Wood was no different. I realized I was no better than the rest of them. No matter how hard I tried to escape, I was one of them.

They all had secrets. I did too.

CHAPTER 4

WHILE DRIVING, I tried to remember the last time I'd spoken to or seen my father. It was on his birthday just a few months earlier. I'd driven home to join my brother and sister to celebrate. We wrapped a few gifts for him—handkerchiefs and grooming products. The center made a cake. Candles were not allowed because fire scared some of the residents.

They decorated the cafeteria with balloons and a banner that all of the staff had signed. Pastel crepe paper streamers were taped haphazardly on the walls as if someone had given up on finding a ladder. Cone hats were given to everyone, but most of the residents lacked the coordination or mental understanding to put them on correctly.

One woman in a wheelchair held her cone hat upside down in her hand and shook it at everyone as if she were a beggar woman. The center was a sad place for those of us who were young and healthy, those of us on the outside.

Since Dad had been in the senior center, I attempted to call him once a week. He had never been much of a talker on the phone, so our conversation usually consisted of simple greetings and then a couple of the usual questions before he was ready to hang up: How was the weather? What had he eaten for breakfast today? Was he winning any of the bingo games?

He'd slowly gotten worse this year. Our weekly conversations turned into every other week. He didn't know who I was when I saw him on his birthday. Even after I told him, I could see the confusion in his face.

He knew Samuel. He knew Melaine. People who were a regular part of his life were easier for him to recognize. But his youngest son, the one who'd packed up and left town as soon as he could, had been forgotten.

The last time we spoke before his birthday, he didn't remember who I was, and he hung up on me. I called him back and tried to get him to remember. I just kept saying, "It's me, Dad. It's Toby. You remember, don't you? It's Toby. Your son." But it was no use.

I was just a memory to him now. Or was I? Could he remember the Toby who was a young boy sitting in his lap or outside playing in the yard? Or was that Toby gone too? It wasn't his fault that he couldn't remember. There was no going back for either of us.

"He might not know who you are, but that's okay. You know who he is," Melaine told me after the party, but it didn't make me feel any better.

"You have to live your life, Toby. Your father lived his," Mom added.

Their sentiments were nice, but they didn't make me feel any better. It was true. I did have to live my life, but I regretted that Dad hadn't been a bigger part of it. There'd been a physical distance between us ever since he'd left—ever since I'd left—but it was my part-ing that had caused the emotional distance. I'd never be able to let go of that.

Dad was lucky. He got to forget.

CHAPTER 5

I THOUGHT picking something to wear was stressful enough, which was why I'd asked Ash to help. When I got to Mom's, Melaine was waiting for me with shoeboxes and albums full of photos. She needed my help selecting an array of pictures of Dad that the funeral home would display on some framed bulletin boards. Mom gave me a long, tight hug and asked how I was holding up. Then she sat down at the table to help us.

"Be thinking about flowers." Melaine opened a box and started flipping through stacks of old Polaroids. "We're going to the floral shop after the funeral home."

"Okay," I said, not wanting to question her.

What was there to think about? Colors? Scents? Types of flowers? Dad's favorite? Did he have a favorite? I realized there were so many things I didn't know about my father.

"And music. We'll need to pick songs for the service," she added, going through her own box of photos and sorting them into piles like jigsaw puzzle pieces.

Melaine had been the unofficial historian of our family's life. She was the one with the camera, always buying film, always paying to have it developed back when that was the thing. She'd kept it up when cameras went digital, editing photos on her computer and printing physical copies, making extras if you wanted one. Because of her, our family had these boxes and albums, these stacks of photos that were tangible proof we existed.

Since I'd left home, my life was a trail of half-decent cell phone selfies. I deleted the bad ones, and the majority were terrible. If there was any other occasion worth remembering, I forgot to take out my phone. I'd never had to be the photographer, so I relied on someone else to take up that duty.

Not every one of Melaine's photos was perfect. There would be a finger in the corner, or the flash was too bright. Our eyes were demon red or closed. Those mistakes didn't matter. Life was full of them. Cameras back then didn't let us cover them up. We didn't even know they'd happened until we picked up the pack of pictures from the one-hour photo mat.

Every Christmas, vacation, and birthday was here. There were fewer pictures as we got older, too old for birthday parties. We stopped taking family vacations. Dad left Mom when I was a senior in high school, so he wasn't in any of the holiday photos after that. He'd send us money in a card. I'd call to wish him a merry Christmas. There wasn't one photo from the past three years he'd spent in the living center. For some reason Melaine had forgotten to take any.

Dad forgot everything.

"This one is nice," Melaine said, handing me a photo of all of us.

"You think?" I asked, showing it to Mom.

"That was Christmas at Grandma and Grandpa Kipton's house," Mom said, smiling.

The photo was a dark Polaroid with *Christmas 1980* written across the bottom in red ink. We were huddled together on a plaid sofa, a photo taken back when uncles, aunts, cousins, and grandparents gathered to celebrate and each immediate family had their picture taken.

I was five years old then. I sat on my father's lap with a hand in my mouth. I was leaning back against his chest as if the camera was too close or I was buckling because I refused to sit still. His legs were crossed in an attempt to corral me. Dad's long arm was stretched behind Mom and across the top of the sofa.

Melaine sat between them with Samuel crouched on the floor. Samuel was the only one smiling for the photographer. Mom's eyes were half-closed. Dad and Mom's clothing had a seventies vibe. Mom's hair was big and brown, unlike the tight gray perm she wore these days. It was a nice photo, much better than the polished family portraits we dressed up and posed for every year.

There were few photos of Dad by himself. They were always of him with Mom or with any combination of us three kids. Melaine found just one picture of him alone. He was working the concession stand at our junior high school for one of Samuel's basketball games. He'd been a PTA volunteer when we were kids, always eager to help the school when parents were needed.

In the photo, he was busy bagging fresh popcorn from the popper, focused on the task in front of him and unaware that someone had taken his picture. Melaine wasn't the photographer this time. Someone had taken it for the school yearbook and given Mom the original copy. It was too bad we didn't always have a family photographer there to capture our lives when we forgot, but some photos were never meant to be taken.

When we finished with the photos, it was almost time to leave to go to the funeral home. Melaine texted Samuel to see if he was ready and could stop by to pick us up.

"Are you coming?" I asked Mom.

My question might have seemed childish, but she'd always been there for us. Why should today be any different?

"No, I think you three should take care of things today," she said.

Despite having told me we'd need to pick music, Melaine had prepared a list of hymns and ballads, and she presented it to us at the funeral home. Neither Samuel nor I protested. Anything to speed up the process. Dad had already picked out his casket. His funeral was paid for with a small burial policy he'd had. Melaine brought the clothes Dad would be buried in—a crisp plaid cotton button-down shirt and a new pair of blue jeans—Dad's daily uniform until he went into the center.

Melaine had also called ahead to the florist. We only had to stop in and pay the bill. There was no lengthy discussion to pick roses or carnations. Samuel and I sat in the car while she went inside.

"What would we do without her, huh?" I said to Samuel.

"Yeah. Sis was on the phone all morning. I told her I could take care of something if she needed help, but you know how she is," Samuel said, his eyes focused on the rearview mirror.

"Always taking charge of things. This is one time I don't mind one bit."

"Me neither."

When Melaine got back in the car, I could tell a burden had been lifted. She even exhaled a deep breath and lowered her shoulders. I didn't know if I should ask her about the flowers or not. I decided to keep my mouth shut so that my politeness didn't sound like I was questioning her decisions. I was sure the flowers would be lovely.

"I think that's everything," Melaine said to us.

"You sure, Sis? You sure we are done?" Samuel said, trying to joke.

"I just want everything to be nice for Dad," she said, not getting his humor.

"It will be." I patted her shoulder. "You've done a great job."

"Let's get some lunch." She exhaled another deep breath.

We ate at Dad's favorite place, a greasy spoon diner on the courthouse square where all the town lawyers and officials ate lunch every day. Dad loved to hang out there after he retired. He would sit in a booth, have breakfast, read the paper, and chat with whoever had something to say. He'd grown up here, so everyone in this town knew him. Anytime we offered to take him out for a meal and let him pick the restaurant, this was where he wanted to go. No questions asked.

After Dad went into the center, Melaine and Samuel—and me too, if I was in town—would check Dad out of the center and bring him here to have lunch. He'd had trouble walking this past year, and it became too much of a liability for him to leave the center, so

Melaine would stop in and pick up something for him before going to visit him.

"Hi, Melaine! You got company today?" a waitress in a sunshine yellow apron said, grabbing some menus and escorting us to a booth.

"Hi, Charlene! This is my little brother, Toby. He doesn't live here. He moved to the city. And you know Samuel."

"Nice to meet you," Charlene said, looking in my direction.

Even though I'd been born right here in Shadow Wood, my family introduced me to strangers as if I had defected to another country. It made me sound exotic, or as if I were a celebrity, or spoke a foreign language. To them, I probably did. I was just an uppity city boy now. My Shadow Wood card had been revoked.

"Need a burger to go for your daddy?" Charlene said.

"Oh no, Charlene! Daddy passed away early this morning." Melaine put her hand on Charlene's wrist.

"Oh, sweetie! I'm sorry to hear that. Lunch is on us today. Just yell when you are ready," Charlene said, patting the top of Melaine's hand. "Sorry for your loss," she whispered to Samuel and me as she left the table.

It was a rarity to share time with just my brother and sister. Dad or Mom had always been in tow. It might have seemed sad since we ate in silence today and Dad could not be here, but I was glad we were sharing this moment together. I wanted to tell them how I felt, but Samuel would have just attempted to lighten the mood by making fun of me. Big brothers were good for that. Living with Ash was no different.

We ordered our traditional burgers and fries, the best in town, and we toasted our father with banana milkshakes, his favorite. We each dug in our pockets for a few dollars and left Charlene a generous tip.

I thought about the last time we'd been there with Dad. I was sure he'd been there today with us in some way. As we walked out the door, I turned to wave good-bye to Charlene, who was already clearing our table. She smiled and waved back. It was a small, polite smile, the kind meant to display remorse.

"Your father was a good man," she said to me. "I miss him."

"Me too," I said, smiling back.

I'd missed Dad for a very long time. I was jealous because it sounded like Charlene knew him in a way that I didn't. Of course she did. He'd eaten there numerous times. Charlene had probably waited on him a lot and shared conversations with him.

I was jealous of her in a way. Maybe even a little resentful. It would have seemed silly, then, to approach a woman who might have known my dad better than me and ask her to admit everything she knew about him.

That would all change after Dad's funeral.

CHAPTER 6

SHE WORE a tight black dress that was maybe a bit too tight for a funeral. It was a fashionable cocktail dress, the kind a well-to-do housewife might wear to a New Year's Eve party at the country club, but no one on this side of town called it a cocktail dress, much less used the word *cocktail* in their everyday vernacular.

Cocktail sounded fancy, and describing something as *fancy* could be a mockery for anything in small towns that stood out from the norm or for anyone who thought they were better than others. This strange woman in the black dress, whom I had never seen before, was definitely fancy.

The dress wasn't even the first thing that attracted my attention. It was the wide-brimmed black hat and the oversized, insect-eye sunglasses. They were the fashionable accessories a bitch heiress to a horse dynasty on some eighties nighttime soap opera might wear when mourning her cheating husband who just died in a freak riding accident. Add a veil, and she could have been playing the part of a First Lady grieving for a dead president. No one wore that around here, not to mourn the death of a blue-collar family man who'd worked for the local meat-packing plant all of his life. She was a blatant anomaly, and I knew that was her intention.

The Devarou Brothers Funeral Home shared its parking lot with a vape shop and a dollar store. The sheriff's department across the street had been under a lot of scrutiny several years back when not just one but four black men brought in on drug charges all committed suicide while being detained there one summer. Riots took place. Someone spray-painted PIGS in neon green on the front of the cinder-block building, with a giant arrow pointing to the front door.

Instead of power-washing the building, they'd painted over it, but if you studied the paint job long enough, you could still make out the graffiti underneath. Family members of the prisoners demanded an investigation, but nothing came of it. People in town joked about not having to carry the bodies very far for their funerals. Just another reason I was glad I'd moved away.

There was an actual pig farm three blocks down the two-lane highway, aptly named Slaughter Pen County Road, which ran in front of the funeral home. The meat-packing plant that employed over half of the town's residents was just a stone's throw down the road from the farm. More jokes abounded about how the pigs didn't have to go far to meet their demise.

Between the smell of the farm and the stench of the plant, the county had a *foul* reputation that it lived up to every summer, especially in late July, when the temperature reached triple digits. Our high school mascot was a bear, but a carefully drawn snout and a curly tail turned it into a hairy pig, which entertained the teens at the rival high school in the neighboring city.

Our football and basketball adversaries squealed and chanted, "Here, piggie, piggie!" at games, which I thought had an odd sexual connotation because of that old Burt Reynolds movie. No one else ever mentioned it, but they did gossip about a deceiving sheriff who supposedly had a love affair with a plump sow of his choosing back during prohibition days in exchange for not arresting the pig farmer for making moonshine.

As an adult, I was embarrassed to admit I was from a town known for its racism and animal cruelty. Every small town like this one had its peculiar stories and legends, and every person in the town knew someone else who could vouch for the tall tales. Their uncle's third cousin was there when it happened, or their neighbor's nephew's son worked at the farm one summer and swore he saw it with his own eyes, and his mother was a God-fearing Christian, so why would he lie about it? The politicians were dirty, the sheriff was crooked, the farmers were poor, and next to church and Walmart, the funeral home was a sacred meeting place.

I knew a dress like the one this woman was wearing was intended to bring attention to herself. She wanted people to know she did not live around here. No one wore attire like that to a funeral or to any other place around here, not even to a wedding. There were no diamond necklaces, no luxurious hats, no Louis Vuitton heels, and certainly no fancy cocktail dresses at the Devarou Brothers Funeral Home. Not today. Not ever.

Here, young men wore tattered ball caps to your funeral. They clipped their gas station sunglasses to the neckline of their best rebel flag T-shirt, tucked into their good Wrangler jeans, which puddled over their sneakers if they didn't have on their manure-stained cowhide boots.

Older gentlemen wore expensive snakeskin boots and leather belts with giant belt buckles that you couldn't see because of their round, protruding bellies. Their cowboy hats were too big for their heads. Their outdated, khaki-colored suit coats were the same ones they wore on Easter Sunday. All the men had pistols in holsters under their coats or under the seats of their oversized pickup trucks.

Wives wore flats and floral house dresses and had overly teased hair with puffy bangs. Their pimple-faced kids wore rainbow or camouflage plastic sandals and had streaks of Kool-Aid-colored hair. Hello Kitty T-shirts were considered suitable blouses. As long as Junior wet his cowlick and wiped the mustard off his Captain America tank top, he was decent enough for church and decent enough for a funeral.

Chubby babies wore diapers—nothing but diapers. There wasn't an infant boy or girl that the whole town had not seen practically nude at the grocery store, a restaurant, or church during the summer. Adults were handed a paper fan when the air conditioner broke down at the Methodist or Baptist church, but fidgety toddlers could strip down to their saggy Pampers and dance in the aisles for Jesus.

The woman in black wore pearls, which I thought were quite elegant. I wondered what type of perfume she might be wearing. The smell of cold carnations permeated the air in the chapel, and I never got close enough to her to be able to smell anything else. Not that day. I was sure it was department store perfume, something with a French name that was never on sale and never came with a free gift. It was not pharmacy-store counter. It was not Avon. It was probably not sold in this town. Women had to go to a department store in the city to make such an extravagant purchase.

She disappeared to the back of the chapel when the service started. I kept my eyes closed while the preacher—whom I did not know and who I doubted knew my dad very well either—read the obituary and said a few kind words. They stayed closed as each song played. If anyone looked at me, they probably thought I was praying. I wasn't. I just didn't want to see anyone. I tried to grieve by myself during that last moment, behind the bleak shroud only my eyelids could provide.

I ignored the music and the words being said. I blocked all of it out. Sitting there mourning my father in the Devarou Brothers Funeral Home was the closest I had ever come to complete meditation in my entire life. Only one thought that I could not block eventually crept in: the woman in the hat.

CHAPTER 7

AT THE end of the service, I opened my eyes to look for her. When everyone filed by the casket to pay their respects before we said our final goodbyes, I noticed the woman did not approach. As we stood to exit the pew and walk by the casket, I looked to the back of the chapel and saw her walking toward the lobby. A funeral attendant, a plump gray man in a gray suit, held the door open for her. He greeted her with a nod and then checked out her ass as she exited.

"Who is that?" I whispered, tapping Melaine on the shoulder.

"What?" she mouthed with frustration.

The preacher had just squeezed our hands and shoulders, offering his last condolences. People were filing out into the blinding sunlight and to the cars lined up around the building. As I looked toward the door at the sun beaming in, I could see thousands of dust particles floating in the air inside the chapel. It was kind of gross, being a funeral home, but it was somewhat beautiful. We were nearing the casket to view Dad's overly-clean body for the very last time. Melaine did not want to be bothered with having to identify a random visitor to me.

"Who was that?" I asked again, a bit louder.

Dismissing me, she just shook her head as she wiped her face. Mom wrapped her arm around my shoulder and took my hand, pulling me so close I felt like I might lose my footing. My emotions stuttered, and my eyes began to water again. I exhaled, noticing for the first time I had been holding my breath for quite some time. I suddenly felt light-headed.

I didn't know how long I was supposed to stand there looking at the stiff hull that had been my father. I felt a wave of heat growing against my chest and in my armpits. I let go of Mom's hand and walked outside—through the dust and into the sun—to get some air. Leaning against a car, I broke down in heaving sobs.

I composed myself when I saw Mom, Melaine, and Samuel exiting the side of the building. Wiping my eyes, I looked around the parking lot. The woman in the hat was not there. Melaine noticed me looking around. She turned her head as if looking for someone too.

I thought about the look on Melaine's face when I had asked her about the woman in black. The muted reaction would have meant she didn't know, but something in her glassy eyes told me she did. She did know the lady in black with the hat and big glasses. She just didn't want to tell me.

The procession had to leave the main highway and traverse several gravel roads, dodging a couple of dead possums and the occasional raccoon, to get to the cemetery. Large black snakes slithered off the hot gravel and into the ditches along the roadside as the cars passed. From the back seat of Samuel's car, I spotted an armadillo pushing through a bank of kudzu. A couple of

turkey vultures circled over a corn field, indecisive as
to which roadkill they should eat today.

Our father had loved to convene with the dead. Before he went to live in the center, he made weekly trips
to his father's grave. If any of us came with him, he'd
remind us that he was going to be buried right next to
our Grandpa Joe. One Christmas Day, I joked that Dad
should lie down on the ground to make sure he'd fit.

The short parade of cars parked across the street at
the church. The hearse parked at the bottom of the hill.
There were steep concrete steps with no handrail set in
the bank. Watching the pallbearers carry our father's
casket up those stairs made me feel tense, and I could
feel myself holding my breath again. When I got out of
the car, I felt light-headed. My last visit to the cemetery
crept into my mind.

It was just after Dad had gone into the center. He
could still walk, slowly, with the aid of a walker, one
of those ones with the tennis balls on the bottoms of its
legs. Melaine and I checked him out of the center, and
we each walked beside him as he slowly traversed the
parking lot. He looked up at the sky as if he had not
seen sunshine in years. It took even more patience to
get him settled into the car.

At the cemetery, he decided to stay in the car. He
knew it would be too much for him to walk up the steps,
much less across the cemetery and back down to the car
again. He just wanted us to park at the bottom of the hill
and sit there for a minute. He looked up the steps and
knew the next time he'd get to go up them would be
when six men in black suits carried him.

Out of kindness, Melaine and I went up to pay our
respects to Grandpa Joe for him. I snapped a photo of
Grandpa's gravestone to show to Dad when we got

back in the car. He'd seen it so many times before, but somehow I felt the need to show him it was still there. His father was still there, waiting for him.

Daddy's oldest sister, Aunt Louise, was the only one left now. She too was battling dementia. Aunt Louise's husband had brought her to the funeral home, and she'd lurked around the room in silence. When she finally approached the casket, Mom spoke to her.

"Louise, do you know who that is?"

"That's my brother," Aunt Louise said.

Mom walked away, content with her answer.

We'd done that to Dad for a bit when we visited him, always asking him if he knew who we were. His nurse would ask him what day it was, which I didn't think was a very good question since every day was the same in the living center. It was something I was prone to forget now myself on the outside. His doctor always asked him if he knew who was president.

"I know who I *wish* was president," Dad would say, smiling at the doctor to let him know he was having a "good day."

Later, all of us—including his nurse and his doctor—stopped asking. His answers were always wrong, and they only made us sad. Aunt Louise was suffering the same fate.

"Who the hell is in the casket?" Aunt Louise said out loud to me not thirty seconds after Mom walked away.

I wanted to laugh—at her bluntness and because I'd never heard Aunt Louise say anything foul. It was so out of character for her, but it also made me sad because I knew it wasn't her. She didn't even know herself. I feared that since Dad and two of his siblings died from dementia—and it was only a matter of time before

Aunt Louise went too—it must be inherited. I'd forget who was in the casket too, or I might forget who I was one day.

I'd forget my name or my siblings. I'd forget where I was, and some nurse or caretaker would find me wandering around the property of whatever care center I'd been banished to, asking me what day it was. Patients with certain forms of dementia forgot their identity, who they were, all the important stuff that really mattered.

You were probably stuck with a head full of the crap—every wrong decision you'd made in life, every word you wished you said in fifty-year-old arguments with your spouse or a relative. The regrets. The secrets. The questions, and their answers. That was why it was so important to try to forget that stuff while we could. It was why Ash told me to move on and not worry about losing my job—to forget about Jacob and Eric—so it wouldn't haunt me later.

Uncle Leonard, Dad's youngest brother, had passed the year before. He'd spent his last year in a senior living center after his wife tripped over their cat and broke a hip, and she couldn't care for him anymore. She blamed herself for his death and made their daughter, Jenny, take the cat because she became angry every time she saw it. In his final months, Uncle Leonard didn't even recognize Jenny, his own daughter, who had visited him every single day.

"I'd never put one of my parents in one of those places," Jenny had said to Melaine three years ago when we had first admitted Dad to the center, before Uncle Leonard fell ill.

"Well, Jenny, I'm glad you don't work and don't have a family and that you can devote every minute of every day to Uncle Leonard's needs. We're not that fortunate," Melaine had said, biting back with a slightly sarcastic tone.

Jenny didn't have a response. She knew better.

Despite their words years ago, Jenny showed up to pay her respects. Having driven in from Arkansas, she'd missed the funeral due to an accident that backed up traffic on the highway, so she stayed in her car and followed the procession to the cemetery. It was hard not to judge her, but we didn't. She could relate. She now knew why we'd done it and what we'd been through. Our silence said enough: *We told you so.*

After the graveside service, Jenny approached me and looped her arm around mine. She snapped a photo of the two of us with her cell phone. Both dressed in black and huddled together, we looked like giant Siamese twins sharing a coat.

My face was blotchy and red. My mouth was a thin line on whatever roadmap my face was becoming. I knew I'd probably never see her again. If she felt the need to commemorate our paths crossing today, in a cemetery after I'd just buried my father, so be it. I looked at the photo and winced. I wanted to forget about it. At times like this, maybe dementia was a blessing.

"Are you going to eat with us at the church?" Melaine asked Jenny.

"Oh no, sorry. I didn't know there was a lunch. I need to hurry back. It was nice seeing y'all, though." Jenny hugged my neck.

"She knew. I texted her," Melaine told me as Jenny walked away.

Melaine and I said goodbye to the few people who had come to the cemetery. Samuel and Mom chatted with the preacher. Funeral workers leaned against shovels in the distance, trying to be invisible. They were anxious for everyone to go so they could do their job and leave. I was tired of being there and wanted to leave too. Grief felt like the same laborious chore.

"See you at the church," Melaine said to me. "You okay?"

"Yeah, I'll be fine."

Waiting for Mom, I stood at the top of the steps and watched Melaine walk across the road. She waved at someone as she approached her car. I looked in that direction and noticed it was Jenny.

Jenny was standing next to a tiny convertible and talking to the driver. She waved goodbye to Melaine and then leaned down to talk to the person in the car. It was the woman in black from the funeral home. She'd removed her hat but still had on the giant sunglasses.

I took my cell phone from my pocket. I turned on the camera and held the phone in front of me with one hand. I wanted to look like I was scrolling or texting, but instead I was taking photos. I zoomed in as close as I could get, but I knew the picture would be grainy. I snapped a few photos and then zoomed out to get Jenny in the frame. That was when I noticed Jenny looking at me. I flinched the way people do when they've been caught staring. I would have felt the same way had Jimmie caught me watching him from the bar window that night.

"Fuck," I whispered to myself.

I did not look up to acknowledge that I knew she'd seen me. Instead, I held my phone out farther and put my other hand up next to it as if trying to block glare from the sun. I even tried to play it up by moving down a few steps and squinting while looking at my phone, hoping my charade worked.

"What are you doing?" Mom said from behind me.

"Oh! Trying to get my phone to work. Service out here is horrible," I said louder than needed, hoping Jenny might overhear me.

"You kids and your cell phones. Always texting and posting and liking and tagging," Mom said.

"You ready to go?" Samuel asked.

"Sure," I said, taking Mom's hand and helping her down the steps. I wanted to tell her I had not been doing that, but I couldn't explain what I had been doing, so I ignored her.

As we crossed the street, I looked in Jenny's direction. She was sitting in her car. The convertible was pulling out of the parking lot, headed away from us.

I wanted to ask my mother and brother if they knew who that car belonged to, but I decided against it. They knew the handful of people who'd been in the cemetery better than I did. Mom would just spend ten minutes trying to mentally count everyone who was there to figure out who was in the convertible. Since the woman had stayed in her car, I decided not to even bother asking. But now I suspected both my sister and my cousin knew this woman in black.

CHAPTER 8

I STAYED at Mom's house that night. I always did when I made my trips to visit for a birthday or holiday. I savored the quiet evenings with her in front of the television as she catnapped with a crossword puzzle in her lap and I channel-surfed, usually settling for late-night *Golden Girls* reruns. My phone got terrible service out in the country, but it was nice to unplug and unwind in our old house.

That house had been our sanctuary, a shrine to our lives together as a family and to all of our memories. Mom had wanted to keep the house when she and Dad divorced. She'd lived there for over fifty years now. The house was a part of her. It was her home. It had been a place of love and happiness to all of us for so many years. For her sake, I hoped it still was.

Ash called me to check in right before bed, a ritual of his every time I came back for a visit. I'd crawl into my bed in my old bedroom and we'd chat as if we were teens again. I would have called him on Mom's phone if she'd still had the one on the wall with the extra-long cord.

I told him about the funeral. He enjoyed every detail and preferred for me to elaborate on the ordinaries of the town and how it had changed over the years than on the methodical routine of a funeral. He'd heard the stories about the pig farm and the crooked sheriff at least a dozen times, but he still savored my recounting as if they were children's bedtime stories. Comparing the eccentricities of our hometowns could have been a drinking game.

Ash's family had disowned him right after high school and made him move out when he announced he was gay. So his hometown stories were not as sacred, which is why I think he enjoyed mine so much. Being a Southern boy from Mississippi, he'd sought refuge in the closest city to his hometown that had any sign of a gay community.

Back then, he'd scored a fake ID at seventeen. He would sneak out of his bedroom window and go to the city in the middle of the night on the weekends with a girlfriend who had a car. He did his makeup and changed clothes in the back seat, and they'd hit all the gay bars just to dance and hang around other people who were just like them. They'd beat the sunrise back to Mississippi, racing to get home and in their beds before their parents woke up. Ash had a relationship with the city long before I did.

"Did you say your mother went to the funeral?" he asked.

"Yeah, she did."

"That must have been nice, her being there and all."

"It was."

I knew Mom no longer loved Dad. He'd broken her heart. He'd walked out on her after three decades of marriage. He'd cheated on her. She'd had time to move on. She'd done well for herself since all of that happened. She wasn't at the funeral for him. She was there for her three kids.

Both of Ash's parents were gone now. He'd been given strict instructions from his older brother that if he couldn't come to see his parents when they were alive, then he could not come and see them when they were dead. But it was his parents who'd kicked him out all those years ago. It was their choice not to see Ash.

Neither of his parents ever made any attempt to mend their relationship. Ash had not done anything wrong and refused to be something he wasn't in their presence. He wasn't going to hide the truth just because they didn't accept it.

When his sister got older—she was ten when they made him move out—she reached out to him. They texted. She mailed Christmas and birthday cards and always included photos of her kids, a niece and nephew he'd never met. She came to visit him once when she drove her kids up to the city for a concert.

She was the one who'd called him to notify him when each of his parents passed. She offered to talk to their brother and convince him to let Ash come home, but Ash told her not to bother. Having them kick him out had been painful enough. He'd already mourned them once and didn't want to do it again.

"How did your parents meet?" he asked me.

"I don't know. I never asked either of them."

"You should."

"Now?"

"Why not?"

"Do you think my mother would want to talk about that?"

"She's a Southern woman. She'll tell you if she wants to talk about it or not. She'll never talk about it if you don't ask."

"I suppose you are right."

"Wouldn't you like to know how your parents met?"

I'd never given it any thought, but now that he had mentioned it, I was curious. It seemed like dated information, secret documents that didn't concern me or that I wasn't supposed to know about since it had taken place before I existed.

But one day I might wonder how Owen Kipton had met Celia Harper, how they'd fallen in love and decided to get married and start a family. By then there might not be anyone around who could answer my questions. There would be no one left who knew the family secrets.

CHAPTER 9

THE FOLLOWING day I asked Mom how long she had dated Dad before they married. Ash had been right about Southern women. Mom was never one to share memories without someone else initiating the conversation. Even when she and Dad were married, she focused on her children and lived in the present.

It was Dad who always shared stories of the olden days, but they were never stories that involved Mom. I had often wondered if Mom, like so many of us who chose not to speak about things, had wanted to forget the past. I knew she had answers to so many questions that she had hoped no one would ever ask.

"Just a couple of years, maybe," she said as we ate breakfast.

Mom was nineteen when they married. He was in his early twenties. She was still in high school when they met.

"Did you and Dad go to prom?" I was trying desperately to elicit a conversation. I hoped my question wouldn't drum up bad memories for her. Maybe Mom and Dad had a tiff, and he'd gone to prom with another girl. Or maybe there was no prom. Or perhaps they weren't dating then and had a short courtship. I was just curious, but I wanted her to fill in the gaps between what I knew and what I didn't.

I was curious about how long they'd dated, but it wasn't imperative for me to know. There were other more pressing questions I wanted to ask later. This one was just a warm-up to see if she would talk about Dad at all.

"I don't remember, Toby. Why does it matter?"

Mom either didn't remember, or she didn't want to tell me. It was probably the latter; Mom remembered everything. Moms, particularly Southern ones, will do that, never admitting they haven't held on to a memory or that a memory just hasn't held on to them. It's usually best not to ask again.

Just like Ash said, she'll tell you what she wants to talk about. I knew it was best to forego my questions and let her take the lead. Mom wouldn't lie to me, and rather than choose to lie about something, it was easier not to talk about it at all.

There were other stories about him she was more than willing to share. Maybe that was because those were pleasant memories. I wondered each time she repeated a memory or story I had heard before if it was because she'd forgotten she'd already told me or if it was because it was so important, she wanted to make sure I didn't forget it. Did Mom know one day she would not remember? Unlike Dad and his siblings, no one in Mom's family had dementia. But old age still tends to take away what we know.

Because of Dad's dementia, stories were often repeated because he'd forgotten that he'd told us before. Or maybe it wasn't the dementia, and that was just his old age. I didn't mind. Dad came alive while telling a story. His eyes grew wide. It reminded me of a child opening birthday gifts and enjoying the splendor of an entire party devoted just to them. I didn't have too many of those moments with him, so I shushed Melaine when she'd try to tell Dad we'd heard the story before.

I decided to try a different approach. I asked Mom how she met Dad. That was a story she seemed more willing to share. Like Dad when he told a story, she let a smile come across her mouth as she started to recall that day. Her face began to glow as she shared that memory.

"He'd gone fishing with a friend. They got a flat tire. They pulled the car in front of our home. Your aunt and I were sitting on the front porch. We walked to the edge of the road to say hello."

"Was Grandpa at home?"

"Oh yes! He quickly came outside to see where his daughters were going. He followed us to the end of the driveway to inspect the situation. When he saw your father and his friend standing there, he knew right away that neither of them knew how to change a tire. So he helped them. Before they left, your father asked me on a date."

"And you said yes?"

"Of course I did. He was quite handsome then, so statuesque," she said, looking at me. I smiled.

"After we got married, we rented the upstairs apartment of a house in town. Samuel was born two months shy of our first anniversary. We bought this house four years later. Melaine was born two years after that, and it would be another six years before you came along. You were born just a few months before my thirty-second birthday. That's it."

That was it? Over an entire decade of my family had been summed up in just a few sentences. Was it so trivial? So unimportant? No, it wasn't that at all. She was growing tired of my barrage of questions and probably tired of talking about Dad. I was tired of questioning whether or not she'd forgotten her memories or if she was just choosing not to share them with me.

Thinking about Dad's own personal battle to remember anything, I tried to recall my own earliest memory. It was of a wind-up mobile that hung over my crib. As I fell asleep, I somehow remembered how much it fascinated me. I decided to ask Mom about it.

"Do you remember that mobile that hung over my crib?" I asked Mom.

"What made you think of that?"

"I don't know. Silly, isn't it?"

"It was a gift from Grandmother Kipton when your brother was born. It had trucks and airplanes on it. When he could stand up, he pulled all of them off and liked to play with them in the crib. Rather than throw it away, I sewed those little felt animals and strung them up myself."

"You made those?"

"Sure did. You and your sister never bothered them."

"Samuel was always the destructive one."

That made Mom laugh. I almost asked her where the mobile was now, but it didn't matter. I didn't need it. It was only a memory turning in my head. But that first memory of how my parents met was different somehow. It wasn't an object someone could dangle over me. It was a keepsake that could be passed down, which was what Mom had probably done with the mobile.

Mom would not have thought of the story of how she met Dad as such now, but it was a memento of sorts to me. It was the very first moment where their lives came together. It's why we were here now—Samuel, Melaine, and me—and how this all got started. I thought it was a harmless question, and I was glad she gave me an answer.

In the days that followed, not all of my questions would be so simple.

CHAPTER 10

KNOWING MY parents' memories, knowing where they came from, helped me understand my own memories and childhood a bit more. At some point in life, people seek to fill in the gaps, or we dismiss what we don't know.

There were many things I didn't know about my father. Suddenly what might have seemed trivial at one point in Dad's life now seemed more important than ever, and I regretted that I hadn't asked my father more questions about his past when I had the chance.

Despite their divorce, Mom knew Dad better than anyone else. She'd been married to him for thirty years. She knew the good and the bad from most of his life, and she had done her best to keep the bad from us for a very long time.

Sure, there were darker, secretive things in every family's past that no one spoke about when there were children in the room. There was gossip overheard while mothers were on the phone with the neighbors. They thought their children were too young to listen.

As we got older and learned more, we might remember something we'd eavesdropped on by mistake. Maybe we couldn't place it. We couldn't remember the whole conversation; we'd only heard part of it. We weren't supposed to remember. If nosy children brought it up later, it was easy for a parent to convince their kid that what they thought they heard was wrong.

I was glad I had asked Mom about when she and Dad met. I was delighted she had been so willing to share, but now some of the bad came to mind, and I debated whether or not to ask her about that too. Some of those one-sided confrontations were a puzzle still missing several pieces. I needed Mom's help to finish putting it together.

So I tried. I asked.

"You were just a kid back then. There was no reason for you to know about all of that," she said. "Why would you want to know about it now?"

As expected, she offered an excuse, letting me know I had prodded too close to information she felt I shouldn't know even now. I could hear Ash's voice in my head repeating what he'd said on the phone: *She's a Southern woman. She'll tell you if she wants to talk about it.*

"I'm not a kid now," I said.

"You were so young back then," Mom repeated.

"Tell me what happened," I said, not letting it go.

"Oh, all right. What do you want to know?" She was exhausted or frustrated that I was digging up the past. It was hard to tell.

There it was—my chance to finally ask more personal questions, to fill in the missing pieces, to learn why our lives had taken the direction they did all those years ago. So I took a deep breath and asked what I really wanted to know.

"Why did Dad leave?"

CHAPTER 11

IT'S ODD how some specific ordinary details escape us, but others haunt us for the rest of our lives. Dementia was almost a blessing when it came to the ghosts we'd always wanted to forget. I knew why. The more something weighs a person down, the more it won't let them forget it.

I thought I could remember the day my father left right down to every detail, every word spoken, every minute that ticked by that October evening after I'd returned home to find he was gone. He'd just walked out. Looking back now, the details seemed just as vague as any other ordinary teenage evening of my life. Maybe we were supposed to forget the bad stuff.

I was a senior in high school. It was Friday night, and I'd gone to a movie. Mom and Dad had gone out to dinner and to buy groceries like they did every Friday evening. This was a weekly ritual the whole family had participated in when my siblings and I were younger and all lived at home.

We'd eat dinner at one of those buffet-style restaurants with a giant salad bar. Mom only ate salad. Dad ordered a steak. I ordered chicken fingers and nibbled off the salad bars, dipping vegetables into ranch dressing. The first time I ever tried cauliflower was at one of our Friday family dinners, and my parents were so proud of me for trying a new vegetable. Every time I see cauliflower now, I think about that. Why did my brain hang on to that tiny, commonplace detail of all things?

Later, Samuel and Melaine grew up and moved out. I was getting close to that point and had become somewhat of a rebellious teenager. It was suddenly uncool to spend Friday nights with my parents, and having my own car during senior year allowed me new freedoms. I wondered if Mom and Dad were finally happy to have their evenings to themselves or if they missed having their children with them as part of that weekly tradition. I secretly wished I'd gone to dinner with them that night. It would have been the last time I'd ever had dinner with both of my parents together. The last time we'd shared a meal before that was a memory I could not recall.

A new movie was opening that weekend about three unlikely college roommates and their semester together in the dorm. I was planning to leave for college myself right after high school and thought the movie, though fictional, might give me a glimpse into what I could expect.

In the movie, a girl with a name that could be mistaken for a guy's was accidentally assigned to the male dorms. She shares a room with a jock and a nerd. The jock falls in love with the girl, but he repulses her. She falls in love with the nerd, and the nerd falls in love with both the girl and the jock. The odd threesome's sexual proclivities build to an intense crescendo as they snub those around them who frown upon their peculiar friendship.

The movie was practically softcore porn and the first time I'd ever seen a bisexual relationship portrayed on the screen. As I sat in the theater watching, I prayed college would be like that, but I knew movies were an escape from the real world and rarely mimicked it. I was so enamored by the music in the movie that I went to the record store afterward and bought the soundtrack on cassette tape before heading home. I played it in the car and relived the scenes from the movie in my head, eager to get home and fall asleep dreaming of a future dorm room affair with my hot new roommate.

When I got home, my father's truck was not there, and the back door of the house that led in from the garage was slightly ajar. When I walked inside, I noticed my father's boots were missing. Dad always took his boots off each evening and sat them by the back door. It was an unimportant detail but a ritual that had always meant he was in for the night. I had never paid much attention to the boots until then.

I walked into the kitchen and found Mom sitting at the table. She was crying. Samuel was sitting next to her and holding her hand. They both looked up at me. Before either of them spoke, I somehow already knew what was about to be said. I was about to ask where Dad was when Mom spoke up.

"Toby, he's gone. Your father's gone," she said.

"What do you mean?"

"He left us."

"Where did he go? Is he coming back?"

I looked at Samuel. Samuel shook his head.

"Why did he leave?" I asked, but neither of them would look at me. No one would answer me. It felt like I wasn't supposed to know, so I didn't ask again. I didn't say anything else.

Now, thinking back, I could not remember any words we'd spoken the rest of the evening. Samuel probably said good night. He lived just a few blocks away and could walk home. Before he left, Samuel hugged Mom. He might have assured her everything would be okay. I remember he touched me on the shoulder and probably said something like, "Call me if you and Mom need anything." Then he'd walked out the door to go home. Or did he? Maybe Samuel did not go home. Perhaps he went searching for our father's truck instead. It's what I wanted to do, but I stayed there with Mom.

"We'll be okay, Mom," I said. Maybe. I couldn't remember my own words either.

It was late, but neither of us slept that night. I was angry at Dad for abandoning us. Two of his kids were adults now and out of the house. I was practically an adult, but what about Mom? She would be alone now, and that's why it still felt like abandonment to me.

Dad returned a few days later. Mom had told me he asked for a second chance. They were going to try to work it out. She asked me not to hold a grudge and to speak to Dad and make him feel welcome. How could I make my father feel welcome in his own house? I told Mom I'd try. When Dad got home from work that afternoon, I made an effort to sit down and ask him how his day went.

"It was good," Dad said. "How was school?"

"Good."

I wanted to ask him why he'd left, but I refrained. I was supposed to pretend that night had never happened, but it was the only thing both of us were thinking about. The conversation died out after that. I had never been very close to him, and I realized we were attempting to create a dialogue between a son and a father that neither of us had ever shared before.

Like anything you try the first time, it was awkward. I assume it was too awkward for Dad. The following day, he did not come back home. He'd left us for a second time. Dad told Mom he didn't think things would have changed so quickly, but they had.

Nothing at home had changed, though. The house was the same. Mom was the same, and so was his youngest son. Dad was the one who had changed. He was the one who was different now. We could all pretend the past few days had never happened, but it was impossible to bury the truth. It was too soon to forget. It would burn in the backs of our minds for months. I would hold my tongue for years, keeping it from asking Mom—or Dad even—why all of this had happened anyway.

"What did you say to him?" Mom screamed at me.

Now it was me who wouldn't answer. I knew Mom was just looking for an escape, for someone to blame this on. She started to cry. I took her in my arms.

"We'll be okay, Mom," I told her again.

Years later, I wondered if Dad could see right through me and could feel the anger burning inside me the day I had tried to have a conversation with him. Dad knew all of this was awkward; I knew it too. Neither of us could hide that. For years, each time I visited him, there was always silence between us when we exhausted our usual topics of discussion. I knew, during that silence, we were both reliving those uncomfortable moments from long ago.

I knew my father leaving us wasn't my fault. It wasn't Mom's fault either. Mom quickly accepted his leaving, and she didn't blame herself. People in the town would gossip, but I never overheard one sour comment toward my mother. Those people, our neighbors, knew better than to blame her for the collapse of their marriage. My ears perked up if I heard mention of Dad, but no one shared any details that I didn't already know. If they knew anything, they kept it to themselves, as most small-town folks are apt to do when those affected are present.

"Your father was a good man," I remember one of my old junior high teachers saying when we crossed paths in town once.

I smiled and nodded, but later, when I had more time to think about it, her remark pissed me off. I wished I'd reminded her that my father was still alive at the time. My father was still a good man, despite leaving his wife. Wasn't he? Did my teacher know something else about Dad that I didn't know? There had been too many situations like this that had caused too much anxiety for me over the years. I just wanted someone to tell me the truth. Why did Dad leave?

After he left, I worried about Mom having to be home alone if I moved out after high school. I chose to attend the local community college for at least two years and live at home with her. It was finally my turn to find adulthood, go off to college, and discover who I was, but I felt like that had been taken away from me. I would resent my dad for years to come for stealing that opportunity from me, but it was a decision *I* made.

I chose to stay. I decided to be there for Mom when I felt she needed me.

No matter how many times Mom told me she'd be okay, I knew she secretly appreciated me being there with her. It had been my decision, and I'd done it for her, but in my mind I still laid the blame on my dad. I was angry at him, and I now hated him for every decision he'd made and every one of my decisions his leaving had forced.

I also hated community college. There were no dorms. There were no roommates. There was no sex. I felt out of place. I didn't want to be there. I wasn't supposed to be there. I was done with high school. All of my other friends were escaping this town. Instead of being positive and reminding myself this was only for two years, I blamed my father. The anger I had toward him grew. The silence between us grew more.

In time, I could see Mom getting better. She moved on. She might not ever forget the past, but she was getting good at ignoring it. It was me who couldn't ignore it. I couldn't let myself forget. Looking back on that, I realized I hadn't changed much. I still wouldn't let myself forget or let go, even when it was my own damn decision that caused my misery.

Through the years, I'd had practice at holding grudges against people I loved. No matter how much I thought it would, moving to the city hadn't changed that. Only the distance between myself and my old grudges had changed. Now, back home, those grudges against my father didn't matter anymore. It was the grudges I held against myself that I couldn't shake.

I would soon learn that the man I thought I knew as my father was someone I didn't know at all. And after losing my job and what had happened with Jacob, I didn't know myself either.

CHAPTER 12

"HE LOVED another woman," she said.

It was Mom's phrasing that hurt the most. It had been twenty years since Dad left, and he was dead now. But that simple phrase twisted my heart into knots. She could have said he had an affair. She could have said he didn't love her anymore. She could have said their marriage fell apart. All of those things would have been true, but Mom bared it all. She hadn't wanted to tell me this, but I asked for it. So she'd told me the truth. Maybe it was even an admission of truth she had never told herself before.

She did not cry. She'd done plenty of that years ago. There were no more tears to shed over this, not now. My anger would not let me cry either.

"He left to be with her?" I asked.

She nodded yes.

I knew it had to be the woman I'd seen at Dad's funeral. I wanted to pick up my phone and show Mom the photos I'd taken in the cemetery. I wanted to ask her if this was the woman Dad had loved. Was this the woman he'd left us for? I was afraid of her reaction. I was also too fearful of the truth.

After Dad left, we were estranged from each other for a time. I didn't speak to him. I didn't want to see him. When I moved to the city, he told Melaine that he'd tried calling me but that I never picked up the phone. I knew this wasn't true because I had Caller ID and voicemail. He never called. He never left messages.

"You should call him," Melaine told me.

I never did. It might have been months or a few years even before Dad and I spoke. I don't even remember the first time I saw him face-to-face after he left. We never talked about it. He never said why he left. He just acted as if our lives had always been this way, as if nothing had changed.

He'd show up at Melaine's house on Christmas morning, and we'd all have breakfast together—this new tradition that felt odd but was somehow supposed to feel like we'd been doing it for years. Then he'd leave and go back to whatever place he called home now, and I'd go back to Mom's house to the place that was home.

We never went to his house. I didn't know where he lived. We never met whoever he was with now, if there was someone. Not at first. Some time passed, and Melaine told me over the phone that Dad would bring a girlfriend with him when he came over to visit. A girlfriend. There were several of them, a different one each year, it seemed. Tammy. Barbara. There were a few others whose names I couldn't remember.

They were younger than him. One had to be close to Samuel's age. They were nice, never mom-like. It was just as if Melaine had invited over an old girlfriend from high school. Dad seemed to ignore them. They never sat next to each other. There were no loving glances or pats, no signs of affection. It was as if they were just friends, or Dad was embarrassed and regretted bringing them to meet his kids. Or maybe he had hoped he could recreate what he had before, but he wanted instant gratification. He knew he was getting older. He was running out of time. There would never be a replacement for Mom. We didn't need one, but he did.

Then it was just Dad again. He'd given up on love and maybe even happiness. Or perhaps he was finally happy and just tired of women, tired of trying. He was through with dating. He'd accepted the changes in his life; he'd grown comfortable with any regrets. Like Mom, he'd moved on—not just physically but emotionally too. He never admitted to us that he regretted leaving Mom. He was too proud for that, but I knew he did. I knew he missed her. He always asked Melaine how she was doing.

I felt sorry for him in a way. I didn't want him to be alone. He deserved love. He deserved to have someone in his life. I just didn't have to know about it. I didn't have to meet them and get a gift card with their name on it every year: *Merry Christmas from Dad and _____* (insert name of whoever he was seeing that year).

I hated these uncomfortable routines. I was thankful I had not been younger when he left and that I had not been caught up in some custody battle. But what we had now felt exactly like that anyway. I had stayed with Mom. I only visited Dad on holidays and weekends. It just felt as if all of us were stuck in a rut like we were waiting for something better that would never come. Then, something did come that changed everything. It changed all of our lives overnight, only it wasn't for the better.

"Dad fell again," Melaine said. "It doesn't look good."

He'd fallen several times. He broke an arm. He twisted an ankle. It was a broken pelvic bone that landed him in the hospital. He went to the senior center for rehabilitation. A few weeks into his therapy, he became erratic. He'd roam the halls in his wheelchair and get lost. He forgot his own name. His doctor diagnosed him with dementia, which was probably the reason for his frequent falls.

Given the earlier diagnoses of his siblings, we were no stranger to that word: dementia. The doctor told us we should consider admitting him to the center as a full-time resident. Dad didn't like doing therapy. He'd given up on walking again, but his doctor was okay with that. He was safe in the wheelchair. Now he just needed a safe place to live, and the outside world wasn't that place. Dad had already given authority to Melaine, but she consulted Samuel and me. All three of us agreed that Dad should stay at the center. That was three years ago. Three short years.

"Are you mad at me for telling you?" Mom asked.

"No. What makes you think that? I asked you. I made you do it. I'd always suspected he left for someone else. You know, Dad and I didn't talk much right after he left, so I didn't know what was going on in his life. I certainly never asked him why he left."

"Now you know. I'm sorry, Toby."

"Don't be sorry. As you said, that was twenty years ago."

All those years had passed since Dad left, but it still didn't make those four little words that Mom had said any better. It made me sad. It made me angry. A flurry of emotions spun through my head, just waiting for me to pick one. I didn't know how to feel. But now I knew why parents kept things from their children. It was because they didn't want us to have to feel this way. It's why, when we were kids, our parents often ignored our questions.

Some things are better off left unanswered.

CHAPTER 13

IT HAD been two days since the funeral. I'd gone to the senior center to help Melaine clean out Dad's room. We donated most of his belongings and clothes to the center. We took some photographs Melaine had hung on the wall for him. Out of kindness, we took the birthday banner that all the staff and residents had signed for him. A small, frail woman with a walker greeted us on our way out and told us how much she would miss our dad.

"Mr. Owen was my friend," she said in a rickety voice.

"Thank you for telling us that. We miss him too," Melaine said, patting the woman's hand.

"I'm sorry for saying this, but I won't miss coming here to visit him," I said outside.

"Me neither," Melaine said. "Do you want to stop by the cemetery on the way home?"

"Sure."

As Mclaine and I drove out to the cemetery, I thought about all those years Dad had taken this drive out there by himself at least once every week. Dad liked the long drives down the narrow gravel roads cut through the corn fields. They reminded him of his youth. He drove slowly, mindful of the lingering wild-life. Some days he saw more critters than on other trips. When I spoke to him on the phone, he enjoyed telling me what animals he had noticed that week.

As I searched the countryside now for any signs of wildlife, I could imagine them peering at him from the side of the road like cautious neighbors wondering who this stranger driving past their house was. He told me he stopped the car once and pulled to the side of the road to observe a mother deer and her baby crossing up ahead. Disturbing them made him feel out of place, like he wasn't supposed to be here. He was intruding.

I wasn't one of those people who stood at the grave of their loved ones and cried or spoke to them. I never even talked aloud to myself, so speaking to a dead person seemed uncomfortable. I had nothing to say. Even saying "I love you" or "I miss you" out loud did not bring me comfort. Like Dad had done when he visited his father, I usually just stood there for a moment, brief-ly trying to recall a happier memory, and then I would walk away.

When we reached the cemetery, we stopped talking, as if we had to be quiet for this ritual, or maybe we didn't want to risk disturbing the dead. We stepped out of the car and traversed the steps up the hill. We stood at Daddy's grave, observing some unneeded mo-ment of silence that felt like it went on for too long, but in reality was only a few short minutes.

I remembered coming here when Mom and Dad were still married. They observed this same quiet cus-tom. Sometimes when Dad was done, we wandered around the cemetery and visited other graves. It was only after we'd had stepped away from Grampa Joe that we started to speak again. Mom liked to look for the oldest dates, years that were barely legible anymore because time and weather had begun to steal the monument's purpose.

Standing there now, I thought about Dad's funeral, hanging on to each detail as if it had happened years ago. I wanted to be able to stow those memories away, to unpack them another day. I had not even looked at the photos I'd taken of Jenny and the woman in black. I wanted to take my phone out now and show them to Melaine, but something didn't feel right.

We stood in silence, looking at Dad's marker, a familiar routine to both of us. I started to step away, thinking Melaine would follow, but she stood in place. I saw her shoulders shaking and walked back to her. She was crying.

"What's wrong?"

"Before we leave, I have something to show you," she said, already digging through the giant purse hanging from her shoulder.

"Okay. What is it?"

"Read this," she said, shoving a tattered envelope at me.

The envelope was yellowed and had a few water spots on the front. Were they tears? Had she cried over this before? The envelope was addressed to Melaine, but it was a campus mail address from when she'd gone to college. That was thirty years ago. There was no return address. I looked at the postmark in the right corner. It was barely legible, but I could tell it was from 1989. The stamp had a price printed on it of twenty-five cents, unlike the Forever stamps of today.

"What is this?"

"Are you going to read it or not?" she yelled as she wiped heavy tears from her cheeks.

"Melaine, what's wrong?"

She sighed and then opened her eyes wide in frustration and pointed to the envelope. I opened it while still looking at her. She turned away and looked back to Dad's grave, as if I needed privacy to read it.

Inside the envelope was a soft piece of paper, folded twice. The two folds had left yellow lines across the paper. I unfolded it carefully and found a typed letter addressed to Melaine.

It read:

> *Dear Melaine,*
> *I just wanted to write to you to say hello. I hope you are having fun and enjoying your classes. Your father told me you are doing quite well at college. He's so proud of you and talks about you all the time. He misses his only daughter, but he is glad you are getting an education. He told me you don't come home as much on the weekends now, and he thinks you probably aren't as homesick as you were in the beginning. Leaving home for any reason can be overwhelming. It gets better with time. I didn't go to college. I went to work right after high school and got married. But things were different back then for women like me. I'm glad you got out of this town and that you are doing something for yourself and trying to make your life better. Take my advice, though, and never get mixed up with a*

*married man. It will cause you nothing but
heartache.*

Take care,
Linda

It was a genial letter until that last line. Out of all
the pieces of advice you could give to a young woman
in college, telling her to stay away from married men
is your shining moment? That seemed tacky. Who was
this woman?

"Who is Linda?" I asked when I had finished reading it.

Melaine took a deep breath. I studied her face as
she tried to find the right words. After what felt like too
much silence, I reached over and wiped a tear from her
face with my thumb, trying to encourage her to speak.

"Do you remember the woman in the hat at Daddy's funeral?" Melaine said, composing herself.

"The one I asked you about when we were leaving?" I reminded her.

"Yes. Black dress?"

"Yeah, I remember. Who is she?"

"That was Linda. She worked with Daddy at the
plant."

"Why didn't you tell me that when I asked you at
the funeral home?"

"It wasn't important then," she said, shaking her
head.

"Okay. And? She wrote a letter to you while you
were in college. Big deal. I wrote letters to you too."

I had many more questions, but Melaine had a
habit of getting emotional and shutting down if you

bombarded her with too many at once. I was trying to push her to get on with it, but slowly.

"Linda and Daddy had an affair!" she yelled.

There it was. That was what I had expected to hear from her.

"An affair? Is that why he left?" I asked.

"Yes."

"Obviously they didn't stay together," I said, thinking of all the women he'd brought to Melaine's house all those years. I didn't think any of them were named Linda.

"No. They didn't," Melaine said.

I folded the letter and put it back in the envelope and was about to hand it back to her, but something still didn't seem right. That's when I looked at the postmark again.

"Wait! This is postmarked 1989. Dad didn't move out until 1993. Was he with Linda for four years?"

"No, they were together for twenty years," she said, tearing up again.

"Twenty?" I asked a little too loud.

I started to cough. I tried to clear my throat. I could feel the blood rushing to my head. All sound left my ears. There was only a faint ringing noise, and then even it ceased. My chest ached from the pounding of my heart. Was I having a stroke? A heart attack? Or a panic attack? Melaine looked at me and could tell something was wrong. My face burned, and then I was the one crying.

"Here," I muttered, handing her the letter so I didn't get it wet. Suddenly I didn't want to touch it. It was as if it had caused all of this. In a way, it had.

Melaine began to claw through her purse. I thought she was just putting the letter away, but she soon produced a small gardening spade. She threw her purse on the ground and fell to her knees.

"Melaine, what are you doing?"

"I wanted you to know. Mom told me never to tell you, but I couldn't keep it inside any longer. I'm going to bury it here. I'm going to leave it with him."

"The letter?"

"Yes."

She threw the envelope on the ground and began to stab at the earth. Although it had only been two days since we buried him, the grassless earth seemed hard and would not relent. She began to cry out with each jab. The spade seemed to bounce off the ground, refusing to penetrate the soil. Her cries turned into screams of anger that echoed across the cemetery and into the surrounding crop fields. I knelt beside her and took the spade.

"Let me do it," I said.

I looked over my shoulder as if making sure there was no one watching, no one to suspect we were trying to dig up a body. Melaine picked the letter up and waited while I dug. When I was done, I looked at her and nodded. She leaned forward and put the letter inside the hole. I put the spade down, and we used our hands to cover it back up.

"Are you angry?" she said as I helped her back up to her feet.

"No. I think I'm sad. For Mom. What about you? You angry?"

"Not anymore."

"I can't believe you never told me until now."

"You were young. Mom didn't think—"

"Don't give me that bullshit! I was fucking eighteen years old when he left, Melaine!" I yelled.

"I know, I know. I'm sorry," she said, in that quiet tone you hope will rub off on the person who is yelling at you.

I tapped the spot again with my foot. Nothing looked out of the ordinary except for the two of us standing there with a spade and dirty hands. Melaine raised her hand in the air and chucked the spade into the nearby field as if concealing evidence. We turned away and walked back to the car. I knew this would be the last time I visited Dad's grave for a while. I had lied to Melaine. I was angry. I was mad at our father. I was angry too that my family had denied me the truth all these years. I could hear Mom's voice in my head: *You were young then. You didn't need to know. It didn't matter.*

"Does Linda still work at the plant?" I asked Melaine as we got into the car.

"No, she's retired. Her husband died several years ago, right around the time Daddy left the plant."

"Her husband! Was she still married? What about her kids?"

"Four boys. I went to high school with two of them. I didn't know who they were at the time."

Did Linda's kids know about the affair? Was it possible one of her boys could be our brother? My questions were adding up, but I didn't want to attack my own sister right here at our father's grave and demand answers. I knew who could answer my questions, though. Linda.

"I guess since she was at the funeral, she still lives here?" I asked.

"Yes, she does. On Maple Street in town."

"Melaine, you have dirt on your face," I said.

"Yeah, I did. Not anymore. That's why I told you. I'm sorry if it seems like I misled you," she said, looking out the window.

"No, I mean actual dirt. Right there," I said, pointing to her cheek.

"Oh," she said, wiping it away.

That made us laugh. It was what we needed after the intensity of the situation, but I needed more. I needed to see Linda again, the woman in black. Maybe talk to her. I needed to know more. If I mentioned it to Melaine, she'd just tell me to leave it alone and forget it.

You were young then. You didn't need to know. It didn't matter.

But it did matter. Mom, Melaine, and maybe even Samuel had had years to deal with this emotionally. I never had that opportunity, so I would have to deal with it now. Burying that letter was good therapy for Melaine, but I couldn't bury the past, especially one I had yet to even know.

Not yet.

Not until I knew all of it.

CHAPTER 14

DRIVING AWAY from the cemetery and back into the civilization of the living, Melaine and I were silent again. It was the shy, quiet, reticent behavior of two teenagers driving around on a Friday night and hoping they were getting away with something.

"How much do you know?" I finally said. It felt like I'd only said it to myself because I'd been thinking it for several minutes.

"Huh?" she asked, looking at me as if she had not heard me or understood. She did, though. "Do you mean about Dad and Linda?"

"Yeah. How much do you know?"

"What do you want to know?" she asked.

"Everything. Where did they meet?"

"At work."

"The meat-packing plant?"

"Yes."

Dad had started working there as a teenager. He ended up there for thirtysomething years. That was another piece of restricted information that had been kept hush-hush or under the table because I was either "too young" at the time or it wasn't something anyone felt the need to talk about. Every time I learned something "new" or a secret was revealed, it only made me angrier.

"Linda was a part-time secretary in the office. Her mother was the office manager. Linda had worked there since high school. After her mother died, Linda took over the manager position. She retired shortly after Dad left," Melaine said.

It all sounded so innocent and pure: a teenage girl entering the workforce, ready for new challenges, earning a paycheck, following in her mother's footsteps. It made me wonder if Linda's mother had been faithful to her husband. I wanted to know when it started and how, but neither of us had been there. If their affair had indeed lasted twenty years, I wasn't even born yet. Did they have lunch together? Or did they sneak off to some cheap motel? Or worse, did they lock themselves in a bathroom stall or broom closet in the plant when no one was looking, the stench of pork on my father's hands as he fumbled with the buttons on her blouse? Thinking of my father in such a pose with a secretary in the dark recesses of a meat-packing plant made me feel dirty.

The processing plant threw an annual retirement party for its employees. There were always pictures in the community section of the newspaper with the names of the retirees listed. The year Dad left, he had not gone to the party. There was no mention of his name in the paper. Melaine said he'd told Mom he didn't want to participate, which was the end of that.

The pictures in the paper always showed the retirees holding up plaques with their names, a nice gesture for their years of service to the company. Dad never brought home a plaque. Melaine believed his affair with Linda had been exposed and that he'd been given a choice to retire or be terminated. It was also possible he and Linda had a disagreement, and she'd caused him to lose his job.

"How did Mom find out?" I asked.

"He messed up. He'd been lying to Mom, telling her he had to work late," Melaine said. "He'd call home right before his shift was supposed to be over and tell her he was going to stay a few more hours."

"Did she go to the plant and look for him?"

"Not right away. When she went to the bank every Friday, she noticed there was no extra money on his paycheck for those weeks he claimed to be working over. That's when she thought he might be lying. So the next time he called and said he was working over, she went to the plant and discovered his truck wasn't in the parking lot."

"Did she confront him when he got home?"

"No, she waited. On another night when he called, she decided to try to catch him in the act. She asked a neighbor to watch us—we were all still young and already in bed. Mom drove to the plant and followed him as he left. He went to Linda's house. Mom wanted to confront him, but she didn't know what to say. She knew he would be angry. He might want a divorce. With no job and three small children, she went home and kept quiet about it."

"That's horrible. I feel so sorry for Mom."

"There's something else," Melaine said, wiping the heavy tears that had begun to form in her eyes.

Shortly after that, a man had called the house and asked Mom if she knew her husband was having an affair. The man on the phone was Linda's husband. He wanted to meet and talk with Mom, but she refused. She told him she didn't meet with men she did not know. He never said what he wanted. Maybe he just wanted to talk. Maybe he wanted revenge and hoped Mom would have an affair with him. It sounded ridiculous, but she hung up and never heard from him again.

"Do you think that was Linda's husband calling?" I asked.

"I don't know. It could have been someone from the meat plant just trying to expose them," Melaine said.

It didn't matter. Linda's husband was dead now. Our father was dead too. Melaine asked me not to bring it up with Mom. There was no reason to bother her about it.

I didn't tell her that it was too late—I had already done just that. But Mom had only told me that Dad left because he'd loved another woman. She hadn't told me that he'd been seeing that woman for twenty years.

Melaine was just like Mom, in a way. Sure. No reason to talk about it now. That's in the past. Let's forget it. Only it's hard to do that when you are just learning about it. She could tell it bothered me.

"Are you mad I told you?" she asked.

"No, but I am mad I didn't know sooner. Not mad at you, just mad at the situation. I feel like I want to be mad at Dad, but that's useless at this point."

"You can love someone your whole life and never really know them," she said.

Her words were thoughtful. Sentimental. Dark, even. But she was right. It did feel like I didn't know our dad.

It felt like I didn't know Mom either.

CHAPTER 15

"You're doing what?" Ash asked.

I had called him to check in and to let him know I intended to stay in Shadow Wood for a while longer. I told him about my father's long-term affair with Linda and about the letter Linda had written to Melaine.

"Do you think that was Linda's way of getting a message to your mom? She knew Melaine would tell your mom, right?"

"Maybe. See, those are the kinds of things I want to find out."

"But you already knew your dad left because he was seeing someone else, right?" Ash asked.

"Yes, Mom told me he was in love with someone else, but she didn't tell me his affair had been going on for twenty years."

"Why does that matter now?"

"It matters to me. I just want to know more."

"I think you should just let it go, Toby. All of that was a long time ago."

"Why does everyone keep telling me that? Jacob, my job, and now Dad's affair. It's hard to drop it and just move on like nothing happened. I hoped at least you would understand that, Ash, so why do you keep saying just to let it all go? "

"I do understand, Toby, but it's over. Your dad's affair is in the past. And it's not your past to dig up. We all miss out on things in life," he said.

"But I have a chance to find out more. I have so many questions, and my family either isn't talking or only knows so much. So I want to talk to her."

"To who?"

"Linda," I said.

"So your mom won't talk about it, and you think it's a good idea to just knock on the door of your dad's ex-lover. Do you know how crazy that sounds?"

"You'll have the apartment all to yourself for a while longer," I said, joking and trying to change the topic. "You can leave your clothes on the floor. You can bring home whoever you want."

"I already do that when you are here," Ash said.

Ash and I had never slept together, but everyone mistook us for lovers. Those who knew us better referred to us as Thelma and Louise, which led to lots of private jokes about us holding hands and jumping off cliffs together. We were inseparable at times. We even joked and said if neither of us had boyfriends by the time we were fifty, we'd just stay together and be old-maid spinsters. The truth was we didn't have to wait until we were fifty. We were pretty much already there. Neither of us had had a relationship that lasted beyond a few months.

We'd been roommates since our midtwenties. We'd met while we were both waiters at one of those posh, upscale movie theaters that served dinner. We'd clicked right away. Both of us were looking for a roommate at the time, so the choice was obvious. When we went searching for an apartment, Ash demanded the place had to have three bedrooms. He was even willing to pay more of the rent because he needed a dressing room. This was how he told me that he did drag on the weekends.

I loved to sit and talk to Ash and watch him do his makeup and transform into "Helen Heels." I didn't mind. I always loved to watch the drag shows at the clubs, though I never personally knew or hung out with any of the performers. That all changed when Ash recruited me to help him backstage in the dressing room, and Ash always had his drag sisters over to help them style a wig or sew a gown.

Ash was fun in and out of drag, which helped get me quite a bit of attention from guys who wanted to know if Helen's friend was single. Who knew that having a drag queen for a best friend could improve your social life—and your sex life—so much?

Neither of us had stayed at the movie theater long. Ash became a professional dog groomer by day, and I entered the office world of phones, faxes, spreadsheets, and con calls. The work was numbing, but I didn't have to work nights or weekends any longer. I started a 401K, had to tuck in my shirt and put on a tie every day, and I finally started making enough money to afford a new car.

I missed Ash now, and for a moment I questioned my obsession with Linda and Dad's affair. Maybe Ash was right. This was stupid. I should go back to the city and start looking for another job. I could find something else to do. I certainly didn't miss the office politics, but I missed the rest of my life in the city, the security and friendship Ash had given me.

I always felt more comfortable in the city, and I felt like I could be myself. I knew Ash missed me too. He rarely spent much time by himself. It felt good to know that someone wanted me in their life. But something was keeping me here, and my fixation with all of this wouldn't let me leave. Not yet.

"Your father is dead, and your parents have been divorced for over twenty years," Ash said. "Do you think this woman is going to talk to you?"

"I don't know, but I'd like to find out."

"I just wish you'd get over this, Toby."

"I think talking to Linda will help me to get over it."

"But your mother got over it, didn't she? Wouldn't she tell you to do the same?"

"Probably, but that's not the point. She didn't even want me to know Dad was with this woman for twenty years. Mom has had time to deal with it. I haven't."

"So now what? You're going to stalk this woman and hope you get the chance to ask her why she did it?"

"Exactly."

"Do you know how creepy that sounds? Don't people have a right to move on from their mistakes? Toby, you know this better than anyone right now. You and your father are alike in a way."

"What's that supposed to mean?"

"You know exactly what it means. Do you want people judging you twenty years from now for losing your job after you slept with a coworker?"

"Two coworkers," I reminded him.

"I don't care if it was the whole office. Do you want the weight of that on your shoulders when you are sixty years old?"

"No."

"Okay, then. Would your dead father want you to obsess over this? Don't you think this woman deserves the same respect?"

"That's different."

"How is it different?'

"I didn't ruin someone's marriage."

"Toby, she didn't either. Your father did that."

"It sounds to me like you are taking Linda's side in this."

"Toby, I'm on your side. I'm worried about you. Will you please just be careful? You were already a wreck before your dad's death. I wish you'd just come back here and try to heal and move on from everything."

"That's easier said than done, Ash. I just need to know more. I need to deal with this right now and in my own way."

Ash was right. I knew it too, but I still wanted answers. I didn't know if this Linda woman could give the answers I needed, but I was going to try to find out.

I told my family that I was leaving and driving back to the city the next day. I said my goodbyes to Samuel and Melaine that evening. I couldn't tell them the truth because, like Ash, my siblings would think what I was doing was wrong. I assumed Samuel already knew everything that Melaine had told me in the cemetery. Maybe he didn't. Maybe he was lucky. Had she shown him the letter?

Melaine might even try to stop me. I could hear her now: "Let it go! Why are you stirring up the past?" I didn't feel like I was stirring up anything. If our father's mistress had the audacity to show up at his funeral, then she should have the heart to tell me what I wanted to know.

The following day, Mom hugged me and walked me out to my car.

"You should stay a while longer," Mom said. She always said this to me at the end of each visit right before I left.

"I would, but unfortunately my work only gives us three days for bereavement," I said, hating to lie but trying to come up with a reasonable excuse.

"How is work?" she asked.

"It's fine."

"And Ash?"

"He's fine too."

"You okay, Toby?"

"Yeah, why?"

"You seem like something's bothering you."

"I'm just sad."

"About your father?"

"Yeah."

"You aren't mad at me, are you?"

"No, Mom. Not at all. Why would I be mad at you?"

"Because of what I told you."

"I asked you to tell me," I reminded her.

"I know. Now you know why I don't like to talk about things."

"Sometimes the silence hurts too."

"I know, and I'm sorry. I guess you kids always had a right to know the truth about him. I just didn't want you to be mad at him for leaving."

Mom was alluding to the fact that she should have told me the truth a long time ago, but she was still keeping things from me even now. I could have told Mom what Melaine had said to me at the cemetery, but

I didn't want her to be mad at Melaine. I didn't want to start an argument. Not now. Not right before I left.

"I'm not mad," I said. "But I should get going."

"Yeah, you've got a long road ahead of you. Be safe. I love you," she said.

We hugged each other. I got in my car and waved to her as I drove away. I did have a journey ahead of me, but it wasn't back to the city.

I was going to Maple Street.

CHAPTER 16

LINDA'S ADDRESS was easy to find thanks to an old phone book I found in a drawer in the kitchen at Mom's house. Maple Street was a long, winding street through the suburbs on the east side of downtown Shadow Wood. Linda's neighbors were the doctors and lawyers of the town. Old money. As I drove down the street and looked for her address, I noticed right away the house next door to Linda's was for sale. It was tempting to buy it, but I didn't want something that long-term.

I didn't need long-term. At least I hoped I didn't. But I did need some time. I could have just stayed with Mom. She wouldn't have minded, but there would have been questions about why I wasn't going back to work.

I didn't know how long this would take—how long before I built up enough courage to approach her—so it was easier for me to hide out and be alone so I could take as much time as I needed. A hotel would have been too expensive. I just needed a house or an apartment, maybe something I could rent by the week.

Ash would kill me if I bought a house here. I'd kill *myself* if I thought there was any reason to move back to Shadow Wood, and I certainly couldn't afford a mortgage. I also didn't want to be too close to her physically or so quickly. I wanted any closeness, any minor relationship that might form between us, to develop naturally and from a distance.

Linda was quite settled in the neighborhood. Like Mom and Dad, she and her husband had bought their house as newlyweds back in the sixties. They'd raised four sons in that house. I knew this because I went to the open house next door, where I met the realtor, who was a woman named Rose. Rose the Realtor. She was very proud of that title. She was very chatty about the neighbors' lifestyle, their property values, and how long they'd lived in their homes.

Buying a house felt so permanent. I'd never dreamed of doing it, not even in the city. Nothing in my life had ever been that stable, so why start now? I never wanted to hear myself saying something like, "I'm ready to settle down." I asked Rose if a sublease was an option, but the owner was determined to sell.

She directed me to a duplex for rent across the street. It seemed much more comfortable to me and more temporary. It had a deep porch with wide columns that I could sit behind for covert viewing, and the large picture window provided the same angle. The owner of the duplex had a flat tire and was running late when I wanted to view the property. He told me where to look for the keys beneath a large rock in the flower bed. The unit next door was empty, so I could look at both and choose the one I wanted.

My binoculars were still in the trunk of my car— an impulsive purchase from back when Ash wanted us to take up hiking—so I brought them inside with me. The unit on the left was a few feet closer to Linda's, but when standing at the window or sitting on the porch, I would have to turn my head just a bit more to the left due to a slight angle where the street in front of the house began to turn.

Even though it was just a few feet, the unit on the right gave me a wider sight line across the bend, and I didn't have to turn my head at all when I was behind the window or on the porch. It would also allow me to use all four porch columns for concealment, since I was a bit farther from Linda's house. I just hoped no one rented the other unit anytime soon.

I asked the owner if he would be willing to let me rent month-to-month; I lied and told him I was a contractor in town for a job and would only be there for a few months. He wasn't too keen on the idea. He was hoping for at least a six-month lease, but when I offered him three months' rent up front and told him he could keep the balance if I had to leave early, he let me have it.

Before I signed my lease on the duplex, I went back across the street to the second open house next to Linda. I waited until Rose the Realtor arrived, and then I rushed to get out of my car before she did. I started walking up the steps to Linda's house on purpose, taking my time and waiting for her to see me.

"Excuse me, sir. Are you here for the open house?" she called out from behind me, right on cue.

"Yes. Yes, I am," I said, turning around.

"It's this house, sir. Next door. Not that one."

I paused and looked at the For Sale sign, putting on my best confused look.

"So it is! Oh, I'm so embarrassed."

"It's okay. Someone did that last week and made it up to the neighbor's porch. It's my fault. I haven't had a chance to hang these balloons. I'm so sorry."

"My fault. I'm early. Here, let me help you with the balloons."

"Thank you. That's nice of you. I'm Rose."

"Rose the Realtor," I said.

"That's right!" she beamed. "Wait, you were here last time, weren't you?"

"Yes, I came back for a second look. Still debating on buying or renting."

"Remind me of your name again."

"I'm... Stephen. Stephen Glass."

"Glass? I don't think I know anyone named Glass in town."

I didn't either. The name just popped into my head. I'd gone to high school with a guy named Stephen Glass, and I had always liked the sound of his name. I hadn't given much thought to using a pseudonym, but coming up with one now seemed like a good idea. Hopefully, the real Stephen Glass didn't still live around here.

"I'm new here," I said.

"Well, welcome to Shadow Wood, Mr. Glass."

While she struggled with the balloons in the back seat of her car, I stole a few brief moments standing there in front of Linda's house to look across the street at the duplex. I wanted to see what Linda could see from her angle. That had been my intention the whole time.

Since the houses on her side of the street were on a small hill, I had the advantage. If someone was on the porch of the duplex, Linda would not be able to see them from the chest up if they remained standing, which meant she would not see me watching her. She also did not have a clear view of the picture window.

"Admiring the neighborhood?" Rose asked.

"Yes, it's quite nice."

All of the houses on Maple Street looked the same at first glance. They were bungalow or craftsman-style houses with wide porches and low-pitched roofs. They were a mix of brick, stone, and wood. They all had pastel exteriors with dark trim. Some of the houses with more recent paint jobs had a third accent color. Small dormer windows overlooked the tiny front yards and the narrow street looking out from upstairs guest rooms or attics. It was a street right out of a black-and-white 1950s TV sitcom. In the summertime, fathers mowing their lawns and kids riding their bicycles in the street probably added to its charm.

Inside, there were wide floor plans, hardwood floors, and exposed beams. Every house had built-in cupboards, bookcases, china cabinets, and telephone cubbies. They had massive fireplaces with wide hearths and narrow mantels, arched doorways, and decorative crown molding. There were signs of that in the duplex, though I could tell parts of it had been remodeled when splitting the house into two units.

Rose was a short, slender lady. Her dress looked too much like a uniform. She constantly adjusted the shoulder pads of her jacket. She was overly tan, and her makeup seemed clownish. I could guess what type of life she led just by looking at her. It was a game I frequently played to entertain myself when I met someone new. The way she sang "Rose the Realtor" told me she thought she had a sense of humor too, but no one ever laughed at her jokes.

Rose spent too much time in the sun by her pool drinking tropical wine coolers. She liked to wear spaghetti-strap tops and show off her freckled shoulders. She had daughters who'd given Rose grandchildren right after high school. Rose's husband was a banker or a pediatric physician who played too much golf. Or maybe he sold insurance or did taxes.

Rose didn't like her work, but she liked the time it afforded her being away from her husband. She was good at her job and had an office filled with awards and framed certificates. She'd been "realtor of the year," or something like that, more than once.

I carried the balloons up the steps while she struggled with her briefcase, purse, and a plate of cookies. I tied a few balloons on the For Sale sign and around the handrail leading up to the porch. Rose thanked me as she climbed the steps. Since I was early, I waited on the porch for a few minutes to be polite, stealing glances at Linda's house next door and what would soon be my new place across the street.

This view was all I had wanted out of today. I almost left, but Rose caught me on the porch just as I thought about walking away. I didn't need to see the inside of the house again, so I quickly asked her about the backyard. It was a clean slate with a small patio, a patch of lawn, and a single-car detached garage that you accessed from the alley that ran behind the house.

From next door, there was a clear view of Linda's backyard, which was a gardener's oasis. Part of her garage had been transformed into a potting shed with a small greenhouse. I already knew she preferred to park on the street out front. Since she used the front door to come and go, I'd be able to see more of her.

She had flower beds that were immaculately pruned. Butterflies and bees flitted all around her yard. I spotted a hummingbird at one of those red nectar feeders hanging from a hook in one of the beds. I could hear trickling water from a fish pond or a fountain. A weeping willow concealed the view of the alley.

"You've got all kinds of possibilities back here. It's a clean slate just waiting for you to start keeping up with the Joneses," Rose said, already warming up her pitch.

"The Joneses have been busy over there," I said, pointing to Linda's yard.

"Yes, Linda loves to garden. She's the president of the local gardeners' club. There's not a board in town she hasn't served on. Cotillion, ladies' auxiliary, school board, you name it. Linda and her late husband used to throw spectacular cocktail parties."

I sensed a bit of hostility in Rose's tone this time as she told me more about Linda. Maybe she was jealous of Linda. She definitely knew something, or there was acerbity between them that I was sure Rose would have gossiped about over lunch at the country club if we were friends. Maybe Linda had slept with Rose's husband.

Rose excused herself to greet a couple who had come inside. Since I was alone, I walked through the backyard to the alley. It was gravel and very narrow. It appeared to be overgrown with trees and bushes that lined the alley. Lazy dads never stepped back there to trim the trees or boxwoods, so the alley had a "backstage" look to it. The rows of tiny garages indicated each of the properties. Trash cans stood nearby.

Most of the properties still had the city-installed chain-link fences between them and matching gates that led to the alley. Others had installed white aluminum or wooden fencing for a personal touch. Linda's property had a low wooden fence, maybe three feet high, with a garden gate. It would have been easy to leap over if you were nimble. I checked the gate, and it was not locked. Most of her yard was concealed from the alley by the branches of the weeping willow. A stone path led from the gate, around the tree, and into her yard, through the flower beds, and past a small Italian garden pool, which explained the water I'd heard.

I set a timer on my cell phone and walked to the end of the alley. When I reached the street, I turned left and headed down the hill and around the corner back to the duplex. More people had arrived for the open house and were loitering on the street and admiring the neighborhood before heading inside. I did not see Rose at the door, so I continued across the street, not worrying about being seen. Too busy with other clients, she'd forget about me or think I left on my own through the front.

When I reached the porch of the duplex, I checked my timer. Three minutes. That was at a regular paced walk. If I had to run, I could probably do it in fewer than two. I thought about that weeping willow and wondered why Linda didn't keep it cut back. Was she not worried about it being a prime place for someone to hide beneath? No, she was not. At the first open house, Rose had mentioned the crime rate on this street was nonexistent. The owner of the duplex had also commented on how "safe" the neighborhood was.

The doorbell cameras on the front porches, including Linda's, weren't there to make them feel safe. They were just the latest gadgets of society. They were there to greet visitors or to spy on Amazon packages being delivered when no one was home. But not one package ever got taken from a porch on this street. So not once had Linda ever worried about that weeping willow being too overgrown.

I doubted there were cameras in the alley, but at some point I'd walk or jog the block and check for myself. Any sensitive cameras that picked up the cars driving by would eventually chime the homeowner's phone, and they'd only see a jogger, that nice man from the duplex. That would be my curb appeal. But just like those overgrown bushes and urban chain-link fences, cameras in the alley might reveal a much different man backstage and behind the scenes. A man now called Stephen Glass.

CHAPTER 17

ROSE SECURED a buyer a week after the open house. From the picture window, I watched Rose add a SOLD banner to the sign in the yard. Linda stepped outside to greet Rose, probably to quiz her about the new neighbors. Rose stiffened, and I could tell that Linda made her uncomfortable. Yet the two women beamed with pleasantries, talking with their hands, pausing and listening to each other with big smiles like two old ladies chatting in the canned goods aisle at the grocery store.

I could tell Linda was the type of woman who liked making other women nervous. It made her feel superior. She touched Rose on the forearm as she spoke to her, letting her fingers rest just below Rose's shoulder, as if she were holding her in place. Each time, Rose would glance down at Linda's fingers like a cat who doesn't want its belly scratched. Linda kept doing it anyway.

I had kept one of Rose's business cards. It might be helpful if I needed someone who prated too much and was willing to share details about her acquaintances. Rose was the type of woman who gossiped without even knowing she was doing it. She could be precarious, but I was pretty sure she only shared the truth. Maybe Linda knew that about her; she'd threatened her. I made a mental note to visit Rose and find out.

A small moving van parked out front a few days later, and a young couple unpacked it themselves. They looked to be in their late twenties, early thirties, possibly newlyweds. They were thin and fit. They wore athletic shorts, tank tops, and expensive white sneakers. He had an unkempt mop of blond surfer hair. He had broad shoulders, veiny arms, and a defined chest. Based on the tubelike crease in the crotch of his shorts, he had much to brag about.

She had a long, tightly pulled ponytail that frequently got in her way when she squatted to lift boxes. She was sickly thin with nice breasts and a shapely bottom. There was something different about her. I didn't know why, but I felt as if I'd known her before. That wasn't impossible in a small town.

They flirted with each other as they unloaded the van. He'd pat her bottom as she passed him; they'd stop on the steps for a quick kiss. It was going to take all day for them to unload that truck. It wouldn't surprise me if they took a break to have sex.

As I stood behind my window and watched them, I imagined them having sex. I liked doing that sometimes if I was people-watching at the mall or the bar and came across an attractive couple holding hands or showing affection in public. It was a game Ash and I played together all the time. Ash obsessed over making up what kinks they might have or what toys we'd find in their nightstand if we were attending a party and decided to snoop through their house. Ash always snooped.

For this couple, I imagined she made him do all the work. I could see her lying there like a dead fish glued to her cell phone while her boyfriend went down on her. She didn't like to reciprocate because he had too much girth. Or maybe she was whorish in bed and wanted to ride him while he pinched her breasts. Maybe she was into anal. Either way, they were young, and I hoped they were having lots of sex, good or bad.

I spotted yoga mats in their belongings and immediately knew everything I needed to know about them. I rolled my eyes, thinking they were probably vegans. Most of their furniture was brand-new in factory-sealed boxes and required assembly, so this must be their first place together.

There were no children and no pets. That was a perk because I didn't need a mouthy dog announcing my presence if I used the alley to spy on Linda. I wondered why a young couple like them would move to a street like this. And what did they do that they could afford a house like that? They were too young to be doctors, and I doubted any medical students chose to do their residency at the nearby hospital.

Their van blocked my view of Linda's house. At one point she must have come outside on the porch to greet them. They put the boxes they'd been carrying down on the front steps and walked over to speak to her. I picked up a book and stepped outside onto the porch. I leaned against one of the columns and pretended to read. I had hoped I would be able to hear their conversation, but I couldn't. Only an occasional laugh. Linda's was a loud and fake cackle. The girl giggled and sounded very nasal, and the boy made a quick and deep sound that sounded like he was saying, "Ha ha!"

What could be so funny? You'd just met your new neighbor, who was old enough to be your grandmother. She was an adulteress who'd wrecked a thirty-year marriage, not a stand-up comedian. She was the queen of bake sales and probably had a killer casserole recipe. She had won blue ribbons for arranging flowers.

They chatted for too long, so I sat down on the steps and took out my phone. Their lengthy conversation led me to believe they knew her. Or maybe they had met before. Perhaps she'd suggested the house to them. I was tempted to walk the block so I could pass by and hear what they were saying, but I wouldn't be able to hear much, and not for very long either. I also didn't want to bring attention to myself. I had not yet made myself known to Linda. I would at some point, but not now.

When I had been parking down the street to watch Linda just before I moved in, a nosey neighbor had already noticed me. I saw him frequently peeking at me through his miniblinds or coming outside to pretend to sweep his porch just as I was doing now with the book and my phone. If I caught him staring at me for too long, I would get out of my car and start walking down the street, trying not to look suspicious. I'd worn gym clothes so that I could look like I was just out for a walk.

I caught him on the porch once and waved to him. The old man frowned and hurried back inside. He was the type of cranky neighbor who yelled at kids riding their bikes down the sidewalk. He probably threatened to call the cops all the time but never picked up the phone. If I'd been a kid growing up on this street, I would have toilet-papered his house at Halloween. I doubted kids did things like that today, because someone could probably get shot. People were so up-tight these days.

After about ten minutes, the new neighbors said goodbye to Linda. There were no handshakes. Linda yelled out, "See you soon," and she went back inside her house. Had they made plans? Did she invite them over for dinner? Did they invite her over?

The girl picked up some of the boxes from the porch and carried them in. The boy came back down to the van. When he reached the street, he saw me. I looked up from my phone, and our eyes met. I smiled and gave a wave. The guy nodded back and stared a bit too long, even looking back at me as he took another box off the van. Did he recognize me? Had we gone to school together?

I was afraid I might find myself tied up in a ten-minute conversation of my own with them, so when the guy's back was turned, I stood up and hurried inside. I went back to the window to continue watching. When surfer boy reached the porch with the box, he handed it to the girl, who was still moving the previous boxes inside. He turned around and went back to the van, looking across the street for me.

He did that several times as if hoping to find me on the porch again. He seemed disappointed. He studied the front of the house a bit each time, and at one point I thought we locked eyes again, but I knew no one could see through the thick curtains hanging in my window.

The more he looked over, the more I wanted to step back out to speak to him. But I didn't want to make niceties. I didn't want to make up details about myself that I'd have to remember later. I didn't want to find out that we did know each other from school or something.

I didn't want to get invited to drinks or dinner. It would be horrible if they invited me to a dinner party and I went only to find Linda had been invited too.

I don't know why, but the couple intrigued me. I wanted to learn more about them, and I wanted to find out if they knew Linda. But there'd be time for that. Coming and going, neighbors always cross paths eventually. For now, I just watched them finish unloading the van, peering at them from behind the curtains like the old man down the street.

There was something comforting about watching the couple move into their home. It was a new beginning for them, and I could tell they were happy.

At first I had no intention of settling in, painting, or decorating the duplex. I pictured a mattress on the floor and a lawn chair facing the window with a milk crate next to it. The only accents would be a lamp on the floor next to the mattress and my binoculars sitting on the windowsill. The curtains I bought to cover the window had changed my mind.

I wanted dark curtains, and though two would have been enough, I bought four so there would be lots of folds, making it easier to hide behind them and hard to see through them from outside. They were midnight blue and made of a velvet-like fabric. There had been a sample hanging in the home décor store, and an employee assisted me by plugging in a lamp and holding it behind the curtain to show how thick the curtains were. I bought a black curtain rod with pinecone finials to hold them.

When the curtains were hung in the front window, they were perfect, but I hated how heavy they looked against the white walls, so I painted the room a dark navy blue. The paint swatch I'd chosen had

"Mysterious" listed as part of the color's name. It seemed fitting.

A blue room with dark blue curtains needed a pop of color, so I added a white love seat and matching armchair. I had some house plants delivered from the local florist, including a giant ficus tree for the corner. I put a can light on the floor behind it and admired the shadows of the branches it threw across the wall and ceiling. It was terrific mood lighting, which enticed me to buy a few more accent lamps, which meant I needed accent tables to put them on.

Ash would have been proud of my work and jealous that he didn't get to participate in a home makeover. I was quite proud of myself too. The living room looked like it came straight from a picture in an upscale home and garden magazine. It was important to blend in, to keep up appearances.

I had no intention of ever having guests, but if a plumber or the landlord had to come inside for anything, at least the duplex was furnished, and it didn't look like I was poor or on a stakeout. Since I was out of a job and had paid the rent I committed to, my bank account and credit cards were getting stretched pretty thin now thanks to the furnishings and the makeover. I wouldn't mind staying longer since the place was comfortable, but I hoped my business with Linda would not take longer. If it did, Ash would kill me.

I'd wasted no time painting and setting up the bedroom with an inexpensive blow-up mattress. I used the dining room as an office and workspace with a desk and chair. I never cooked much, so the small kitchen didn't require much attention other than a few plates, glasses, and silverware.

The new neighbors finished with the van just as the sun was setting. They drove it away and must have come back in their car and parked in the garage, because I didn't see them out front again that night. Instead, the lights in the house came on, and I could see them behind their windows moving around in the front of the house, shifting boxes and unpacking them.

As night fell, the lights in the front of their house went out. They hung blankets over the naked windows. Lights came on in the back of the house. They might have been assembling their new bed, or maybe they'd sleep on their new mattress on the floor tonight.

I took an evening walk and cut through the alley, hoping for a look, but they'd covered the back windows too. It made me think of that night outside the bar and looking in at Jimmie, but I knew that street and that place very well. Something here felt different. It felt dangerous. I was out of place. I knew I wasn't supposed to be here.

After all the years I'd lived here, I realized I'd never walked through the suburbs of Shadow Wood. Living out on the country side of town, I didn't have any friends who lived within the town proper. Sure, there were kids from high school who probably lived around here, but I never went to their houses after school. They were just classroom acquaintances.

This was the first time I'd ever felt like a stranger in my own hometown. Suddenly I was the barkeep dancing to the jukebox while sweeping up, and the people in their houses were the ones keeping their eyes on me.

The lights in the couple's home stayed on late into the night as they unpacked and set up their "forever" home. Even though the duplex was temporary, I still felt sad and alone that no one had been there to share in it with me.

Despite all of my work to make it feel like a home, I could never move back here permanently. I didn't have much of a life in the city, but I liked the life that I did have. Thinking of Ash now made me jealous of the couple across the street. They had each other. They weren't alone.

CHAPTER 18

I HAD not intended to spend much time studying the agenda of the young neighbors. I focused on Linda instead, but I found myself writing down the couple's schedule in a notebook where I also recorded Linda's daily routine. Neither was fascinating. At first.

The blankets the young couple had placed over their windows that first night were replaced with sheer curtains, the kind passersby could see right through if the lights were on inside the house. The curtains were pulled back and left open until they turned out the lights and went to bed. They put their television in the front room, where they spent evenings cuddling on the sofa with only the bluish, flickering light from the television filling the space.

Due to the hill on their side of the road, I couldn't see them from my window once they sat down, but a large mirror hanging over their sofa offered a clear view of what they were watching on the television. It was just sitcoms or crime dramas. On some nights, it was reality show trash. They turned the television off and went to bed after the late-night talk shows.

On more than one occasion, I caught a glimpse of their tan and bare glistening bodies from the waist up. They'd stand up from the sofa, having paused their lovemaking to move into the bedroom. She'd pull her long hair out of her face, check her reflection in the mirror, and leave the room. She'd have one forearm angled across her breasts, covering her nipples as if she was aware their curtains were open.

He'd walk over to the window to close the curtains. She'd probably told him to do that before coming to bed. He often paused at the window for a bit too long. I felt like he was looking across the street at times. My lights were off, even the porch light that I never burned, although everyone else on the street left theirs on all night.

I felt he wanted to be seen. He wanted someone to be watching. He'd scratch his chest, and his fingers would linger at his nipples for a bit too long. His other hand was hidden below the windowsill, as was his erection, which I imagined he was fondling while standing there. Even after drawing the curtains, he'd stand there for a minute longer between them, giving the neighborhood one last glimpse at his round pectoral muscles and tight abdomen like a proud creature preening from his perch over his kingdom.

I sat out on the porch one night in the dark as this charade played out. Unbeknownst to the neighbor, our eyes met briefly. Or maybe he knew I was there. Maybe he could see my silhouette against the brick column or my moonlit shadow against the house. If so, he did not stay at the window any longer than usual. I felt like a predator. I was now the creature lurking in the bushes, out of sight, but still there, in the dark. Something dangerous. Watching.

They were not early risers. I never saw any indication they were up before 8:00 a.m. The girl opened the curtains again and then drank a cup of coffee on the front porch in her pajamas. Cell phone in hand, looking down, she scrolled through whatever social media posts she'd missed during the night. She smiled and laughed to herself. She held her hand over her mouth as her phone entertained her.

Her boyfriend never joined her on the porch. I assume he stayed in bed or did his social media check inside the house. After she'd caught up on Facebook and finished her coffee, she went back inside to get ready for work. She left the house just before ten dressed in tight gym clothes with a logo on the breast. She worked at a local gym and fitness center. I had followed her once. She taught yoga or a cycling class, or maybe she was an aerobics instructor. She came home for lunch every day.

They did not have a second car. He must have worked from home if he worked at all. The house remained quiet and still while she was gone. He greeted her at the door when she came home on her lunch hour. After she went back to work, he liked to jog to the local park and back. I had followed his route once as well. I was careful not to take one of my walks at the same time because I did not want to cross paths with him and risk introductions or small talk.

After his jog, he liked to watch porn in the front room. I knew this thanks to that damn mirror above their sofa. He had a taste for bisexual stuff with two men and a woman, which might have explained a lot about his voyeuristic display in the window each night or the reason he'd looked over at me so much during their move-in day.

Maybe they were kinky, or at least, perhaps he had a kinky side. The longest the porn ever played was around four minutes. I hoped for her sake he lasted much longer in bed. Later, he began closing the curtains in the afternoon. I wondered if he'd figured out the revealing mirror on his own or if someone else passed the house, caught the action taking place, and alerted him.

They'd taken to parking their car out front, which I appreciated because now I could watch them coming and going. A walk through the alley one day revealed the side of their garage had been damaged. The wood had splintered just a few feet above the ground, possibly from a car's bumper. Walking down the sidewalk on their side of the street that same day, I saw a scratch and some white paint on their car bumper, which would have matched up with the puncture to the garage. She'd turned too wide when pulling the car out one morning.

I saw them in the grocery store once. It caught me off guard because I hadn't been following them, so seeing them in a place I wasn't expecting them felt like they were following me instead. It made me uncomfortable, but such accidental meetings were common in a small town. When I was a child, quick trips to the grocery store with Mom could turn into lengthy affairs because she'd run into two or three people she knew and proceed to carry on fifteen-minute conversations with each of them.

I guess I'd forgotten you were apt to run into someone you knew around every corner. As I was watching them from a distance, I noticed Melaine entering the grocery store. She had not seen me, but it startled me. If I ran into an old neighborhood friend, I could just say I was visiting my family, but I didn't have a good excuse for being here if I ran into Melaine. Luckily, she seemed to be on a mission and headed for the customer service counter possibly to pay a bill or return something.

I loitered near the back of the store, attempting to keep one eye on the couple while also watching out for my sister. It didn't take Melaine long to wrap up her business and leave the store without shopping around. The couple had not noticed me either. Instead, they lingered in the produce department, picking out tomatoes.

Their shopping must have taken forever, just as long as it took for them to move in, because she seemed very indecisive, holding up pieces of fruit and studying their shape. He appeared to make most of the final decisions, and he only had the use of one hand because his other was wrapped tightly around her waist or caressing one of her buttocks.

After the perfect tomato or apple had been chosen and bagged, they gave each other a brief celebratory kiss. Their public romance was both charming and exhausting. More than one old lady rolled her eyes at them. Old men took a second and third glance, grinned, and shook their heads in admiration or jealousy.

Though Linda was retired, her schedule was just as active, but not so precarious. She kept her curtains pulled day and night. She never wasted much time selecting vegetables at the market, but she did meticulously prune the plants and shrubbery in her front and back yard. She stayed inside her house most mornings, maybe sleeping in even later than her young neighbors. Or maybe she read the paper or watched the news in the mornings.

At precisely ten every morning, she came outside with pruning shears and hedge clippers in hand. She put on a pair of yellow gardening gloves and a sun hat and trimmed whatever stray leaves and twigs had dared to sprout overnight. Her gardening was frequently interrupted by her cell phone, which slowed down the trimming because she would pause to talk to the person on the other end, waving her hand in the air to emote the conversation, though the caller could not see her.

If there wasn't one long call delaying the chore, there were several short calls breaking up her morning work. She once spent thirty minutes clipping at just one bush, and the result was only three or four cuttings. She bagged what clippings there were. She never completed all the bushes and hedges in one morning, especially when there were numerous phone calls. Ash would have found the repetitive entries in my notebook to be comical: *Linda trimmed her bush.*

As it got closer to noon, she rushed back inside to change clothes and leave for lunch. She drove a small, sporty Miata, always with the top down. She ate lunch every day with various people I did not know. They were women around her age or younger. I did not recognize any of them from the neighborhood. They dined at the country club, the golf course, or at one of the many local restaurants about town. Lunch consisted of several martinis and fancy salads that they never finished. Servers faked smiles and rolled their eyes when their backs were turned.

Linda and her lunch guests were pretentious and needy. They asked for extra dressing. They dropped their napkins and needed a clean one. Their fork had spots on it. The ice in their water glass, which they rarely drank from, had melted. They snapped their fingers in the air to get the waiter's attention.

Her guests had long stories to tell her, and Linda listened intently, never interrupting. She had a very therapeutic quality about her. She even reached across the table to pat their hands. They feigned annoyance when the server returned to refill their drinks or interrupted them with the check. I would have thought Linda was a therapist had I not already known she'd spent thirty years as the secretary at the meat-packing plant.

After her long lunch dates, Linda ran errands around town. This was when she did her grocery shopping. She paid bills. She dropped off or picked up clothes from the laundromat. She went to the library, the florist, or one of the numerous antique shops around the courthouse square. On Thursdays, she had a routine hair appointment.

She was quite dull during the daylight, occupying her afternoon with the same mundane movements and appointments each week. But it was during this time, these several hours each afternoon when she remained gone from the house, that I wanted to take advantage of if I was going to learn more about this woman.

I would use this time as a chance to get inside her house.

CHAPTER 19

DUE TO her hair appointment, Linda was gone a bit longer on Thursdays. I knew that would be the best day to try to get inside her house. I'd spent time studying the alley each day as she left. After she finished her daily yard ritual and pulled away in her Miata, I went out my back door and walked the block, then entered the alley behind her house from the far end. I looked for other neighbors on that side of the street who might be outside in their backyards at the same time or who might leave at the same time as she did.

By then I wasn't too worried about being seen. I'd walked the entire neighborhood enough for neighbors to recognize me as "just the new neighbor taking a walk." No one had a perfect view of the alley because of their fences, garages, or, in Linda's case, her weeping willow. There were no security cameras on the sides of the garages. There weren't very many home-installed security lights either. The alley wasn't very appealing, so there was no reason to want to see it.

I looked through the glass panels of Linda's green-house and could see a lawn mower, weed eater, and all of her gardening tools. No plants were growing in the greenhouse. The potting shed was just storage for empty flower pots. It was the open space beyond the willow, between the shed and her backdoor, that worried me. Any neighbor who might be in their backyard for any reason and who might look in that direction could see someone from the waist up standing in Linda's backyard. It was only about fifty feet, but I decided I would try to crawl from the willow to her back door just to be safe.

I tested it by seeing how fast I could crawl across my living room floor, through the dining room, and back. Then I tried it in Linda's yard the next day, traversing between her flower garden beds and along the garden pool. I arched my neck up to look around to see if any of the neighbors on either side had a clear view over the fence looking down into the backyard. Neither of them did, and I was thankful the voyeuristic neighbor didn't spend any time on his patio while his girlfriend was gone. Other than his daily jog to the park, he wasn't much of an outdoor person. I was able to crawl to her back door and back to the willow in just under one minute.

There was a small sun porch on the back of her house with a storm door that did not lock. Inside, the back door to the house had a single key deadbolt and knob. I knew the predictable habits of Linda's generation all too well. The chances of there being a spare key somewhere in the sun porch were very high. I just had to find it, and I hoped it was not in the potting shed or the garage.

I soon adopted a routine of my own: watching Linda leave, observing the neighbors, hiding beneath the willow, and then crawling to her sun porch to look for the spare key. I meticulously reconnoitered my surroundings each day, expecting a hiccup at any time. Maybe Linda forgot something and would return home unexpectedly. Maybe her young neighbor decided to hang out in his backyard before prepping lunch for his girlfriend. Perhaps a lady from down the street decided to cut through the alley on her daily walk. The lack of disruptions was too good to be true.

On the first attempt, I looked for the key in the most obvious places: under the sisal doormat, above the doorframe, along the window ledge. The sun porch was cluttered with terra cotta pots, some of them empty and some of them containing various houseplants she'd moved outside. I lifted each pot to check underneath. Some of the pots had drain dishes; I checked inside and under each of those too. I set a timer on my phone again, and I never spent more than three minutes looking for the key before giving up and crawling back across the lawn. I was careful each day not to check the same places twice.

On the third attempt, a large spikey snake plant caught my attention. It had the largest pot of any of the plants on the sun porch, and it was the only pot that had polished river stones in the top surrounding the plant. One stone was not so polished, and it reminded me of the rock that had hidden the key to the duplex. When I picked it up, I discovered it was not a stone but a fake rock with a plug in the bottom. I removed the plug, and there inside was a key. I tried it in the back door. It worked.

I pushed the door wide open and waited. No beeping sound came from inside. I studied the frame of the door but found no sensor. Linda had one of those doorbell cameras at the front of the house like everyone else, but it appeared there was no alarm. I didn't want to take any chances, so I locked the door, returned the key to its hiding place, and crawled back across the yard. I returned to the duplex and waited to see if Linda or the police appeared, just in case an alarm had been triggered. No one showed up until Linda returned home later that afternoon.

On Thursday I was inside Linda's house just ten minutes after she'd left for her hair appointment. I had not given much thought as to what I would do once I was inside. I didn't know what I was even looking for. I didn't want to steal anything. I thought it might be humorous to rearrange her furniture, but I didn't want to do anything to give away my presence. Even though I knew she'd be gone for a few hours, I planned to stay no longer than ten minutes, so I set another timer on my phone.

Standing in her house, I immediately began to think about my father. I tried to picture Dad and Linda sitting at her breakfast table in the kitchen or cuddling on her sofa. These images were not easy for me, not because they made me angry, but because I knew Dad was not a very affectionate man. I'd seen him give Mom a quick kiss on the lips plenty of times when they were together, but I never saw them hold hands or cuddle. I could not imagine my father was any different with Linda. Maybe he was, though. Perhaps that's why they'd carried on their affair for so long.

There were several leather-bound photo albums stacked on the coffee table in the living room. I opened one of them and thumbed through photos of her husband and sons. I watched the four boys grow and mature into men as I turned each page, changing from young, pale-skinned boys with toothy grins into mature, dark-eyed men with solemn, closed-mouth smiles.

There were birthday parties, vacations, and Christmas gatherings. Each album appeared to be at least a decade's worth of photos.

I hoped there would be some evidence of my father amongst the photos, but there wasn't. I doubted a photo of him with Linda had ever been taken. It would have been evidence, something tangible, something she could not deny if confronted with it. At some point in their lives, maybe each of them had denied it. My family wanted to forget and move on. That's what Ash had told me to do. Now that Dad was gone, it's what Mom would have told me to do had she known I was obsessing over this woman, this woman who'd slept with her husband and played a part in ruining her marriage. But Linda had shown up at the funeral; maybe she had not moved on.

Mom had moved on, but it was easier for her. She'd known about Linda much longer than I had. That was why I was there. That's what I kept telling myself. That's why I was standing in the middle of Linda's house and nosing through her photo albums, her life. This was my way of dealing with it, my way of processing my father's infidelity, no matter how crazy it would have seemed to Ash or Melaine. It was me who needed to find proof, to find an explanation, to get closure. It frustrated me to know there wouldn't be any. Not there, not in Linda's house.

I thought of my last night back in the city and the few moments I'd spent standing outside the bar and watching Jimmie through the window. I remembered how it had made me feel somewhat aroused to be in a place where I shouldn't be, watching something I wasn't meant to see. I felt that way now—in a way—but for a completely different reason.

One of the photo albums still had its plastic sleeve over the cover, as if it had been recently purchased. I opened to the middle of it, and its pages were empty. I flipped back to the first page, and there was a newspaper clipping of my father's obituary. A flower had also been pressed beneath the plastic sheet, probably one she'd somehow taken from his funeral, or maybe she'd returned to the cemetery after everyone else was gone. She'd stood there over his grave, just the two of them again. She'd spoken to him. She'd wept.

This was it. This was what I had been looking for. This was somehow the validation I sought. Wasn't it? I wanted to take it, to steal it from her as some kind of revenge, taking something that I felt she was not worthy of having, but that seemed childish. It was just a piece of paper and a dead flower. Without the satisfaction of seeing her face when she realized they were missing, taking them was no good to me. No, I needed to be face-to-face with her. I needed to speak to her.

I had a few minutes left and decided to look at the rest of the house just for the sake of knowing what she might be doing inside. I looked at the photos of her family hanging on the wall. Each of her four sons' senior photos sat on the mantel. Their brown suits and feathered hair dated them as having graduated in the '70s or '80s. Two of them had made sad attempts at growing mustaches. Samuel had had the same faint charcoal fuzz above his lip when he graduated.

There was only one photo of Linda's husband, and it was also dated. It was a professional family photo taken when all four boys were younger. Linda had a silken dress and beehive hairstyle. Her husband had been a handsome man. He wore a checked suit that looked too small for him. He could have been a doctor or a lawyer. I wasn't sure what he'd done, but it made me wonder why she'd cheated. For the most part, all four boys looked just like their father, probably a sad reminder of him to Linda. I was thankful for that. For a moment, looking in the photo albums on the coffee table, I wondered if one of Linda's sons could have been my brother.

There were no signs of men in the house now. It had a very feminine vibe with pastel-colored furniture and lots of silk floral arrangements despite all the fresh flowers she grew in her backyard. There were only three bedrooms, so the boys must have shared rooms when they grew up here, just like Samuel and me. One of the bedrooms had been turned into an office. Maybe it had been her husband's space at one time. A half-empty cup of coffee sat on the giant desk in the middle of the room, a sign that Linda still used the space.

A large day planner lay open on the desk. I looked at it and was surprised at how much it mimicked the exact schedule I'd penned in my notebook while observing her from my window. Her planner filled in some of the gaps, like her doctor's name and the names of her lunch dates. I took out my phone and snapped photos of the pages to remember the names in case I needed them later.

On the first Friday of the month, she'd written at the bottom of the square for that day: *Milieu 8 p.m.* The Milieu was the name of the restaurant inside the Common Loon Hotel and Spa, named for the water birds that migrated through Shadow Wood each winter, leaving their breeding grounds in Canada and headed for the Gulf of Mexico. A whole week of festivities was dedicated to the event each year: bird-calling contests, art exhibits, and guided tours. Bird-watchers congregated at the hotel to catch glimpses of the birds as they passed through.

Beneath this entry, she'd drawn a red arrow that went through each of the Fridays right below it. I looked at previous months and found the same thing. It was the only entry made in red. Everything else was written with black or blue ink. I was so well acquainted with her daily habits that I had not paid much attention to her nightly ones. Did she have dinner at the Milieu every Friday? If so, did she dine alone? Unlike her lunch dates, this entry had no names written next to it. I wanted to know more about this weekly Friday night itinerary, and since today was Thursday, I would not have to wait very long to find out.

CHAPTER 20

I THOUGHT Shadow Wood was full of loons, especially common ones, and I didn't mean the birds that
migrated through the town either. I often swore the
town was some kind of psychiatric community, and everyone was lingering about in a comatose state, waiting
for a bed to open up. Small towns were havens for drug
abusers, rapists, alcoholics, racists, and men who beat
their wives. All of this took its toll on the mental health
of the community.

Not to mention the lack of education and the abun-
dance of faith that kept dirty politicians in charge. All
an incumbent or candidate had to do to win votes was
mention he was a born-again sinner and that Jesus had
forgiven him—oh, and that he was against abortion—
and the locals would overlook the fact that he had raped
his cousin when he was a teenager.

The Common Loon Hotel and Spa was just as odd
as the townspeople. It was the only hotel in town that
wasn't a chain. There was a cluster of cheap name-brand
hotels and seedy motels just outside of downtown, loitering near the highway in case someone passing by

needed a place to stay and might choose Shadow Wood to be their stop for the night.

The Loon was their wealthy classmate who didn't associate with them in public. Instead of prostituting itself on the outskirts of town beneath a neon sign in the sky, it had been built in the heart of downtown. It had more of a bed-and-breakfast vibe with its posh suites, expensive food and banquet center, hot towels, and massage services.

Local kids called it the Loony Bin. It's where all the proms and award banquets were held each year, so I was well acquainted with the inside. It was a bit dated, with its large murals of the hotel's namesake. Several taxidermy loons hung on the wall behind the front desk. Only in a small dull town would someone celebrate the life of a bird by killing it and hanging it on the wall.

The hotel's restaurant was originally called the Bird's Nest but had to rebrand itself due to several food-poisoning cases back in the '80s. Whoever owned the hotel leased the restaurant out to a corporation that ran a chain of Milieu Restaurants in hotels across the country. I felt the distinction of the place was lost, and it was only a matter of time before the hotel itself turned into a Holiday Inn.

When I was growing up, the place always seemed "fancy," as Mom would have called it. Teens took pride in having their dances there but would have been just as content if the formal was held at a community center or in the school gymnasium. Now that I was an adult, the place had lost its appeal and was only still in business thanks to bird-watching tourists who stayed there and got excited about snapping photos of themselves in front of the sign out front that was shaped more like a duck than a loon. When I later discovered what was happening inside the hotel each Friday night, I was not surprised.

Linda left her house Friday evening at seven thirty. She wore a heavy trench coat. I thought that was odd, but women always wore coats out of season, especially to restaurants or venues that might be cool inside. She did not button the front, and I could see what appeared to be a cocktail dress underneath. It might have been the black dress she'd worn to Dad's funeral. She also wore black heels, an indication that maybe she was going to something worth dressing up for.

She arrived at the hotel at 7:40. I stayed back a bit so that Linda would not see me when she got out of her car. I noticed before she went inside that she'd removed her coat and left it in the car. Linda hadn't worn the coat because she was worried about the temperature in the restaurant; she'd worn it to conceal her outfit between her house and the hotel, even though she hadn't stopped anywhere in between.

The restaurant had a separate entrance, but Linda didn't use it. She went through the front door of the hotel instead. Maybe she was meeting someone who was staying there, which was why she'd chosen that entrance, but based on her calendar, I doubted they were staying there every Friday. Maybe it was a lover from out of town, but why wouldn't they stay at her house?

After she was inside, I found a parking space that gave me a good view of the restaurant's entrance and anyone coming and going. I could also see the separate entrance to the hotel. Through the outer windows, I saw Linda enter the restaurant. I wished I'd brought my binoculars, but I would have looked suspicious. No one else coming or going from the hotel or the restaurant looked as if they were dressed for any type of special event, especially one that was hosted every week based on Linda's calendar.

A woman, who looked close to my age, walked across the parking lot. She was dressed in black pants and a teal button-down shirt, the stiff uniform of the restaurant employees. As she approached the entrance, I saw a name tag pinned to her chest, confirming she was indeed an employee.

I rolled down the window to speak to her. "Excuse me."

She froze and looked around, not immediately seeing who had spoken.

"Over here," I said, waving my hand.

"Can I help you?" she asked, staying on the sidewalk.

She had that immediate defensive look on her face, the cautious look of a woman caught off guard by a stranger trying to speak to her in a parking lot. It was the same stern look any retail worker or server has when a customer speaks to them and they are off the clock.

"Sorry to bother you. Can you tell me what's going on here tonight?" I smiled, an attempt to let her know I was harmless.

"What do you mean?" she asked, not relenting to my casual demeanor so quickly. I didn't blame her. After all, I was sitting in my car in a hotel parking lot. Why would I ask someone instead of going inside myself?

"I saw some people all dressed up going inside. Is there a wedding or something?" I asked.

"No, sir. No wedding."

"A banquet or dance, maybe?"

"No. Not tonight."

"Okay. I was just curious. Sorry to have bothered you."

"No bother. Have a good night, sir."

"You too," I said, rolling the car window back up.

Throwing her hand up in a quick, dismissive wave, she continued walking toward the restaurant. When she reached the door, she turned and looked back at me for a moment as if replaying our conversation in her head or trying to place how she might know me. I smiled and waved at her and then looked down at my phone to avoid awkward eye contact.

I wondered what she was thinking, what wheels were turning inside her mind. I glanced up and saw her looking inside the restaurant and then checking her watch, debating on how much time she had left before her shift started or break ended. I rolled my window back down, anticipating that she was going to approach the car. That's exactly what she did.

"Are you Toby Kipton?" she asked as she walked up to my car window.

"Maybe. Yes. Do we know each other?" I asked, suddenly forgetting all about my pseudonym.

"We went to high school together. Well, not together. I was a year behind you."

"What's your name?"

"It's Parker. Parker Ambrose."

"You were on the newspaper staff, right?"

"Good memory," she said, smiling.

I actually didn't remember. It was just a good guess. If she looked athletic, I might have said track or basketball. If she'd had visible tattoos or multiple piercings, I might have asked if she was in the drama club.

"You didn't date my brother, did you?" I asked, joking. It was a way to get her to trust me, though I didn't think that would be a problem.

"Ha! No. Why?"

"I run into a lot of his bitter ex-girlfriends around here."

"Every small town is full of those," she said.

"Very true," I said with a grin. I liked her sense of humor.

"So, what are you doing here?"

"I could ask you the same thing," I said, then immediately regretted it.

She indicated her name tag and smirked.

"I was just about to compliment you on the shirt. Teal isn't your color?"

"No, and I don't normally wear a duck-shaped name tag either."

"It's a loon."

"It makes me look like a loon," she said, rolling her eyes.

"Well, you do work at the—"

"—Loony Bin," we said in unison.

"Are you a reporter?" Parker asked.

That was a strange question out of nowhere.

"No. Why do you ask?"

"Lots of those always poking around."

"Really? Why's that?"

"C'mon, it's no secret. A certain clientele is here every Friday night."

"A certain clientele?"

"Yeah, I don't want to say too much. You never know who's around," she said, looking over her shoulder to make her point.

"So there *is* an event here tonight?" I asked.

"Let's just say it's not an event scheduled with the hotel, but yes. They are here every Friday."

"They?"

"Yep. Hey, I have to go. My shift starts in a few minutes. If you want to know more, next week park in the back. Sooner or later you'll see what they all have in common. It was nice chatting with you, Toby," she said and walked away.

At the door, she brushed her hair back out of her eyes and looked over at me once more. She smiled, waved, and went inside. I waved back.

I waited there in my car for a few minutes, contemplating what she had said. I watched more couples walk inside. Besides that they were heterosexual, I couldn't tell what they might have in common that would require them to come to the hotel each Friday. It must have been some sort of club or society function.

I went back to the duplex and waited up for Linda to arrive home. It was after midnight. She was alone. She had the coat on again as she walked up the steps and went inside. She had taken her heels off and carried them in one hand. She did not stagger as if she was drunk, but given how many martinis she could put away at lunch, I was sure she'd had drinks this evening.

The lights inside her house, which she had left on, went off one by one. Since I'd seen the inside of her home and was familiar with the layout now, I could imagine her traversing through the house to her bedroom.

I sat down to contemplate what to do next. I thought about what Parker had told me, something about parking farther back to see what they all had in common. Was that supposed to be a riddle? Did they wear something in common? Did their cars all have something in common? Was that supposed to be a pun or a play on words since the hotel was called the Common Loon? I knew from Linda's calendar that next Friday night I'd have a chance to find out.

CHAPTER 21

I DID not feel the need to go back into Linda's house the following week. Instead, I kept a watch on both her and the young couple. Linda's routine was much the same as before. The neighbors were also developing a predictable schedule, with one exception.

On Friday, instead of following Linda, I went to the hotel earlier in the evening. I scored a parking space near the back, just as Parker had suggested. I wanted to watch some of the other cars arrive. I wanted to study the people who got out of the vehicles to see what they might have in common. I'd brought a notebook to write down anything I noticed. So far it was just a bunch of couples, men in clean jeans and women in skirts or dresses, who appeared to be arriving for a nice dinner. My neighbors were one of those couples.

He had on black pants and a lime-green silken dress shirt that clung to the curves of his upper body. She had on tight jeans tucked into boots and a sparkly floral blouse. These were the clothes of young couples out on the town or going to a dance club. If you added cowboy hats, they could be country line dancers.

The only problem was there weren't any good nightspots or dance clubs in Shadow Wood. The bars were on the outskirts of town and catered to rough trade—tattooed bikers and beer-gut truckers. They were one-room cinder-block joints with nothing more than a pool table and a dartboard. The motorbikes parked out front cost more than those places made in a month.

There was no reason for people dressed up like this to have dinner here in town and then drive all the way to the city just to go dancing. They'd have opted for a better steakhouse closer to their midnight destination. So I had a feeling it wasn't their clothes they would have had in common with other couples going inside the hotel.

I didn't see Parker that evening, or I would have just come right out and asked her. I got bored and went back to the duplex. I waited up to note what time Linda arrived home. It was just after midnight, the same as the week before. I wanted to wait up for the couple, but I fell asleep on the sofa.

About two hours later, car lights gleamed across my ceiling and woke me. I looked at my cell phone and noted the time. I stood up and checked the window. It was indeed the couple arriving home. Since I had not stayed at the hotel and they were arriving back much later than Linda, I assumed they'd left the hotel earlier in the evening and gone somewhere else, possibly to that nightclub that they seemed to have been dressed up for.

They both slammed their car doors. He was yelling as they got out. His words were loud but slurred, so I could not make out what he was saying. She kept quiet as they went up the steps. They'd forgotten to leave their porch light on. I could tell that she was attempting to climb the steps with caution, either because of the darkness or because she'd been drinking too.

She stood in the yard and fumbled through her purse, maybe for the house key. He grabbed her by the chin to get her to look up at him. She slapped his hand away. He started yelling again. He was drunk, but his mannerisms made me wonder if he was abusive toward her when he was sober. I thought about calling the police, but I waited.

She found what she was looking for and hurried up the steps to open the door. She was able to unlock the door in the dark without hesitation. She rushed inside. He went in after her, leaving their front door standing open. He was inside only for a few seconds before coming back out onto the porch. He sat down on the steps holding his head in his hands, either regretting his words or too intoxicated. I thought he might have fallen asleep.

This was the first time I'd felt sad for spying on them, the way you feel when you might witness a random public argument between two people at the grocery store. One loses control and gets loud. The other speaks in a whisper and hopes their partner will calm down. I felt sad for her. This was a part of their relationship they wouldn't want anyone to see. She'd raced to the door and found her keys so fast because she wanted to move the argument behind closed doors even though it was late into the night.

It was over now. That was why he'd come back outside. He wanted to distance himself from it, from her. He wanted to calm down. It was apparent she was not going to come back outside. She would go to bed but lie awake. He would go inside and try to make amends. After at least ten minutes passed with him sitting there unmoving, I got tired of watching. I stepped away to make myself a cup of hot tea. While the water was boiling, I flipped on the television and surfed through the channels. I got caught up watching a terrible infomercial selling some kitchen gadget.

The salesman was a bit too excited about how quick and precise he could chop an onion with the gadget. The audience oohed and ahhed. They applauded his handiwork as if he were a magician. *It slices. It dices. But wait! There's more!* I wondered who else was up at this early hour watching this crap?

I turned it off and checked the time. It had been an hour since the couple arrived home. I got back up to look out the window to see if my neighbor was still sitting outside. When I pulled back the curtain to have another look, he was gone from the porch. Their front door was closed. The lights inside their house had all been turned out.

That was the last time I saw my neighbor alive.

CHAPTER 22

WHEN I awoke in the morning, I walked to the window to look across the street, expecting all to be quiet. The sun was coming up, and I was sure any aggravations from the night had dissipated or been forgotten. I was wrong.

There was an unmarked cop car parked out front, a black car with one of those single blue lights sitting on the dash above the steering wheel. At first I thought the girl might have been hurt, but there was no ambulance. I made coffee and stood at the window for a bit, watching the activity from between the folds of my curtains. I wondered how many other neighbors up and down Maple Street were doing the same thing.

Soon I saw the girl walk outside with a cop. She'd been crying. She was wearing a tank top and lounge pants, so she'd gone to bed last night, or at least she'd dressed for it. I stepped out onto the porch with my coffee to enjoy the morning. I wanted to try to overhear their conversation but was unsuccessful.

The postwoman appeared, walking across my lawn, so I announced myself so I didn't frighten her if she stepped up onto my porch.

"Good morning," I said.

"Good morning! What's going on over there at the Perkins house? Everything okay?" she asked.

"I was just about to ask you the same thing," I said.

This was the first time I'd ever spoken to her, and already we were acting like we knew each other. I had not listed the duplex as my address for anything, so she usually skipped me on her daily route and used my yard as a quicker path to the next neighbor's house.

In a way, the postwoman knew everyone on the street: their names, bills, and magazine subscriptions. Just doing her job allowed her to accomplish more than I had been able to do during my short time here on Maple Street, and I'd broken into someone's house.

"Nate okay?" she asked, looking across the street.

"Nate? Oh! I haven't seen him this morning. Only her."

"Christine looks upset."

Christine and Nate Perkins. I smiled. At one time I'd thought of walking up on their porch and taking a piece of their mail to find out their names. Just in case someone saw me, I'd knock on the door to hand it to them. I'd tell them it had been delivered to my house by mistake. All that just to find out their names. After I'd witnessed the man's antics through the window, I avoided any contact with them.

There were other ways to find out their names, but I didn't need to know. I didn't even know why I'd paid attention to them. I supposed it was because I'd seen the inside of their house too, possibly even before they had. I'd watched them move in because they were in the way, the only thing between me and my motive for being here. So they held my curiosity.

But Linda was my focus. She was the reason I'd rented this place on Maple Street, and I still wasn't sure why'd I'd even done that. I could have easily stayed at my mom's, but I would have had to explain why I wasn't working. Having the duplex allowed me to blend in and take my time. I certainly didn't care about any of the other neighbors.

Now I didn't have to steal anyone's mail to learn their name. It was the postwoman who'd given me their names anyway.

"Hopefully everything's okay," I said.

"I'll find out and let you know. Enjoy your week-end," the postwoman said, and she walked to the next house to continue her route.

She sounded very sure of herself. I admired her resolve. I stayed on the porch until the cop car pulled away. That's when I noticed the empty spot in front of their house. Their car was gone. Maybe something had happened during the night after I went to bed, and the man, Nate, had left. Something had happened—something serious enough for the cops to show up and assist.

I watched as the postwoman continued her route across the street. When she reached the Perkins household, she knocked on the door. Christine answered. She handed Christine her mail, and the two of them spoke for several minutes before the postwoman moved on to Linda's house. She continued on to each home and back to her mail truck parked at the end of the street. I waved as she drove by.

I'd hoped she might stop and share the news, but she had work to do. I thought about following her to the next street to ask what she'd learned, but I didn't want to seem too interested. Instead, I'd make an effort to run into her on Monday and ask if she didn't find me first, but I would not have to wait until then.

The following morning I awoke to someone knocking on my door. I looked out the window and noticed it was the same police officer who'd been at the Perkins house the day before. I held my breath. My chest tightened. Why were the police at my door? I thought of ignoring him, but I'd been so careful with everything. Someone could have seen me, though. Maybe Christine or Nate had filed a report against me, but for what? I'd had no contact with them. Had they seen me looking at them through my curtains? That wasn't a crime. Maybe the cop was just here to scare me.

Or had Nate Perkins seen me go into Linda's house on Thursday? Maybe he had been peeking through his window. He could have told Linda, and she called the police. Perhaps he told her on Friday night at the hotel. The cop had shown up yesterday to take a statement, but Christine was at work that day and couldn't have seen me. It would have been Nate giving a statement. But why was Christine crying yesterday when the cop was at her house? She *was* crying, wasn't she? And it had been over a week now since I broke into Linda's house. If he was here for that, why wouldn't they have reported me sooner?

All of my thoughts were nonsensical. Both the postwoman and I had noticed Christine had been crying. The postwoman had even said it out loud. The officer had to be here about something else. I exhaled and reminded myself to keep my composure as I went to the door. I opened it just as the officer raised his hand to knock a second time.

"Good morning. Sorry to bother you so early on a Sunday," he said, lowering his hand as I opened the door.

"No bother. I've been awake for a while now. How can I help you?" I said.

"I'm Officer Tom Harland. Are you familiar with the Perkins household across the street there?" he asked, turning to point to the house.

"No, sir. Not really. They've only lived there for a few weeks, maybe. I remember seeing them move in. I'm new here myself and haven't met them yet."

"Were you at home Friday evening?"

"Yes, sir. I was."

"Notice anything strange that evening?"

"Nothing out of the ordinary. This is a pretty quiet street. Is everything okay?"

"Mrs. Perkins reported Mr. Perkins missing yesterday. She hasn't seen him since late Friday night. He left in their car early Saturday morning after a quarrel. He hasn't called or texted."

"Oh no. I hope he's okay."

"I'm sure he'll turn up. Do you have any security cameras on the premises?"

"No, sir, I don't. Why's that?"

"We're thinking of asking people to check their doorbell cams to see if they picked up anything. Since you live directly across the street from them, I thought I'd check with you first."

"Oh, that's a good idea. No, I haven't thought about installing one yet."

"Well, thank you for your time. Here's my card if you think of or see anything."

Nate Perkins had been missing less than forty-eight hours, but cops were already checking security cameras on the street. That seemed odd to me. Those doorbell cameras only kept a record for so many days, so maybe they were just being thorough before the recordings disappeared.

I chose not to tell the cop that I had witnessed the quarrel because I had not heard it, and I had not seen Nate leave. I didn't want to subject myself to numerous questions or lengthy interviews later on. I didn't want to seem like the nosy neighbor who was up late peeking out the window, though that's precisely what I had become.

I could have partially told the truth or lied about what I had and had not seen, but I didn't want to risk forgetting details I'd made up if I had to be subjected to a second or third round of questioning. I'd already presented a pseudonym, if only to Rose the Realtor. A name was easy to remember, but other details could pile up and be harder to keep in order.

It was just best to avoid any questions if I could. It was essential to remain silent about what little I had witnessed. I wanted to go unnoticed, so I knew I should ignore the business of certain neighbors and continue to focus my attention on others as I intended. I could continue being Stephen Glass but needed to avoid the possibility of other inquiries from anyone, especially cops.

I took the officer's card and watched him turn and walk back to his car. He got in and drove away. He said he was checking my house first, but why had he not continued up the street to check others? Why just me?

As I made breakfast, I thought about Officer Harland. I'd seen his face before, or maybe it was his eyes that were familiar. Tom Harland? The name didn't sound familiar, but perhaps we'd gone to high school together. No. He was older than me. Maybe he had been a friend of Samuel's and been to our house before to hang out as a teenager.

His face or voice felt like a memory from a long time ago. I'd seen him somewhere, or maybe I'd seen a photograph of him from when he was younger, from a yearbook or a newspaper. It was those eyes that were unforgettable. I wondered if he had recognized me.

I looked at his business card again and was curious why he had not asked my name.

CHAPTER 23

ON MONDAY the postwoman didn't know much more than what the officer had told me. Christine had told her that Nate left the house early Saturday morning and had not returned. He was not answering her calls or texts. The postwoman presented these details without any surprise. I imagined she'd already repeated them several times to other neighbors up and down the street who relied on her for the Maple Street chatter.

I checked the local newspaper, the *Shadow Wood Gazette*, online, and Monday's edition didn't even mention it. No police had shown up at the Perkins household again, but neither had Nate or the car. I didn't see Christine Perkins leave the house all week. I couldn't see any activity in the windows, and the house remained dark at night with the curtains drawn, so she might have been staying with friends or family.

A reporter by the name of Celeste Lowery had new details to share in Wednesday's edition.

The missing car was found late Tuesday night in a vacant lot near the park where Nate Perkins liked to jog each day. It was locked, and the keys were inside. Witnesses had seen him in the park the previous Friday afternoon. Speculation was that he'd left his home and gone to the park to jog on the night he'd last been seen. Still, I knew this was just Mrs. Lowery coming up with her own theories to build up the story, or reporters trying to piece events together themselves because the police weren't talking.

I had never seen Nate go jogging at night. He only went in the afternoons, and only once a day. He never drove to the park because Christine drove their car to work. If he had decided to go jogging that night, I doubted he would have taken the car at all, and why would he have parked it in a vacant lot across the street from the park?

The park had its own car lot and wasn't gated after dark. There was a sign by the park entrance stating no entry after sundown and that violators would be ticketed, but since I knew he'd been drinking, I doubted Nate would have obeyed the sign and parked across the street had he gone to the park that night at all.

The paper believed he'd locked the keys in the car by accident and disappeared while walking back home.

But the park was just a few blocks away at the end of Maple Street, so why had the vehicle not been found until four days after Nate went missing?

If it had been there since Saturday, Christine or the officer who'd been to her house would have seen it, because everyone drove to that end of Maple Street when leaving the neighborhood. This meant the car had not been parked in the vacant lot this whole time. Someone had left it there sometime between Nate's disappearance early Saturday morning and when it was found Tuesday night.

Celeste Lowery painted a very clear picture of the disappearance, and not once did it quote a police official. It read as if Lowery had insight into what had actually happened to Nate Perkins and was using her position with the paper to tell investigators what someone wanted them to believe had happened. It was all too neat, and I was anxious to see how the story would play out. I didn't recognize Celeste Lowery's name as anyone I might have known from high school, but it might be a nom de plume. I knew someone who could help with that.

"You're back," Parker said, spotting me parked at the Loon that Friday evening just after seven.

"I took your advice again and parked in the back this time."

"I see that. Slow night tonight, though," she said, looking around at the rows of cars between the restaurant and us.

"Slow? The parking lot's full," I said.

"Yeah, I meant something else."

"You told me last time that sooner or later, I'd see what they have in common. Does that have anything to do with it being slow tonight?"

"Yes, actually," she said, smiling at me. I could tell she was savoring the fact that she had information she knew I wanted.

"Why would it be slow tonight, then?"

"You heard about Nate Perkins disappearing last Friday?" she asked.

"Yeah, I saw that in the *Gazette*."

"He was last seen here Friday night."

"Yeah, I was here that night. I saw him and his wife go inside."

"Yeah, that's Chris."

"Do you know them?"

"I didn't know Nate, but I knew Chris. Sorry. I guess I should say Christine."

"Why are you sorry?"

"You don't know?"

"Obviously not. Care to enlighten me?"

"Do you remember Chris Harland from high school? Long hair, kind of effeminate, everyone made fun of him back then?"

"I don't think so," I said, trying to place the name.

"Well, now she's Christine Perkins."

"You mean he's a woman?"

"*She's* a woman. Yes. Not sure if she's fully transitioned, but she goes by Christine now."

"Transitioned? Oh! Chris is transexual?"

"Yes, but the correct term is transgender."

"I'm sorry. You are right. Okay, so I'm confused. Please tell me what Nate and Christine would have in common, as you said, with everyone else here. Why would they have come here on Friday?"

"Why do you come here?" Parker asked, giving me that peculiar smile again.

"I don't go inside."

"Are you married?" she asked.

"No."

"Seeing anyone?"

"No. Why?"

Parker walked to the back of my car and looked at the rear windshield.

"What are you doing?"

"Looking to see if you had a sticker."

"A sticker? What kind of sticker? A bumper sticker?" I asked.

"Look around," Parker said, almost in a whisper.

I studied the row of cars in front of us. That's when I noticed it. Several of them had a small sticker on the left side of their rear window. It was a pink poodle. It was a silly cartoonish sticker of just a poodle's head with frilly cotton-candy ears, a pearl necklace, cynical eyes, and a tongue sticking out of the corner of the mouth. It was the stereotype of a snooty, rich french poodle in television cartoons.

"Pink poodles?" I asked.

"Bingo!"

"What's that about?"

"You don't know about the Pink Poodle Club?"

"Obviously I don't."

Parker leaned down and crossed her arms across the top of my open car window. "The Pink Poodle Club is a swingers' club that meets here every Friday," she said in a low tone.

"A swingers' club?" I asked.

"Yep."

"You're serious?"

"Yep."

"Who are the members?"

"Pretty much the upper crust of Shadow Wood. People with money, city officials. The sheriff."

"The sheriff?" I asked, raising my voice.

"Shhh, not so loud. Yes, the sheriff and a lot of other people who might surprise you."

"Were Nate and Chris—I mean Christine—members?"

"Yes, I think so. Only one way to be sure."

"What's that?"

"See if they had a sticker on their car."

"The poodle sticker?"

"Yeah, it's how they identify each other around town."

"Like a secret password or code or something?"

"I guess so."

"Do you think Nate's disappearance has something to do with this poodle club?"

"Oh, yeah. Definitely."

Parker had to start her shift, so I said goodbye and left.

I decided not to wait around to spy on Linda or anyone else. Suddenly this swingers' club shed a whole new light on things. I wondered if my father might have been a member when he was seeing Linda.

While driving home, I tried to place the name Chris Harland. I parked on Maple Street and looked over at the Perkins house. It was dark and quiet.

Inside the duplex, I made myself a nightcap and sat down at my desk to think about everything I'd learned from Parker. I wanted to look for Chris Harland in my old high school yearbooks. I looked down at my desk and noticed the police officer's business card: Officer Tom Harland.

Christine and the officer were related.

CHAPTER 24

I TEXTED Ash to see if he was at home or had a drag show that evening. Instead of texting back, he called me. The sudden ringing of the phone caught me by surprise, and I almost dropped it. I was glad he had called. I wanted to hear his voice.

"What's up?" Ash said when I answered.

"No show tonight?"

"Nah, didn't feel like it."

"You okay?"

"Oh yeah, I'm great. How are things there?"

I had not told Ash about renting the duplex. I had not set a time limit on how long I planned on sticking around, so I didn't want to scare Ash or make him think my stay was permanent. It definitely wasn't. I hadn't stayed more than four days in Shadow Wood since moving away.

"Things are getting weird," I told him.

"Oh? Why's that? Have you spoken to Linda yet?"

"Not exactly."

I didn't tell Ash I'd broken into Linda's house. I kept specific details from him because I didn't want him to panic or scold me. His roommate had lost both

his job and his dad in just a few weeks. Telling him
the extremes I'd gone to so far to learn more about my
father's affair would make it sound like I was losing
my mind. I'd questioned if that was happening myself.
I didn't need him doing it too. Instead, I told him how
I'd been following Linda around town. I told him all
about Nate and Christine Perkins and about how Nate
had gone missing.

"What do they have to do with Linda, besides being neighbors with her?"

"Well, I found out they are members of a local
swingers' club."

"What? A swingers' club? So that's why you are
sticking around there!" he joked. "How did you find
out all of this?"

"I ran into an employee at the hotel that I went
to high school with, and she told me everything. Her
name is Parker."

"You think she's telling the truth?"

"She has no reason to lie to me."

"And Christine is a transgender woman who went
to high school with you?"

"That's right."

"Lord, that small-town drama is deep, honey," he
said, breaking into his Helen Heels demeanor.

"Yes, it is."

"Do you think it could be a hate crime?"

"I don't know. Parker thinks it's related to the
swingers' club."

"So now what?"

"I'm going to see what Linda does the next few
days. I also want to find out her role in this swingers'
club."

"I could bring Helen to town if you want to join the club," he said.

"Too risky. There's already one missing club member in the headlines."

"You're no fun."

"Sorry."

"How's your mom?" Ash asked.

"Oh, she's fine. Melaine is too. She said to tell you hi," I said, realizing Ash still thought I was staying with Mom.

"How about you? You okay too?" he asked. It made me wonder if he knew I was lying.

"I'm fine. Why do you ask?"

"Well, you recently lost your job. Then you lost your father. You found out he had a long-term affair. Now you are following his mistress around town. Oh, and *she's* involved in a sex club that may be linked to a missing man. This all sounds very dangerous, Toby."

"I knew I shouldn't have told you any of this," I said, growing defensive. It was the same reason I hadn't told Melaine what I had planned to do, and why I knew I couldn't stay at Mom's house while doing it.

"What's that supposed to mean? You don't think I should be concerned about you?"

"I appreciate your concern, Ash, but my family has had longer than me to process all of this. I knew Dad had an affair, but no one told me it lasted for twenty years. I guess this is just my way of finding out the truth and working through it."

"Okay, and while working through it, you've become a stalker and have stumbled onto a sex club and a missing neighbor," Ash said.

"Just another day in small-town Shadow Wood, right?" I said, hoping to lighten the mood.

It was true I was becoming just as curious about Nate and Christine's situation as I was about Linda and Dad. There was a silence between us. Ash never had a problem filling a conversation before, but somehow I knew Ash wanted to ask when I was coming home. I hoped he wouldn't, because I didn't know the answer.

"I miss you," he said instead.

I paused. Words felt heavy in my head, and I couldn't make sense of them. Not yet.

"I miss you too," I said.

I'd never had feelings for Ash before, but hearing his voice tonight stirred something inside of me. It was probably just my longing to return to the city. Ash was my best friend, my comfort zone. Yet something tonight felt different. After we hung up, I went to the window to look out. There was a single light on in the Perkins house, and in the Reyes house too. Each of us—Linda, Christine, and me—was alone tonight, and for entirely different reasons.

CHAPTER 25

ANOTHER WEEK passed. I'd spent it following Linda around town, but there was nothing new or noteworthy in her schedule. On Friday I went back to the Loon parking lot. Parker didn't have any new information to share. I gave her my number and told her she could text me anytime she wanted. Her first text came that following Monday. She asked if I'd seen the morning paper. I had not, but I pulled it up on the computer before texting her back.

The nude body of Nate Perkins had been found in the park where he was rumored to have gone jogging the night he disappeared. His body was lying in some overgrown brush near the edge of the park. City workers were cutting it back and came across the body. The story in the newspaper didn't mention that the park had been searched by policemen with dogs just a few days after Nate went missing. I had driven by and seen them searching. The park wasn't that big, so how could they have missed the body?

I, along with half the town, knew someone had dumped Nate's body there, wanting it to be found. Once again, reporter Celeste Lowery painted a different story. She presumed Nate was drunk and had wandered off the jogging path, fallen, and hit his head. That didn't explain why he was nude, and some readers must have called her out. In a follow-up story the next day, she stated he might have gone skinny dipping in the pond in the park.

Reporters from other out-of-town papers and news stations camped out on Maple Street to no avail, hoping for a statement from Christine Perkins. As I watched from behind my curtains, I wondered if Celeste Lowery was among them. Christine herself had disappeared, at least from Maple Street. She had returned home briefly one night. It looked as if she'd come for some clothes and other possessions. She was in the house and gone again in less than an hour.

I didn't want to go to Mom's house to get my yearbooks. I'd never paid her a surprise visit before. I could have called and pretended I was coming to town to get them, but that would have required at least an overnight stay. I had a key to her house, but another stakeout just to learn when she wasn't at home so that I could sneak in and get them was too much.

I decided to call my old high school. They told me copies of each yearbook were available to the public at the local library. I called the library, and they told me I could view the yearbooks online. I thought this might require some sort of membership or library card, but since I was an alumnus, the lady who answered the phone gave me an online passcode that was good for five days.

It didn't take long to sign in and navigate the library's website. I found my senior yearbook in just a few minutes. I looked through the pictures of the juniors to find Christine. She was Chris Harland back then, and

I recognized her right away. I purposely avoided a look at my own senior photo.

Chris had been the skinny emo kid with purple bangs and no close friends. Back then, she wore eye and lip liner without shame. She dressed in tight black pants with lots of zippers and Erasure, Pet Shop Boys, and Culture Club T-shirts. Today the shirts would have been a clear indicator that Chris was gay, but back then other kids just thought they were goth bands.

Jocks called Chris a fag or a queer. They pushed Chris into the lockers when they passed her in the hallway. Others whispered about Chris behind her back. They said Chris worshipped the devil, just like they did about every kid who wore makeup or dyed their hair a different color back then. Chris gave them all the finger, and they laughed at her. She skipped physical education class and volunteered in the library. She hung out with kids who were older than her and from another school.

One of those kids had a convertible and picked Chris up after classes a few days a week. Chris would leap over the door like an escaped prisoner, and they'd drive off. Chris and her friends looked like the cast from *The Breakfast Club*. Thinking back, I wondered where they went after school. I never saw them hanging around town. Did they hang out in someone's basement and smoke pot and listen to music? Did they drive to the city to go to a mall? What kind of teenage life had Chris led outside of school?

I had never seen Chris smile except for when she was getting into that car and riding away. Even her yearbook photo presented a tightly closed mouth that looked as if it had never felt a smile one single day in her life. But in that car she could relax. She could smile because she was happy. She was free from those who didn't understand her and didn't want to, and she was around her own kind. She was safe. She was accepted.

I felt sorry that I'd never spoken to Chris in high school, but that had been years ago. High school was cruel, but it still didn't prepare you for the cruelty that life was about to hand you. In school kids were bullies. Life became your bully after graduation. It was too late to make up for the past, to change it. Chris had changed his—*her* future. She'd become her true self, maybe who she'd always been: Christine. It was me who'd stayed the same. I had not changed at all. I didn't even know who I was anymore.

"Did Chris always want to be a woman?" I asked Parker in the hotel parking lot on Friday night.

"Chris was always a woman. Transgender people change the outside to match the inside. They want to fit in, and they want to be accepted by society, but they also want to be comfortable and accept themselves."

"I don't think I follow," I said.

"Look, did you always know you were gay?" Parker asked.

"Of course."

"Is that why you left Shadow Wood?"

"Maybe. I don't know. I know I wanted to find others like me. I wanted to be able to be myself."

"So does Christine."

"Ah! I get it."

I'd never known anyone who was transgender. Growing up gay in a small town was my own struggle. Hearing about Christine's personal battle to be her true self suddenly made my plight feel so easy.

"You never told me why you are here," Parker said, changing the subject.

I looked at her. She raised her eyebrows. I kept quiet, trying to think of a logical excuse. There wasn't one. She sighed and pretended to look at an imaginary watch on her wrist.

"I've been stalking someone," I finally admitted.

"What? So you *are* a reporter!"

"No. Not a reporter. Just messed up in the head, I suppose."

"Welcome to the Loony Bin!" she said.

"After my father died, I found out he'd had a long-term affair with another woman."

"How long?"

"Twenty years."

"No! And your mom didn't know?"

"She knew. She tolerated it. Anyway, I've been trying to make sense of it myself, so I've been following her around town. Stupid, I know."

"You've been following your father's adulteress?"

"Yep."

"I thought you said your father was dead."

"He is."

There was a pause. I looked at Parker. She looked toward the restaurant and then back at me again. She was either confused, or she totally understood and was just processing it. A slight breeze blew her hair in her face.

"I get it," Parker said, brushing her hair back.

"You do?"

"Yeah, that's messed up. Shame on your dad. Sorry, I know he's dead, but—your poor mom."

"Thanks."

"So, can I ask who it is?"

"Linda Reyes."

"No way!"

"Yep. So I guess that means you know her?"

"Know her? Uh, yeah! She runs the Pink Poodle Club," Parker said in a huff as if I should have known all along.

"She runs it?"

"Yep."

"Do you think she had something to do with Nate Perkins disappearing?"

"No, but she probably knows who is responsible."

"You think so?"

"I know so. Linda knows everything about the club's members."

"Members? Nate and Christine were members?"

"Yes, silly. You didn't know?"

"It seems like there's a lot I don't know. Care to enlighten me?" I asked.

"Are you asking me on a date?"

"No."

"I get off work at eleven," Parker said.

"I can pick you up then."

"Nah, let's meet somewhere. I don't want anyone to see us together."

"Gee, thanks," I said.

"Sorry, I didn't mean it that way."

"Why someplace else, then?"

"Isn't it obvious?" she said.

"No."

"I told you. You never know who's watching or listening around this place. I've already said too much," she said, looking over her shoulder for effect.

I'd never thought about the Loon being a dangerous place. Parker indicated someone might be watching or listening. Was there someone else watching us right now?

"True. I guess this place is part of the crime scene or investigation or whatever," I said, looking around to see if I could see anyone else sitting in their vehicle.

"Yeah. With everything going on, I think it would be better if we met somewhere else."

"You can come to my place," I offered.

"Where do you live?"

"Right across the street from Nate and Christine."

"What?" Parker yelled out. She caught herself and put a hand to her mouth. "Sorry. You live on Maple Street?" she said in a wide-eyed whisper.

"Yes, I'm renting a place."

"Talk about being near the crime scene."

"Christine hasn't been staying there."

"You know who else lives on Maple Street, don't you?" Parker asked.

"Um… yeah."

"Then why did you pick a place there?"

"Isn't it obvious?"

After Parker went inside, I drove through the parking lot and looked for anyone sitting in their car. There was no one. There weren't even any security cameras on the outside of the building, at least none that I could see.

Parker had lived in Shadow Wood her whole life. She'd grown up in a small town where your neighbors were always watching and listening. They were always sticking their noses in one another's business. They were always talking. I'd grown up here too, and now I was doing the same thing. Maybe that's why I had gotten so excited about watching Jimmie through the bar window that night.

I'd left Shadow Wood to get away from such behavior, thinking I was better than these people, but now
I was back in town and acting the same way. I guess it
was true what they say: you can take the boy out of the
small town, but you'll never take the small town out of
the boy.

CHAPTER 26

I GAVE Parker the address. She told me she'd be there by eleven thirty. Not having stocked my fridge with anything other than ice, I asked what she might want to drink. She liked gin and tonics. So did I. Instead of waiting in the hotel parking lot again to observe who was coming and going, I went to the liquor store.

"I can't believe you rented a duplex right across the street from Linda fucking Reyes," Parker said, standing at my picture window shortly after she arrived. She opened the curtains wide to look out. I almost felt the need to scold her in case someone was watching, and because I never opened the curtains, but it didn't matter. She'd changed out of her uniform and into a pair of nice jeans and a blouse. She'd put on makeup. Maybe she thought this was a date.

"Me neither. I'm not working right now, so please don't remind me what a waste of money this is for me," I said, handing her a gin and tonic.

I admitted to her I had still never met Linda in person. I told Parker how Linda had shown up at my father's funeral. I told her about the letter Linda had written to Melaine and about when I first found out how long her affair with my father was.

"So here I am," I said. I quickly finished my drink and made another.

"You're like a spy or something!" Parker said with a dramatic tone.

"I guess so." I shrugged off her excitement.

I showed Parker my notebooks where I'd recorded Linda's daily routines. I also showed her Nate and Christine's activities.

"Why were you writing down what they did?"

"I don't know, honestly. I looked at their house when it was on the market, since it was so close to Linda. Being across the street, this was much more convenient. I was here when they moved in and just started writing it down."

"You know this could help the cops figure out what happened to Nate, right?"

"I don't think so, and I don't want to bring any unwanted attention to myself."

"Why?"

"Well, I did something," I said.

I didn't mean for that to sound so bizarre, but it did. Parker raised her brows and twisted her mouth.

"What does that mean?" she asked.

"If I tell you, you can't say anything to anyone."

"Was it illegal?" she whispered like a child.

"Ha! Yes, it was definitely illegal."

"I won't tell," she said, crossing her heart with a single finger making a sharp jab across her chest. "But first, I think I'm going to need another drink."

My glass had also run dry, so I mixed another round of gin and tonics.

"So, tell me," she said.

"Well, I've been inside Linda's house."

"What? Oh my God! No!"

"Yeah, it was brief. And no, I didn't take anything."

"What did you do?"

"I just looked around. I guess I was looking for signs that my dad had been there."

"Did you find anything?"

"The planner on her desk had the Milieu written down every Friday. That's what led me to the restaurant," I said, not bothering to tell her about the copy of Dad's obituary I'd found in Linda's photo album.

"You should go back. I could go in with you," Parker said, a little too excited about the possibilities of such a mission.

"Nah, sorry. I admit I had no business going in the first place, but two people would be pretty risky."

"You have to go back in!"

"Why?"

"I'm pretty sure she has a logbook or a list of all the members. If we found it, we could give it to the cops!"

"That's clever, but they'd want to know how we got it, and didn't you say the sheriff is involved with the Pink Poodles?"

"Damn it!" Parker yelled out after a few seconds of thought.

I shared in her frustration. I didn't say it out loud, but her idea made me want to go back inside Linda's house just to see if I could find any records of the Pink Poodle Club. I had not known about it before. At least now I would know what I was looking for if I went inside again. I didn't mention my thoughts to Parker because she'd been too keen about tagging along.

I could tell Parker was eager to accomplish something right now. She suggested we go down to the park to look at where Nate's body was found. I didn't want to go back out. We'd each had a few drinks, so driving was out of the question.

"You live so close. We could walk," she said.

I agreed, only because for the first time in quite a while, I felt very carefree. I had not felt like this since the night I went home with that guy, something with an S, from Backstreet. Parker was beginning to feel like a friend, and I could use one of those right now in Shadow Wood.

Despite my slow gin and tonic buzz and feeling like a mischievous teenager with no curfew as we walked to the end of the street, I checked the windows of the neighboring houses out of the corners of my eyes. I looked for any movement from the windows, someone peeking through the blinds, or the slight shift of a curtain being drawn. I checked for anyone sitting out on their porches or in their vehicles in the driveways.

As we walked, I asked Parker why she had stayed in town, just to give her something different to talk about in case someone did come outside and overheard us.

"I never thought about leaving," Parker said. "I never thought about staying either, for that matter. I've always just lived in the moment and gone wherever it takes me. It's never taken me very far. What about you?"

"I always wanted to leave right after high school, but I waited two years," I said.

"Why's that?"

"I felt like my parents' divorce held me back. My dad left us halfway through my senior year. I worried about my mom being alone, so I stayed here and went to the community college."

"You went to Shadow Wood Community College?"

"Yep."

"So did I! What do you think you would have done had you stayed here?" Parker asked.

"I don't know. Killed myself? Sorry, that's a horrible thing to say. I guess I never thought about that since I never wanted to stay."

"I was the exact opposite. I never thought about leaving."

"Not once?"

"Nope. Never did. I mean, I guess if the opportunity presented itself, I would have gone. I just never went looking for it."

"You always planned on staying right here?"

"Toby, I've never planned anything. I've always just sort of lived day by day. Call me crazy, but life is just easier that way for me."

"But don't you think we all crave consistency in some way?"

"Oh yes, too much of it, even. That's why we are always planning out our whole lives instead of just living them, isn't it? Get out of high school. Move away. Go to college. Get a job. Get married. Have kids. It's all too much, don't you think? I stress out now just thinking about all of that."

I envied her for being able to do that. She was probably happier because of it. I'd never been able to do that, just let go and not worry about anything. I was always planning ahead. I couldn't imagine not having that uniformity in my life, even though I didn't have it now. I, like most people, did crave it. It was because I'd always had it and even the most minor bump that knocked everything off course felt like a colossal disaster.

It was why I felt guilty about losing my job. It was why I was obsessing over my father's affair. It was why Parker and I were going to a park where a dead man's body had been found after midnight. It's also why Parker wasn't too worried about who might be watching us, but suddenly I was.

I knew this was the most exciting thing Parker had done in a very long time, possibly ever. It felt that way to me too, thanks to the gin.

We'd reached the end of Maple Street. I pointed out the vacant lot where the car had been found. No cars were coming down the highway in the distance now, but we rushed across the street and into the park to avoid being seen.

"Isn't this exciting?" Parker chirped as she grabbed my arm. "Wait! What do we do if a cop shows up?"

"Run and hide?"

"Good idea! And then meet back at your place? If I'm not there by sunrise, then you know I've been caught. Or I might be dead."

"Don't say that!" I said, loosening the grip she had on my arm.

"We need a signal in case we get separated. Can you make a bird sound?" Parker asked, followed by, "*Ka-kaw!*"

"Shhh! No bird in Shadow Wood has ever made that sound."

"You're right! What sound *does* a loon make? I'm not sure if I've ever actually heard one."

"No bird noises! Let's just be quick and have a look around."

Had I been sober, her banter would have irritated me. This was exciting for me too. It reminded me of how much fun I had with Ash and how he lived in the moment sometimes. It made me feel like a teenager again, one who never worried about consequences. It made me wonder if Parker had ever been to the city— or if she'd ever been outside of Shadow Wood, for that matter.

We rounded the lake and could see a long strand of yellow police tape in the distance, tied around the trunk of a tree. The tape had been cut. It dangled at the base of the tree. I glanced over my shoulder just to make sure we weren't being followed. You always get that feeling that you are being watched when you are in someplace you shouldn't be in the middle of the night. Intuition, I guess.

Parker fell quiet as we got closer. Her grin faded. It reminded me of how me and Melaine had grown quiet when visiting the cemetery. I pointed out where the weeds and brush had been trimmed back for the investigators to search the outlying area where the body had been found. A cluster of flower bouquets surrounding a teddy bear formed a makeshift memorial just off the running path. A half-deflated mylar balloon strangled the bear's neck and flapped against the ground like a fish out of water. We both stood still on the trail, too afraid we might desecrate the location by stepping into the grass.

"Is it just me, or do you kind of wish there'd been a chalk outline?" Parker finally asked.

"I think that's only in movies," I said.

There was a reflection or a glimmer near the ground on the other side of the path. At first I thought it might be another balloon, but it was too small and rectangular. Then I recognized it. It was the moonlight flickering off the front of someone's cell phone.

"Did you see that?" Parker whispered.

I started to whisper back, but then Parker called out in a loud tone, "Who's there?"

Twigs snapped. Leaves rustled. What looked like a shadow to me was indeed a person in dark clothes, now sprinting away from us. Someone else had been there. My intuition had been right. Someone had been watching us.

CHAPTER 27

"Do you think we should—"

I started to speak, but Parker was already running off the path and across the park, chasing after the person who had been watching us. I kept my own pace and let Parker run ahead of me. I was afraid the person might have a gun, or they might hide behind a tree and ambush us. At this point it was too late to talk Parker out of it, and there was no use calling out for her to slow down. It seemed she had a habit of reacting in the moment. The gin was probably to blame.

There was a concrete ravine at the back edge of the park. If we'd stayed on the path, it would have led to a bridge that allowed you to cross the ravine, though it was very shallow. There was a small parking lot on the other side tucked between the park and a grove of trees.

"Shit! Shit! Shit!" Parker called out just as I caught up to her.

I heard splashes of water. She had foregone the bridge and gotten her feet wet. When I caught up to her, red taillights were already fleeing the parking lot.

"Did you get a good look at the car?" I asked.

"Yeah, and based on the size of the driver, I think it might have been Christine. Whoever it was, there was a pink poodle sticker on the window," she said, bending over to catch her breath.

"We should get out of here," I said.

Going back the way we came, we cut back across the park. We were quiet during the slow walk back to my place. It took a while for Parker to stop breathing so heavily. I asked her several times if she was okay. She'd just close her eyes and nod. It was either the gin refusing to let go, or she was sobering up and realizing how scary all of this had been.

"That was crazy," she finally said as we neared my duplex, having caught her breath.

"You wanna know something even crazier?"

"What?"

"Look over there," I said, pointing across the street.

"Fuck me!" she said in a loud whisper.

Christine's car was parked on the street in front of their house. I looked up the hill, and there were lights on inside. I could tell Parker wanted to jet across the street and knock on the door. I grabbed her arm and steered her toward my porch.

"Let's sit out here and see if anyone comes out. I bet she's just grabbing some things and intends to leave again. Is that the car you just saw at the park?"

"Definitely," she said.

We watched as the lights in the house went out one by one. They had left the porch light off. Someone stepped out and locked the door. They hurried down the steps to the car. It was someone dressed all in black. They were wearing an oversized hoodie with the hood pulled up to cover their head and face. They were carry-ing a duffel bag. Based on their size, it could have been

Christine, but when they reached the car, they pushed their hood back, and we could see it wasn't Christine.

Parker looked at me. I held a finger to my mouth just in case she had the urge to call out to them. The man got into the car and sped away. Seeing Christine in the park and back at her house would have made more sense, but I'd never seen this man before.

"Who was that?" Parker said.

"I don't know. Do you think that's who was in the park?"

"Definitely, but why were they there?"

"It's someone who knows Christine. They are driving her car. They had keys to the house."

It was getting late. I didn't mind Parker being there, but I didn't want to waste time obsessing over another person who had been introduced to the drama. I wanted to know more about the swingers' club at the hotel, so I asked Parker to tell me what she knew about it. Now that she was away from the hotel, she was much more willing to talk.

It had been going on since the late eighties, when the hotel was on the verge of closing due to lack of business during the off-season. It seemed our banquets, proms, and the community's local happenings weren't enough to keep it afloat. It needed more consistent revenue. My dad's affair with Linda had started in the seventies and ended in the early nineties. This led me to believe he probably wasn't involved in the club.

To become a member, you had to be willing to pay for a complete block of rooms. At first, couples might have to pay out two or three times a year. There were enough members now for everyone to split the cost of the rooms with another couple and only have to pay once a year.

"How many couples are there?" I asked.

"Oh, at least sixty or so," she said. "There might have been at least seventy couples once."

"Wow! That's a lot of swingers for this town."

"Not all of them are from here. I think Linda has recruited them from neighboring cities over the years."

"So Linda started the club?"

"I'm not sure if she started it, but she's in charge of it now. Makes sense. She's been on every board or served on every council in town. Why not this one too?"

"How does Linda benefit from it? I don't think she's seeing anyone, so she doesn't participate."

"I'm pretty sure the hotel gives her a kickback for bringing in business, but I'm not sure."

Parker explained that the rooms—always with two king-size beds—were booked months in advance. Couples arrived early in the evening and usually had dinner in the restaurant, which was also good for business. Then they mingled in the hotel bar afterward. Key cards were drawn at random from a bowl throughout the night to determine which couples would share a room for the evening.

"It's kept totally random to prevent couples from taking a preference to one another. Two couples can share the same room two weeks in a row, but after that, you're encouraged to mix it up and move on to someone else. Two couples share partners and stay in the same room rather than going off with someone else just to avoid issues of jealously."

"How do you know all of this?"

"Various sources over the years, but one very reliable source once worked at the hotel."

"This all just blows my mind!"

"There have always been reporters poking around. Remember, I thought you were one. I don't think anything has ever been printed, though. None of the members have been exposed. Everything is kept pretty hush-hush, and it's managed to go on without a single spectacle that I'm aware of until now."

"You mean Nate's death?"

"Yes."

"Did you ever see who Nate and Christine shared a room with?"

"No, I only work in the restaurant. I'm never in the bar, so I rarely see the couples split off together unless I'm on a break and pass through the lobby late in the evening. That's why I think you should go back inside Linda's house."

"Why?"

"She keeps detailed records of who ends up together each week."

"What?" I couldn't believe what I was hearing.

"Yep. I told you. It's not just people showing up to have an orgy. It's pretty detailed. There are rules. They don't condone rule-breakers."

"Has anyone ever been kicked out of the club?"

"I'm not sure, but I've worked there a long time, and I've seen couples come and go. Some couples who you get used to seeing just stop coming. New couples aren't allowed in very often. There seems to be a pre-ferred number of members, but I don't know the ins and outs of that. Everyone on the inside is pretty tight-lipped about all of it, and anyone working at the hotel doesn't ask questions. So, yeah, I'm sure someone's been kicked out at some point."

"Do you think if I could get my hands on Linda's record books and we could see who Nate and Christine hooked up with, one of those might be the killer?"

"It's a good theory, especially if we could determine if that person had been kicked out of the club."

"If they were kicked out recently, then there's a good chance Linda might know they killed Nate. Or she'd at least know why someone would have it out for him."

"Yep, and if Linda keeps records of the members and who they sleep with, I'm sure she keeps a logbook of who leaves the club and maybe even why they left."

"Okay," I said. "I'll do it."

She looked at me and smiled. She raised her eyebrows. She started clapping like a giddy child when I told her I'd go back into Linda's house. I told her she couldn't go in with me, but she could be my eyes and ears on the outside if she wanted to be a part of it. I was perfectly okay with handling this by myself. I'd done it before, but not at night. So it didn't hurt to have Parker's help.

"Okay. Should we get earbuds or hidden communication devices? I know a guy."

"We could just use our cell phones," I said.

"That works too. When do we do this?"

"She goes out to lunch almost every day. She gets her hair done on Thursdays and is gone for a bit longer. That's when I went in the last time, but I think I might need more time. Friday night would be our best chance. We know she's gone most of the night, and it would be dark outside."

"I'll take off next Friday, then. That work?"

"Okay, next Friday works."

"We're going in," she said in a serious tone.

"*I'm* going in," I stressed.

"Right! You're right. You'll go in, and I'll be your eyes and ears from here."

I said good night to Parker and waited on the porch to make sure she got to her car okay. I wasn't convinced that involving her in this was a good idea, but my own involvement also seemed nuts. I'd only hoped to find out from Linda why she had an affair with my father. I still wanted to find that out. Yet instead I'd somehow taken it upon myself to investigate a murder and infiltrate my hometown's sex club.

Yep, this was definitely nuts. I kept thinking about what Ash, or even my mother, would think of me for doing this. I had to block them out if I was going to go through with it. I'd let my guilt defeat me for my erratic behavior in the past. Something else was taking control of my actions now. I felt no shame or guilt whatsoever.

CHAPTER 28

THE FOLLOWING week I monitored Linda's house to make sure her schedule stayed the same. I debated on going into her house on Thursday, like I'd done before, just to get it out of the way. It felt like a good idea because I wouldn't have to involve Parker. However, I knew Parker would be disappointed, so I waited until Friday as planned.

Linda's schedule was by the book, except on Thursday, after getting her hair cut, I followed her to the florist, where she purchased a small wrapped bouquet. I had a feeling I knew what she was going to do with the flowers, and I was right. Her next stop was the park. I sat in my car and watched as she got out and walked the path to where Nate's body had been found.

The park was crowded with some other people also adding flowers and stuffed animals to Nate's memorial. Linda didn't seem to mind who saw her there. She didn't speak to anyone and patiently waited her turn on the walking path behind other mourners. She waved at someone she knew; they waved back. She laid her flowers near the others and then walked back to her car.

When I returned to the duplex, I checked the *Shadow Wood Gazette* and learned that Nate's funeral was being held today in Arkansas.

On Friday, Parker showed up right on time. The sun was setting, and Linda had just left to go to the hotel. Parker was dressed all in black, including black sunglasses and a black beret. Minus the white face, she looked like a mime. She was carrying her purse and a paper bag.

"What are you wearing?" I asked with a slight laugh.

"Too much?"

"Just a bit. You look like a cat burglar."

"I wanted to look the part."

"What part? I told you I'm going inside. I just need you to keep watch on the outside."

"Am I going to hide in the bushes? Should I have worn camo?" she asked.

"Ha! No! You're going to stay here and watch from the window," I told her.

"Oh. Well, shit."

I could tell she was disappointed.

"Guess we won't need these, then," she said, holding up the bag.

"What is that?"

"I borrowed my dad's walkie-talkies."

"Hmm… it might be quicker to use those over texting," I said. I was being honest, but I also wanted to cheer her up.

"Yes!" she shouted, throwing her fist into the air.

She turned on both transceivers and made sure they were on the same channel. She spoke into one and then talked back in the other. She assured me they were on a private channel and no one else could hear us.

I explained to Parker that Linda parked on the street out front. I told her how I'd used the alley to access her backyard and went into her house through the back door. I wasn't too worried since Linda had never come home early on a Friday. I didn't tell Parker what time to expect Linda because I wanted her to keep a watch for me at the window since I'd never done this at night before. I promised Parker I'd turn on the walkie-talkie as soon as I entered the house.

We agreed it was too risky for me to steal any club logbooks if I found them. If Linda discovered they were missing, she might suspect a burglary and get the cops involved. Instead, I planned to take photos of the entries. I would look for all of Nate and Christine's entries and determine who their hotel roommates were if they were listed. I was also hoping to find out if my dad had ever been a member early on, but I kept that part to myself.

I left Parker at the window, tucked behind my curtains with my binoculars. I'd changed into sweats and tennis shoes to look the part. I walked the block just as I'd done many times in the past. I didn't come across any neighbors outside, but I still wanted to look like I was just out walking in case someone was watching. I walked the length of the alley to see if there was anyone outside in their back yards that might see anything. All was quiet as usual.

I knelt beneath Linda's weeping willow, crawled across her backyard, and was standing at her back door just like before without any problems. I checked my phone. It had only been seven minutes since I left the duplex. Parker was already texting and asking for an update. I checked to make sure the spare key was still in the potted plant. It was. I texted back, letting her know

I'd just reached the door and was about to go in. She reminded me to turn on my walkie-talkie as soon as I was inside.

"I'm in," I spoke into the radio.

"I just thought of something," Parker said.

"What?"

"We should have come up with code names."

"We're on a private channel, right? We don't have to use our names."

"I still want a code name."

"We'll do that next time."

"Oooh, you think you might need to go in again?"

"I will if we don't stop talking so I can hurry up and look around."

She went silent.

"You there?" I asked.

"Yes. You said we should stop talking," she said, sounding defeated.

"How are things looking outside? I need an update," I said, hoping to bring her back up. It worked.

"Good! No signs of anyone. Over and out."

I clipped the radio onto one of my belt loops and then carried on through the house. All of the photo albums I'd looked at before were still in place. I checked the one that had my father's obituary in it. Nothing had been added. I moved on.

"I'm in the office," I said into the walkie-talkie, attempting to keep Parker engaged.

"Is there a large filing cabinet or a bookshelf? What do we do if the logbooks are in a safe? I've got a crowbar in my trunk."

"No crowbar! Give me a minute and let me look around."

"Over."

There were bookshelves, but the contents were mostly romance paperbacks and a few mysteries. There was no visible safe. I checked behind the photos on the walls and didn't find one there either. If there was a safe, it was probably in her bedroom.

I checked the top of the desk. Her calendar was still there. I noticed it was propped up. Something had been slid underneath it. I raised it and found an address book. I checked the front cover, and there was a pink poodle sticker stuck to the front. I grabbed the radio.

"I think I found an address book of all the members," I said.

"Check and see if Nate and Christine are listed."

I turned to the latest entries. Nate and Christine were there, with only one new entry after them. As I looked at the entries, I noticed Linda had written "PAID" and a date in the column next to the names. Some entries had more than one date listed. These must be the dates they paid for the rooms at the hotel. I snapped a few photos with my phone and sent them to Parker.

"Sending you photos," I said into the radio.

"I got them! Over!"

A small two-drawer filing cabinet with a lock was under the desk. I had not noticed it when I came here before. I tried one of the drawers and discovered the cabinet was unlocked. When I bent over to open it, the walkie-talkie came unclipped from my belt loop and fell on the floor. I tried to grab for it, but I must have bumped the knob and knocked it off our channel. It emitted a loud, screeching noise as it hit the floor. I grabbed it, turned the volume down, and then sat it on the desk.

The top drawer was filled with hanging files labeled HOUSE, CREDIT CARD, UTILITIES. It was the typical everyday-life stuff you'd expect to find in a filing cabinet under your parent's desk. I flipped through the files to see if anything stood out that could be related to the club. There was nothing, but the bottom drawer made up for it.

"Found the logbooks!" I texted Parker.

"Jackpot! Send photos!" she sent back.

The bottom drawer contained a stack of notebooks. I expected them to be elaborate captain's logbooks like they used on a cruise ship or something; these were just plain old spiral notebooks, the kind every high school kid used. Inside them, though, Linda's notekeeping was meticulous. One page was devoted to each Friday. Everything was dated. Room numbers were listed. Under each room number, four names were written: two men and two women. It had to be the couples who shared a room each Friday night.

It struck me that Linda might carry the latest notebook with her to the hotel each Friday, but there was also the chance it might get lost too, and it contained relatively private information. Maybe she recorded the information on her phone or a piece of paper and then transposed it into the notebooks later.

My theory was correct. The notebooks were in order by year. I pulled out the latest and turned to the most recent page. Tonight's date had been written at the top, but the rest of the page was blank. I flipped back a few pages to find Nate and Christine. Their names were listed only three times, which seemed accurate since they had not lived on Maple Street very long. This meant they weren't members before moving into the house across the street.

I grabbed my phone and snapped photos of each page. The couple they'd shared a room with were the same on their second and third weeks, but a different couple was listed next to Nate and Christine on the first week. I recognized the names and was stunned. I was just about to text the photos to Parker when the beams from a car's headlight hit the office window. I ducked down and crawled to the window to look outside. It was Linda!

Why had Parker not told me? That was when I remembered I'd dropped the walkie-talkie. She'd probably been trying to communicate with me. I put the notebook back in the file cabinet. I hesitated for a minute. I had not had a chance to look back at the older logbooks to search for my father's name. I quickly thumbed back through the logbooks and pulled out the one from the year Dad had left Mom. I also pulled out the one from the year before that. I tucked them under my shirt.

I grabbed the walkie-talkie and raced through the house and toward the back door. Part of me thought I was going in the wrong direction. It felt as if I was moving in slow motion, or perhaps I was forgetting things. I knew I was just a few feet from the back door, but suddenly I was in a carnival fun house and struggling to get out.

Were there lights I should have turned off? Had I left any muddy footprints Linda might notice? Did I close the filing cabinet?

Where's the fucking walkie-talkie? I picked it up! It was right here in my hand! I patted my pockets to make sure I had my phone too. I did.

I had always been this cautious guy who had to check to make sure the stove was off before leaving the apartment, even if I had not used the stove in days. But there was no time to let my OCD kick in now. I had to get out!

I heard someone's footsteps!

They were just my own.

Was that a door opening? Had Linda made it inside yet?

No! It was just me—trying to open the back door!

I fumbled with the knob, trying not to make a noise in case Linda was coming in the front door right at the same time I was going out the back.

I ran across the yard, not bothering with trying to crawl across the yard to avoid being seen. Once I was past the willow tree, I turned back to look at the house.

All was quiet—except for my heart frantically beating against my chest and the sound of rushing blood coursing through my ears.

In the alley, I knelt with my hands on my knees to catch my breath. I looked around again for a sign of anyone. I was alone.

I jogged to the end of the alley, anxious to get farther away from Linda's house as fast as I could. I reached the cross street and began walking back toward Maple Street. As I got closer, I heard voices.

It was Parker. She was on the sidewalk in front of the duplex. She was next to her car and talking to Linda from across the street. Linda was standing on her side of the street in front of her house. I couldn't make out what they were saying. They weren't whispering. It just sounded like friendly talk, any conversation two neighbors might call out to each other when they crossed paths while out getting the mail or taking out the trash. *Oh, hey, neighbor! How's life treating ya?* It even sounded like they knew each other.

I waited for them to say good night and for Linda to walk up the steps to her house. I checked my phone. There were still no texts from Parker. Why had she not warned me?

I watched as Parker closed her car door and walked back up the steps to the duplex. She'd slipped a coat on over her black outfit. She had her phone in her hand and was texting as she went inside my front door. My phone pinged. I knew it would be from her.

Her text read: *Linda!*

I sent back: *Saw her car. Got out in time. On my way back now.*

The timing was off. This was all very strange. I turned right, away from the duplex. I circled the block at a quick pace. I decided to go back to the duplex through my back door instead of through the front. I didn't want Linda's doorbell camera to catch me, just in case.

I had tried to be careful inside her house, but I could have left something askew or knocked something over while rushing to get out. I rechecked my pocket to make sure I had taken the walkie-talkie. Had I closed the file cabinet? Did I lock the door? It was too late to worry about any of that now.

What I did worry about was why Parker had not warned me sooner. I knew the walkie-talkie not working was a good alibi. I bet she'd say she had texted earlier but that it had not gone through, even though I saw her texting me while going back inside and I got that text message just fine.

As I reached my back door, something else occurred to me. I'd thought about the logbook. It was Parker who had suggested that Linda kept a record of the members. Earlier I had wondered if Linda took the logbook with her to the hotel. After seeing the contents of the filing cabinet, I knew she didn't.

But how did Parker know that Linda even kept records? She said she only worked in the restaurant. She said she never saw anything. Parker knew a lot, and I thought she'd shared all of it with me. But now I was pretty sure there was more that she had not shared.

I didn't think she had set me up, but maybe she'd lied about what she'd known. Perhaps she knew Linda and had told her our plans. That seemed odd, but maybe I'd trusted Parker too soon. I wanted to be wrong about all of this, but now I just didn't know.

As I walked back, I looked at the photos of the names I'd seen listed next to Nate and Christine. For their second and third weeks, it was Hunter and Celeste Lowery both times. I recognized Celeste's name from the local newspaper right away. It was the names listed next to them on their first week that had shaken me. It was my sister-in-law and my brother, Samuel.

CHAPTER 29

PARKER WAS standing in my kitchen pouring a drink when I came in the door. She looked at me, and her eyes grew wide.

"Oh my God! That was intense!" she said.

"Yes, it was. Pour me one of those," I said, trying to study her demeanor to see if anything seemed different.

"Coming right up!"

We sat down on my sofa, and I asked her about what had happened. As I anticipated, she said she tried to reach me on the radio, but I wasn't answering. I told her I had dropped it and messed up the knob or lost the channel. I told her how I'd seen the lights from Linda's car and looked out the window.

When she didn't hear back from me, she ran outside to try to stall Linda. I was glad she did. Parker had pretended she was getting her coat out of her car. She told Linda that she was new to the neighborhood, and they just exchanged polite hellos.

"You don't think she recognized you from the hotel?" I asked.

"I don't think so. It's dark out. She rarely eats in the restaurant. I don't think I've ever had to wait on her."

Parker said she had also tried to text me several times before running outside to stall her. I showed her my phone. There was only one text, which I assume I saw her sending when she was going back into my house. I told her I got that one after I was already out of Linda's house and headed back. She showed me her phone, and she had indeed texted several times. I had not received any of those earlier texts yet, but my suspicions about Parker started to fade. I felt she was definitely on my side and could be trusted.

"So? Did you find Christine and Nate in the logbooks?" she asked.

"I did."

I picked up my phone to pull up the photos. It started to ping over and over again as all of her texts came through at once.

"There they are," Parker said. "Damn cell phones."

I was relieved. I still wondered how she knew about Linda's logbooks, but I decided not to ask. It didn't matter if she knew Linda or not. She had indeed tried to warn me, and she had stalled Linda so I could get out. I was just glad I had not agreed to let Parker go in with me.

"At least I got out in time. Thanks for stalling her. Look at this," I said, handing her my phone after I deleted the photo that showed my brother's name.

I explained how there was a notebook for each year, and each page was devoted to a Friday, listing the names and room numbers. As she looked through the photos, I told her about the address book marked with who had paid for the rooms for the night.

"Christine and Nate were only listed on two recent Fridays, so I don't think they were members before moving here. I didn't have time to look back at any other dates further back. So this is the couple who shared a room with them on both of those nights," I said, showing her the phone. I intentionally lied and said I'd only seen Nate and Christine listed twice.

"Oh my God! Do you know who this is?" Parker said, reading the names.

"Yep. It's the reporter."

"Hunter is her husband. They've been Pink Poodle members for a while now."

"Should I know them? Did either of them go to school here?" I asked.

"No, Celeste went to a private school and graduated from Union University in Jackson. She and Hunter met there. I'm not sure where he's from."

"Why come back here to work for the *Gazette*?"

"Her parents own it."

"What does Hunter do?"

"A banker or something to do with finance."

If I didn't already know about the sex club, I would have known exactly what kind of people Hunter and Celeste Lowery were. I could even guess how they voted in the last election. Wealthy conservatives always afforded their children the best schooling money could buy. They didn't blink at the two-thousand-dollar monthly tuition for their teen's private school education. Anything so their precious Graham or Camila wouldn't have to mingle with poor people at recess. Even though Union University was an hour away, it was still a Christian college.

Yet these children grew up and remained closed-minded, just like their parents. That's why they came back home and lived in a bubble. They'd never been exposed to anything in the outside, real world. They'd been around people just like them their whole lives, and they weren't about to take risks and make changes even if given a chance. Their hometown, their rich family, and their arrogant friends were all safe to them.

They hated people like me, even though I was from here. I was everything their parents had shielded them from their whole lives. I didn't have a lot of money. I'd grown up in the country outside of town. I'd left and moved to the city. I wasn't a conservative. I never voted Republican. I was a homosexual.

If Hunter wasn't from here, that was okay. I'm sure he was born and raised in another town just like this one. Celeste had refused to follow him home. She'd told him on their first date that she was going to move back home and work for her parents. Moving to Shadow Wood was the only way he'd get to be with her. These women always got their way.

I knew what they looked like too. I knew how they dressed. I knew what names they'd give their children. Boys got a cowboy name: Logan, Dylan, or Austin. Girls always got clumpy names that were never spelled how they sounded: Ayn, Cate, or Alyse.

These young couples didn't move to Maple Street, which was why Nate and Christine had seemed like such an anomaly at first. No, the houses on this street were either too small or too old for the Lowcrys. Couples like Hunter and Celeste wanted bulky new homes in some subdivision where all the houses looked the same. If their parents had land, they built a new house near them. They never strayed far from their flock.

While the house was being built, they'd make changes to the number of bedrooms or where the bathrooms were located. They hired interior decorators and painters. They had maids and gardeners. They took extravagant vacations abroad or on private yachts.

So why the sex club? Whose idea was that? My first guess was Hunter. Maybe he didn't come from money. Perhaps he was a city boy. I found that hard to believe, but it was possible.

"Do you think Celeste will talk to us?" I said.

"I doubt it. We already know too much. She'd shut down, especially since she works for the paper. You've read what she wrote about Nate."

"Yeah. Pretty one-sided. Lots of information that sounded like she either knew something or was leading the police on."

Parker was right, and girls like Celeste were good at keeping secrets. With her being a reporter, we'd have to play a game of quid pro quo to get any information out of her, and even then she might lie or be very selective in what she said. But if her husband was the reason they were involved with the Pink Poodles, he might be a bit more impartial.

We finished our drinks, and I walked Parker to her car. I offered to take the couch and let her have my bed if she wanted to sleep over, but she had an early shift in the morning. As she drove away, I hurried back to the porch. I was anxious to be closer to the house and under its roof, shielded from the night or from some imaginary outsider who might be lurking in the bushes. Suddenly I was a child afraid of the dark and clinging to their security blanket, or a horror-flick girl stopping to look over her shoulder because she feels someone watching. I had reason to feel that way.

On the porch, I turned to look over at Linda's house before going inside. The light in her office was on. I could make out her silhouette standing at the window. The curtains were slightly parted.

Linda was watching.

CHAPTER 30

I DON'T know why I cared about Parker seeing my brother's name listed in the logbook. Deleting the photo and not telling her was just a habit, that mentality again that's embedded in everyone who grows up in a small town. You pick it up from your parents. No one teaches you. It's one of those unspoken lessons to attempt to keep things private or secret.

It's why a small town like Shadow Wood was so full of secrets. We gossiped about each other when a secret was revealed, but we did everything possible to avoid "airing our own dirty laundry," as adults used to say. Parker and I were deep in the town's soiled undergarments, yet I was still hiding my own.

Samuel and I were not very close. He was much older than me. He'd moved out of the house and married his high school sweetheart, Blythe, before I was done with junior high. I could not recall the last time I'd had a conversation with him on the phone, if ever, but it wasn't hard to come up with an excuse to call him now.

"How are you doing?" I asked.

"Hey, Toby. I'm good. You?"

"I'm fine. I thought I'd call you and Melaine and see how you were doing."

"I haven't talked to Melaine in a few days, but I'm sure she's okay."

I tried to talk about Dad, hoping that might spark a conversation between us. Samuel didn't have much to share. He was just like our father, who had always been more of a listener on the phone. He gave a quiet laugh to a few of the memories of Dad I shared. He listened with patience, but I knew he didn't like talking on the phone all that much, so I got to the point.

"I heard Nate Perkins was murdered. You remember him?"

"No, not really."

"Did he go to school with you?" I said, sounding just like our mother. Nate was younger than Samuel, so I knew they had not gone to school together. I was just trying to come up with something to see if Samuel would admit they knew each other.

"I don't think so."

"Everyone's been talking about his murder here. It's all over the news."

"Yeah, it is here too. There's something about it in the newspaper every day."

When I mentioned the Pink Poodle Club, it was hard to judge my brother's reaction by phone. His conversation was already stiff. He wasn't hiding anything. He was like that in person too, a quiet Southern man of few words, rarely speaking unless spoken to. If you didn't know him, you might think he was angry or that he was ignoring you, but he was always the more cognizant man in the room. Listening. Learning.

"A friend of mine thought she saw you and Blythe at the hotel," I said, not sure where to go from here.

"Oh yeah? Who was that?"

"Just an old friend from high school. She works in the restaurant."

"We've had dinner in the restaurant a time or two. Good steaks."

"You and Blythe aren't involved in the Pink Poo-dle Club, are you?" I asked, not believing what I had just said. I felt like a teenager who'd been building up the courage to ask their parents to borrow the car.

"What makes you think that?"

"Just curious."

"Toby?"

"Yeah?"

"Why don't you stay out of your brother's business, and I'll stay out of yours."

"So you are—"

The line went dead. He'd hung up.

I wasn't mad at him. How could I be? I still couldn't believe I'd had the audacity to call and ask him that. What did I expect him to say? It helped that I lived, usually, in another town that was several miles away. I deserved his response. It was my fault for prying into his business. A part of me felt like dialing Melaine's number just to ask her if she knew what our brother had been doing, but I knew she didn't. It was just me revert-ing back to how I would have acted as a child wanting to tattle or gossip. I called Ash and told him instead.

"Oh my God! Seriously?" he said when I told him.

"Yep."

"And how did you find this out?"

I should have lied and told him I saw Samuel at the hotel, but that would have just sounded like specula-tion. Feeling like an antsy teen again, I went ahead and told him the truth.

"You are going to get arrested, Toby! Who are you? Breaking into people's houses? C'mon!" he scolded.

"I'm not going to do it again. I don't have any reason," I said, trying to assure him, but I knew I sounded stupid.

"You didn't have any reason to do it before or the first time you did it, for that matter."

Silence.

"So, what have you been up to?" I asked, trying to turn the conversation away from me.

"Don't try to change the subject, Toby. This isn't like you, and you know it."

"This isn't like me? What's that supposed to mean?"

"You know exactly what it means. If there was anyone else listening to this who didn't know you like I do, they'd think you were crazy."

"Oh, you mean like my family?"

"Especially your family! I feel like you need a intervention or something."

"Don't you dare tell my fucking siblings or my mother what is going on here!"

"Why are you yelling at me? See, Toby, this is what I'm talking about. This isn't you."

"I'm sorry. I'm sorry. I didn't mean to lose my temper."

"It's okay. Just promise me that you'll be careful."

"I promise."

Ash was right, though. I wasn't this person. This wasn't me. I had never done anything illegal in my life. Nothing about any of this appealed to me. There were no temptations. I just needed someone—anyone—to tell me the truth, to give me answers.

Answers.

That was all I wanted.

I sat down at my desk and opened the top drawer where I had put the logbooks I'd stolen from Linda's house. That night, I'd waited until Parker had left before taking them out of my shirt. I didn't want to show them to her. She would have questioned why I had taken the logbooks from earlier years, and I didn't want to explain my reason. I also didn't want her to touch them. I figured the fewer people that handled them, the better.

I thumbed through the books, checking each and every page of the two years I'd taken. My father's name was nowhere to be found. I had hoped that would give me some sort of relief, but it didn't.

I could forget about Nate and Christine. I could forget about the Pink Poodle Club or Celeste and Hunter Lowery. I could even forget about my brother and his wife being involved in the club. But I couldn't forget about Linda's relationship with my father.

I still wanted to reach out to her. I still needed answers. I still felt like Linda was the only one who could give them to me.

CHAPTER 31

In Shadow Wood, if you want to know something about a person, you don't have to throw a stone very far to find someone you can ask. That's why I decided to call my sister. I was not going to tell her about the conversation I'd had with Samuel. I did tell her that I'd called him just to say hello so that if they compared notes, they'd know I had indeed called both of them just as I said. My main reason for calling her was because I wanted to ask if she might know anything about Hunter Lowery.

I'd been living in the duplex for several weeks now, and I had managed to avoid crossing paths with any of my family. I had to remember that now with Melaine and tried my best to sound miles away. It had been easy to do that with Samuel. I also couldn't come right out and ask her about Hunter; she was smart and would be suspicious. I had to build up to that just as I had tried to do with Samuel.

"Ash says hello," I told her.

"Tell him I said hi."

"She says hi," I said, holding the phone away from my mouth to pretend Ash was there. It felt juvenile, but it worked.

"You doing okay?"

"Yeah, just busy with work and stuff. It helps to stay busy," I said. I hated to lie to her, and it was a poor way of trying to make her think I was done grieving. I wasn't.

"Same here," she said with a heavy sigh, not wanting to talk about her own grieving either.

"I heard about that body they found in a park up there. Man, that's crazy."

"Nate Perkins. Yeah, the whole town is freaked out about it."

"I bet. Do they have any leads?"

"I don't think so. I only know what I've read in the paper."

"Yeah, I've been reading the coverage online from some reporter named Celeste Lowery," I said. This was going to be easier than I thought.

"Ha! Don't believe anything you read from her."

"Oh? Why's that?"

"She doesn't know anything. She's just a rich bitch. Her family owns the *Shadow Wood Gazette*."

"Did she go to school with any of us?" I asked, feeding her along.

"Nah, she's too good for public school."

"Is she married? What about her husband?"

"He's VP of Shadow Wood First National. I don't think he's from here. They met at college or something. There was a huge wedding announcement a few years ago in the paper, of course. He comes from money too. His family owns the Bacon Me Crazy fast-food chain."

Bacon Me Crazy had been a staple in our childhoods. Back in the eighties, their Crazy Kids' Meal came with a cheap plastic toy that always broke shortly after you started playing with it, destined to be lost and forgotten in the back seat of your mom's station wagon. It was still a special treat for well-behaved children when Mom was out running errands.

Their soft-serve ice cream and homemade milkshakes made them a go-to on the downtown strip for a quick drive-through dessert. There was a rainbow-colored playground both inside and outside the building, so they frequently hosted birthday parties attended by their mascot, Pork Chop, a pink pig wearing a chef's hat and apron. A giant neon sign out front showed Pork Chop chowing down on a burger, pointing to the building and beckoning you to pull in. It was fun until you realized Pork Chop was pretty much a cannibal.

There were two locations in Shadow Wood. One of those was the first location ever built. There were sixteen other franchised restaurants throughout the state, including four near me back in the city. Hundreds of other locations were scattered throughout the South, catering to your conventional red states because the restaurants were closed on Sundays. I hadn't been to one of them since moving to the city but frequently got dinner to go at least one night when I went back to Mom's house for a visit. It was a taste of home, and I'd always loved their sweet-and-salty fries.

After I learned from Melaine which bank Hunter ran, it wasn't hard to find him. The Shadow Wood First National Bank was the only one in town with its own parking garage. Hunter had a parking space on the first level reserved for him with BANK VICE PRESIDENT on a plaque on the wall. He drove a large black Land

Rover with dark tinted windows. He arrived at the bank each morning wearing a tailored suit. His black hair was spikey and plastic-looking from too much hair gel. He had a fake tan and a fake veneer smile.

Hunter left the bank by four each day and drove to the gym, the same one where Christine Perkins worked. He carried a large duffel inside with him. He worked out for about an hour. Since I did not have a membership, I sat in the parking lot and waited for him to leave. Most days he left the gym in a tight muscle shirt and shorts with a gym towel wrapped around his neck. Rings of sweat circled his neckline and armpits. His face was red. Once or twice a week, he must have showered inside, because he left in designer jeans and a striped polo or crisp T-shirt.

On the sweaty days, he drove straight home from the gym. I had been right about the subdivision. He and Celeste had a house in a gated community out near the lake. On the days that he showered and changed clothes, he made one stop before heading home. It was this stop that might have explained their swingers' club membership.

Hunter drove to the outskirts of town near the highway, past the truck stops and the last hourly motel, to a two-lane sideroad. He pulled around to the back of a rectangular cinder-block establishment known as Jake's. Its parking lot sparkled with green and amber glass from broken beer bottles. There were no outside windows. An obese man with dark sunglasses stood by the front door and guarded the parking lot. The surrounding area was a dense forest of rusted corn stalks.

Jake's was a porn shop, one of the oldest and most lucrative in this area. It supposedly still had a peep show arcade inside. One of those roadside signs with plastic letters and a flashing light bulb arrow on top announced LI E DANCERS and HAPPY OUR.

I'd never been inside, even when I was one of those bored teens. Back then, when I first got a car, I drove by plenty of times. I thought about going in, especially after I turned eighteen. With friends out riding around with me, I crept by and we searched the crowded parking lot for people we might know. We giggled like curious boys seeing a boob for the first time in one of their dad's porn magazines or on cable television.

Jake's was always crowded, making it easy for me to avoid the security guard's attention as I followed Hunter into the parking lot. I backed into a parking spot and waited, searching the corn in my rearview mirror for any lurid activity. I hoped I wouldn't have to wait very long. A man sitting in his car in a porn shop's parking lot could undoubtedly attract unwanted attention.

Hunter pulled up right in front of the back door. He left the Land Rover running, a bold move for a place like this, but I guess he wasn't too worried since he didn't stay inside longer than a few minutes. He came right back out carrying a banker's deposit bag.

I could believe that Jake's was in debt to the bank, but I doubted the bank's VP was out collecting money. I suspected that Hunter or his family owned the place.

"Have you ever been to Jake's?" I asked Parker.

"The porn shop? Yeah. Once. But it was a long time ago, right after high school. It's like a rite of passage for high schoolers around here, isn't it? Didn't you go?"

"No. Never. What's it like on the inside?"

"Exactly what you'd expect. Dark and seedy. There's a bar with a pole for dancers in the front with a store that sells porn mags, movies, and sex toys. The rest of the building is the peep show and movie arcade section. You have to pay to go in there, and you have to buy tokens to watch the shows. I doubt it's changed much. Why do you want to know?"

"I've been following Hunter Lowery. He stops there about twice a week and picks up a banker's bag. I think he might own the place."

"Really? Wow! That explains a lot."

"Yeah, I was thinking the same thing."

"You think someone there might know something?"

"Yeah, but I don't know if they'd talk to us."

"I know how we could find out," Parker sang, looking at me with wide eyes and raised brows.

"Stakeout?" I asked, carefully anticipating her reaction.

She smiled and rubbed her hands together, the look of a child getting ready to blow out their birthday candles. She'd read my mind. She offered to get a hidden mic in case one of us was to go inside, but I politely refused.

I parked in the same area as before but closer to the road, so we could see the front and the back of the building. I figured it was safer not to have any cars behind us, and any perverts creeping through the corn wouldn't want to be detected anyway. Parker kept looking out the window into the cornfield. She was just as nervous as I had been when I came here by myself.

"Makes me think of that horror movie about the kids who—"

"Uh-huh, I tried not to think about that the last time I came out here."

"How can you not think about it?"

"We can leave if you don't feel safe," I said.

"I'll be okay," she whispered.

I hoped she was right.

We sat in silence for at least thirty minutes with not much activity going on. One or two camo-wearing, stick-figured men stumbled out of their trucks. They skulked toward the door of the building, checking their pockets for their wallet, cigarettes, or ID before disappearing inside.

It was the shimmer of sequins at the back of the building that caught our attention.

A leggy woman had stepped outside the back door. She leaned against the building, smoking a cigarette. She wore a green trench coat over her work attire. Neither of us wanted to get out of the car to approach her as if we were bird-watchers who might frighten a rare species away. Parker suggested I drive around the building so that the woman was on the passenger's side, and she could roll down the window and speak to her.

"What are you going to say?" I asked.

"I'll ask her if Hunter is here tonight."

"Do you think she knows who he is?"

"Only one way to find out. Drive!"

I circled the building as quickly as possible. The security guard at the front was too busy looking at his phone to notice. The woman was still leaning against the building when we pulled around. She leaned up as if she'd been waiting for a ride when we pulled in front of her. Parker was ready with her window already rolled down.

"Hey there!" Parker chimed.

"Hey," the woman said, lifting her chin to blow a stream of smoke in the air. She stayed near the building.

"May I ask you a question?" Parker said.

"You lost?" she asked, folding her arms and puffing on her cigarette. "I'm not from around here, so I'm not good with directions."

"No, we aren't lost. We were just wondering if Hunter was here tonight," Parker said.

"Who?"

"Hunter Lowery. Doesn't he own this place?"

"Who wants to know?" she asked after a long huff of smoke.

Parker turned to look at me for direction. I was already digging in my pockets to pull out my wallet. I handed her a ten-dollar bill. Parker held her hand out the window, the money cupped in her hand as if she was feeding an ostrich at one of those drive-through safari parks. The woman stepped forward and reached out for the money, still avoiding getting too close to the car. She avoided eye contact with Parker, keeping her eyes focused on the distance beyond the corn.

"Yeah, he owns the place. He's not here. He's never here," she said.

"Do you know Christine Perkins or Nate Perkins?" Parker asked.

"Parker! Shit!" I whispered, tapping her arm.

"What?" Parker turned to look at me. "I don't know what else to say to her."

"Who wants to know?" the woman said again, looking away as we both stared at her.

I handed Parker another ten, and she offered it to the woman.

"So you know Christine?" Parker urged.

"You guys cops?"

"No, we're not cops. Honest," Parker said.

The woman finally turned and looked at us. Parker crossed her heart with her finger.

"Will you do me a favor?" the woman said, pitching her spent cigarette butt down. She approached the car and leaned down to look inside.

"Umm, depends. We can try," I offered.

"Will you run me up to Bacon Me Crazy and back? I haven't eaten all day, and I don't get off till morning."

Parker looked at me for confirmation.

"I don't do drugs or nothing," the woman added.

I shrugged and nodded.

"Sure. Get in. Do you have any money?" Parker asked, obviously not thinking.

"Umm, yeah! Yours!" the woman said. She opened the back door to the building and yelled at someone inside that she'd be back in a few minutes. Then she climbed into the back seat of the car.

"What's your name?" Parker asked.

"Mitzi," she said. "My stage name is Delilah."

"That's pretty," Parker said.

"I used to be Coco. Delilah was my mama's name. She died about a year ago."

"I'm sure she'd be proud," Parker said, sounding sarcastic.

"I'm Stephen. This is—Enid," I said, cutting off Parker in case she blurted out our real names.

Parker flattened her lips and crossed her eyes at me. "Enid?" she mouthed.

Enid was my grandmother's name. It was the first thing that came to mind.

"So, how long have you been working at Jake's?" I asked.

"About three years. I was gonna leave a few months ago because they cut our hours. I was going to try to get on at Platinum's over the river, but then

Geraldine retired and I picked up some of her shifts. Geraldine was the mother hen."

"Mother hen?" I asked.

"Yeah, the lead girl, usually whoever's been there the longest," she explained as she leaned up in the back seat to talk to both of us.

As we drove away from Jake's, Mitzi continued to talk. I imagined she was appreciative of a connection with someone who wasn't a groping trucker. She told us she didn't have any kids. She lived in a trailer park with her grandmother across the highway and either walked to work or got a ride with one of the other girls. She even told us all about how the peep shows worked before we'd reached the drive-up window at Bacon Me Crazy.

I drove under the speed limit just to give her a chance to talk. At the window, I pulled up so she could order for herself from the back window. She got two combos, one with a large soda and the other with a large coffee. I was sure it was all for her unless she planned to save some for her grandmother. I gave her another ten to get a couple of milkshakes for Parker and me and told her she could keep the change.

"So you know Christine?" Parker asked while we waited in line at the window.

"She used to be Chris, you know?" Mitzi said.

"Oh, we know. We went to school with Chris," Parker added.

"Chris used to work the Romeo Room. Did you know that?"

"The Romeo Room?" Parker and I said in unison.

"It's one of the peep shows in the back of the club where guys dance. Occasionally there's a bachelorette party, but the customers are mostly old gay guys now. That's where she and Nate met."

"Really?"

"Yeah, Christine started transitioning shortly after that. Boobs. Hormone shots. Stuff like that. Told us Nate was paying for it, but we knew she was lying."

"Who paid for it?" I asked.

"Hunter did."

"Were Hunter and Christine having an affair?" Parker asked.

"Nah, Hunter ain't like that. He gave Christine a personal loan, but then Christine wanted to start working up front with the girls after she transitioned. Hunter wouldn't let her. He wanted her to stay in the Romeo Room. Thought the customers would enjoy a—you know. But Christine didn't want to do that, so she quit."

"Did Christine pay Hunter back?" Parker asked.

"I don't think so. That's probably what got Nate killed. You guys want some of these fries? I should have got the medium," Mitzi said. She'd already eaten both burgers by the time we were back at Jake's.

"Do you think Hunter Lowery killed Nate?" I asked Mitzi just as she opened the door and started to get out.

She hesitated, looking toward the door to the club. She took a huge sip of her soda and then got back in the car. She pulled on the handle, making sure the door was closed tight. "No, but I wouldn't be shocked if he had Nate killed. Retribution and all, ya know?"

Parker gave me the side-eye. I raised my eyebrows, careful not to let Mitzi see me.

"Thanks, Mitzi, you've been a big help," Parker said.

"Thanks for the ride, and for the cash and all. We done here?"

"Sure. If we have any more questions, can we swing by again and pick you up?" I asked, trying not to sound like a john.

"Yeah, just don't mention you heard any of this shit from me. Okay? I don't need no trouble. Nobody fucks with Hunter."

"No trouble at all. We won't say anything. Don't worry," Parker said.

Mitzi nodded. She opened the car door and stepped out.

"I'm here every night except Tuesdays and Wednesdays," she said, slowly pushing on the door as if she didn't want it to slam. It was the focused actions I imagined a prostitute might carry out late at night as she traversed between customers in the parking lot.

Parker waved as we rounded the building and drove away, but Mitzi didn't see her. When we were out of the parking lot and back on the highway, I rolled down the back windows, hoping to air out the stench of Mitzi's cigarette smoke.

CHAPTER 32

ASH HAD texted once or twice a day ever since our last conversation. He was eager for any soap opera details I could provide. I knew he was also constantly checking in because he was worried. I didn't mind. I liked hearing his voice, and it only made me more eager to get back to the city. When I got back from Jake's, I wasted no time calling him.

"You took a hooker to Bacon Me Crazy? I'm jealous! You've never even taken me there!" he said.

"Not a hooker. She's a dancer."

"Her name *is* Mitzi," he stressed.

"Okay, she might be a hooker."

"You did pay her for services," Ash said.

"In a way, yes."

It helped to rehash what Mitzi had said just to get it straight in my head. Parker and I had compared mental notes in the car. It was quite a bit to analyze. Once again I felt bad for Christine and embarrassed by any judgment I might have had back in high school. None of that mattered now. In was in the past, but like everything else I should have left behind, I couldn't let it go. The anxiety was still overwhelming.

"So if Christine owed Hunter for her implants, why would they share a room at the swingers' club?" he asked.

"Maybe Hunter was willing to accept some other kind of compensation?"

"Maybe. Do you think Nate slept with Hunter's wife?"

"No. I don't think Celeste or Nate was in the room that night. Honestly, I don't think their meeting was even about sex."

"Yeah, if it was, that sounds odd. Didn't Mitzi tell you that Hunter wasn't like that?"

"Exactly. She did indicate he was dangerous, though."

"So why the argument afterwards?"

"I think Nate found out about their meeting, and that's why Nate and Christine were arguing outside of their house that night. He found out Christine went to a room with Hunter, and then Nate went back to confront Hunter after they left. Nate and Hunter probably had an argument or something worse, since Nate never came back that night."

"So now what?"

"Parker and I want to find Christine."

"Where do you think she is?"

"I think she is staying with her dad. He's a police officer. Parker isn't so sure. We saw some with short hair, a man maybe, come to the house in her car, so we think she might be staying with someone else."

"Have you confronted Linda yet?"

"Not yet. But I will."

"And then?"

"And then what?"

"You'll come home?"

I liked how he used that word. *Home*. He didn't say *come back to the apartment*. He said *home*. It made me think of how Mom's house had always been home before, but I'd now lived in the city longer than I had lived in Shadow Wood. This town wasn't home anymore. My home was with Ash.

"Yeah. Then I'll come home."

"And you'll take me to Bacon Me Crazy?"

"I'll take you to dinner anywhere you want to go," I said.

"Anywhere?"

"Yep. You get to pick."

"Olive Garden."

"What? Why there of all places?"

"They have the hottest waiters."

"We're not going there for the waiters," I said. I knew he was just joking around, though what he had said about the waiters was true.

"I know, but don't forget they also have endless breadsticks."

"I do love the breadsticks."

"Olive Garden it is then!"

CHAPTER 33

I CONTINUED to follow Hunter and Linda, but neither of their schedules strayed much, at least nothing out of the ordinary. Like Linda's, Hunter's daily routines formed a predictable pattern in my notebook.

I also kept an eye on the Perkins household, but neither Christine nor the strange man we'd seen in the park had returned. Sitting at my desk, I came across the business card for Rose the Realtor and decided to call her to see if we could meet. She invited me to stop by her office, a converted one-car garage attached to her house.

She met me at the door and invited me in. I was surprised to find the inside didn't look like a garage at all. Drywall and carpet had been installed. The garage had been divided up into two rooms—a sitting area and Rose's office. One wall was decorated with various re-altor awards, another with photos of properties. A cof-fee maker, cups, creamer, and a small container of sugar packets were neatly arranged on a side table. A slotted magazine holder hung on another wall filled with inte-rior decorator magazines. There were no typical garage smells. A candle burning on her desk filled the air with the soft scent of vanilla.

Had her husband done all of this for her so she could work from home? Maybe he wanted her to raise the kids and balance her career? Or maybe she'd taken charge because she now had a space to herself where she could devote professional time to her clients and work from home. It didn't matter. I had no right to judge. I'm sure she'd been subjected to that enough by other women in Shadow Wood. I could see that Rose had done well for herself.

"Mr. Glass, how are you?" she said, extending her hand.

"Oh, please call me Stephen," I said, shaking her hand. "I'm great, Rose. How about you?"

"Doing well, thanks. So, how are things on Maple Street? Are you in the market for something more permanent now?"

"Possibly. I had some questions about the house across the street."

"The Perkins house?"

"Yes, the one next door to Linda Reyes that I looked at before."

"Oh yes. How did you know it was going back on the market? Did Christine tell you?"

I didn't know that it was going back up for sale, but I had a good follow-up, at least.

"No, Christine hasn't been staying at the house, but I've seen people there a few times, and they are always packing stuff up and taking it. After what happened to her husband, I guessed she was moving back out."

"You are correct. I haven't talked to Christine either. A lawyer has been handling all of this for her."

"So she is selling the house?"

"If you're interested, just be patient. There are a few steps to take first—legal stuff—since they just bought the house. But then it will be back on the market in a few weeks. Just some paperwork to file. Given the situation with Nate's death, the previous owner was very understanding and willing to work with her."

"It's terrible what happened to Nate and all," I said.

"Yes, a tragedy. Did you know they think someone poisoned Nate?" she said, whispering the word *poisoned* as if someone might overhear her.

"No, I had not heard that."

"Don't tell anyone I told you, okay? The lawyer told me. Nate and Christine went to the Milieu for dinner earlier that night. They think someone put something in one of his drinks at the bar. Can you imagine? I haven't eaten at the Milieu in years, but I told my husband we definitely won't ever be going back," she said.

"Wouldn't the hotel or the restaurant be under investigation?"

"Maybe they are, but yeah, the toxicology report showed poison in his system."

There might have been poison in Nate's system, but this didn't explain why he'd gone missing, why the car had been abandoned, or why his nude body had been found in the park several days later.

I didn't want to get into a debate with her about any of that, so I didn't mention it. She had to have known about those details too; they had been in the newspaper. I was convinced her poison theory was only hearsay. A lawyer would never have told her that anyway.

"And you believe that?" I asked.

"Honey, I've lived here a long time, and I believe almost everything someone tells me these days. True or not, there's a little bit of honesty in every story you hear in this town."

She had a point. After all, she was just repeating what someone had told her. She had no reason to embellish or add her own opinions. She didn't seem like the kind of woman who would lie or spread falsehoods on purpose. That lawyer had probably told her about the poison in confidence. I assumed it was a real estate lawyer, so they had not heard about it from Christine. They weren't involved in the murder case. So who told them?

"So, tell me more about Linda Reyes," I said.

"Ha! Where do you want me to start?" She crossed her arms. It wasn't a defensive gesture; I could tell she was more than willing to talk.

I decided to start with my father.

"Do you know a man named Owen Kipton?"

She squinted and looked at the ceiling, a child's mannerisms for trying to think of an answer to the question.

"I can't place the name. Does he live around here?"

"He used to. Not important, though. I was just curious."

"Did Linda ruin his marriage?" she said, sounding smug.

"She did, actually."

"Well, let me tell you, Stephen. There's a lot of Owen Kiptons walking around this town."

"Really?"

"Yes, sir. And if Linda Reyes didn't personally ruin their marriage, she had something to do with it."

"Are you referring to her club at the hotel?" I asked.

"Oh, so you know about the Pink Poodles?" She uncrossed her arms. She moved her hands to her hips and leaned forward so that she was closer to my face.

"Yes, I've heard about them."

"Did you know the hotel has to give her a cut each month? I mean the audacity of that woman. She knows that hotel is running on fumes. She thinks her little sex club saved it from having to close down. Maybe it did. I heard she slept with the hotel manager just so she could extort him for money."

"Blackmail?"

"Of course! So that she has something to hold over his head in case he decides to stop paying her commission. There are two kinds of men in this town, Stephen."

"Oh?"

"There are the men who owe Linda Reyes money and the men who owe her a favor."

"Well, I'm happy to say I don't fit into either one of those categories."

"That could change if you move in next door to her," she said, tilting her head and widening her eyes.

I knew she meant that as a joke, so I just smiled. I wanted to ask Rose which category her husband fit into, but that would be rude. I thanked her for her time and told her I'd be in touch again if I decided I was still interested in the Perkins house.

She had gotten up to walk me to the door when we were interrupted by a sweaty basketball player. He was shirtless and glistening in gym shorts, with a basketball tucked against his side.

"Mom? Oh, sorry, I didn't know you were seeing a client." He stopped at the door.

"It's okay. I was just leaving," I said.

"Stephen, this is my oldest son, Spencer," Rose said.

"Sup?" Spencer gave that typical straight-guy head nod as he stepped inside. He took the ball from his side and held it in both hands to avoid a handshake. I didn't mind since he was covered in sweat. His outdoorsy smell immediately overshadowed Rose's vanilla candle.

"Oof, Spencer, you smell!" Rose waved her hand in front of her face.

"Yeah. Sorry," he said with a grin, raising his arm and giving his own pit a sniff.

"Spencer is wrapping up med school this fall," Rose said with pride.

"Oh really? Here in Tennessee?" I asked.

"Yeah. Knoxville," he said with a grin as he scratched at one of his nipples.

"That's cool. Congrats. Well, I should be going," I said, doing my best to avoid eyeing his taut body.

Spencer stepped back out and held the door open for me. I thanked him.

"I'll stop by if anything changes on the Perkins house," Rose said.

"Oh, no need to do that. I can call him. I mean, I'll call you."

"You still have my card?"

"Yes, I want it," I said. "I mean, I have it. I do. I do still have your card." I realized I was stumbling over my words. Spencer's hypermasculinity was turning me into a nervous mess.

"You thinking about buying that dead guy's house on Maple Street?" Spencer dribbled his basketball from hand to hand a few times, showing off his coordination. I was more impressed by his defined abdomen.

"Spencer!" Rose slapped his arm.

"What?" he said with a shrug as he grabbed the ball before it got away from him.

"Yeah, I'm thinking about it," I said with a nod, so he didn't feel embarrassed. He oozed confidence as he stood there. I knew he probably rarely felt ashamed of anything. He liked having eyes on him. In a way, he reminded me of Nate, and the way he'd acted while standing at his window. Now I also wondered if Jimmie had indeed known I was watching him outside the bar that night, and he was putting on a show for me.

"Stephen lives across the street from the Perkins house now," Rose added.

"I see," Spencer said. Now he was the one looking me up and down. We exchanged glances. He didn't seem to mind. Instead, he gave a wink. I smiled back at him.

"Well, goodbye. Nice meeting you, Spencer. Thanks again," I said, waving to them as I raced to get back in my car.

Just Spencer's presence had begun to make me sweat too. It made me wonder what Rose's husband looked like. If I still lived here, Linda and I would probably have a lot in common when it came to our bedroom manners.

CHAPTER 34

THE NEXT day Celeste Lowery reported that the case to find Nate Perkin's murderer had gone "cold." I didn't believe that. It was too soon to be a cold case; the police probably just didn't have any leads. It was sloppy reporting, but it was what I'd come to expect from Mrs. Lowery. Her article didn't even ask anyone who might have information to contact the police. I doubted anyone was talking, but it's still a nice gesture if the local newspaper seems like it is trying to assist.

Another story in the paper, this one about the Bacon Me Crazy restaurant, caught my attention. It said the original flagship store in Shadow Wood was going to be torn down and rebuilt. When we took Mitzi through the drive-up window a few nights ago, I had noticed a sign out front that read *Closing for Renovations Soon*. I had not thought much about it at the time.

The article said that they would tear down the old restaurant to rebuild a more up-to-date modernized version in the same spot. I hated to see that happen. I had always liked the nostalgia of the current location, with its neon exterior lights and fifties soda-pop atmosphere.

The new site would only have a playground on the out-side and have a more "adult feel" inside.

I dismissed the story until Parker said she wanted me to meet two people who were former employees at the restaurant. I didn't know why that was important, but I told her she could bring them by my place that evening. They agreed, but she said they would park in the alley and come in the back door.

"This is Ali," Parker said, introducing me to a teen-age girl. She looked to be still in high school.

"It's short for Alison." The girl stuck out her long, bony arm for me to shake her tiny, clammy hand.

"And this is Lucas," Parker said. A boy entered close behind Ali. He gave a quick nod, keeping his hands deep in the pockets of his jeans.

Before they arrived, I had prepared a tray with ice, lime soda, gin, and four glasses. I had not been expect-ing teenagers. As they stood at the door waiting for me to let them in, I tucked the gin back into the pantry. I could tell by their clothes that they came from blue-col-lar, working families. They weren't poor, but they cer-tainly weren't rich either. They both had on tight, faded jeans with holes in the knees. Their expensive sneakers were dirty and worn. Each wore a hoodie. Ali's teeth were bleached white but crooked. Lucas had acne scars on his temples, and his mop of hair was oily and needed to be cut and combed.

Both stepped in and waited for direction. I picked up the drink tray and motioned for them to follow me into the living room. Staying close together, they sat down on the sofa at the same time. I let Parker take the chair, and I remained standing. I set the tray down on the coffee table in front of them, and they immediately poured themselves some soda without asking. I didn't mind. I bet they came from households where soda was a treat, or their mother watered it down to avoid her kids from being too hyper on the caffeine.

"Nice place," Lucas said, looking around. He picked up a glass paperweight from the coffee table to examine it. He didn't look like the type of kid who would steal it. He was just curious. As a child, I bet his mom always slapped his hand for touching things.

"Thanks," I said.

"Lucas and Ali both worked at Bacon Me Crazy, right?" Parker said, nodding as if trying to get the kids to agree.

"Not anymore," Lucas said.

"The one they are going to tear down?" I offered, just to add to the conversation.

"Yep," Lucas said, looking at Ali as if he'd already said too much.

"They were both recently fired. Do you want to elaborate on that?" Parker said.

"Huh?" Ali said. "Oh, yeah. Lucas and I got fired for going into the freezer. At first it was just a write-up, which was stupid. It's not like we hadn't gone in there a thousand times before. I already had two write-ups for being late, so maybe that's why. Anyway, they asked us if we saw anything in the freezer. I was too afraid to admit it. I think they knew, but they fired us and told us not to tell anyone about anything we saw."

"You went in the freezer?" I asked, still not sure what all of this was about.

"Yeah," Lucas said. "You see, the freezer is in the basement."

"Why would they fire you for that?"

Ali and Lucas looked at each other. Parker told them it was okay to tell me. Lucas sat the paperweight down, as if needing both of his hands to tell his story.

"You see, only managers have keys to the freezer, but sometimes they are busy, so they leave it open so employees can go down there and get boxes of fries and burger patties when they need them. So I went down there on my shift to get some more fries. I couldn't believe what I was seeing. It was freaky, so I went back up and grabbed Ali," Lucas explained.

"What did you see?" I asked.

"We saw some blood on the floor," Ali said.

"And there was a big lump wrapped in a white sheet in the back of the freezer near the blood. They told us it was just meat waiting to be processed," Lucas added. "I didn't think anything about it, but Ali said all the food comes in freezer trucks and it's already prepared, so she knew they were lying. Makes sense, right?"

"What do you think the lump was?" I asked, still unsure where this was going.

"I don't know, but it disappeared right after that man's body was found in the park near here," Ali said.

"Nate Perkins," Lucas said to her.

"Yeah, him," Ali said.

Parker looked at me. I didn't know what to say.

"It didn't stink or nothing. You'd think a body would stink, right?" Lucas said, but we ignored him.

"You think there was a body in the freezer?" I asked.

"Yup," they both said.

I would have thought this all sounded bizarre had I not known the Lowery family owned the restaurant chain. Maybe Hunter had killed Nate, and he'd stashed the body at his family's restaurant until he could figure out what to do with it. That would explain where Nate's body was while he was missing, but it seemed very risky to stash it in a restaurant freezer where employees had access.

"Do you know when the lump, or the body, got removed?" I asked.

"No, the manager that was on duty that night got fired too," Ali said.

"For leaving the freezer unlocked?" I asked.

"Yup," Lucas said.

"Do you think them remodeling the restaurant has anything to do with this?"

"Yeah, I think they are trying to cover up some DNA or something?" he said.

It seemed pretty far-fetched, but nothing in this town surprised me anymore. Tearing down a restaurant to conceal the DNA of a dead body was a bit unbelievable, but so was using its freezer to hide the body. The Lowery family tearing down an entire restaurant to conceal a crime scene was just as unusual, but given the amount of money they had, I guess it was conceivable.

"And both of you think it was a body?" Parker added.

"Yeah, I do. Like in those crime shows or a movie where you see a body wrapped in a sheet, it looked just like that," Lucas said.

"Yeah, it looked just like that," Ali repeated, nodding at Lucas. He nodded back, as if he was happy that he'd thought of that.

We sat in silence, contemplating all of this. It was a bit too quiet for the two teens. Lucas began to bounce his leg up and down and tap his knee, a typical fidgety teenager growing tired of sitting still. He picked the paperweight up again and tossed it back and forth between his hands like a baseball. I didn't say anything because I didn't want it to seem like I was scolding him.

"You guys aren't going to tell anyone, are you?" Ali asked, finally speaking up.

"No, not at all," Parker said.

"Yeah, don't worry about that. You guys just keep quiet and be safe. I'm glad you told us, though. I'm sorry you lost your jobs," I said.

"It sucked anyway," Lucas said.

"Yeah, I always went home smelling like grease. So gross! But I'm starting a new job at the mall next week as a makeup consultant. I'm so excited," Ali said.

"What about you, Lucas?" I asked.

"A buddy of mine is gonna try to get me on at the movie theater. He works in the concession stand. Or Parker said she might be able to get me a busboy position at the Milieu," he said with a yawn, putting the paperweight back down. He emptied his glass of soda, dramatically holding it up in the air so the last drop could fall into his mouth. He was ready to leave.

That was it. Both of these kids had lost their jobs because they'd gone into a restaurant freezer where they might, or might not, have seen a dead body wrapped in a sheet. They weren't upset by this. Neither of them seemed shaken up or worried. They had not gone to the cops.

Teens were pretty unresponsive to things these days. The internet has made all of us a little less sensitive. It was just an ordinary detail of their lives absent of any emotion. There was nothing they could do about it. They knew no one would believe them. Maybe teenagers had learned it wasn't worth wasting their time or effort to get anyone to listen to them.

I felt like I needed to be cordial and ask them about school or their college plans, but I always hated when adults did that to me back when I was their age. I refrained from saying anything, realizing now just how creepy it was. I assumed they were juniors or seniors if they were already working. It wasn't my business. Maybe they didn't intend to go to college. Now, as an adult, I hated how adults immediately forced that expectation on kids.

Parker admitted that bringing them in the back door had been her idea, not theirs. She just felt the need to protect them after she'd heard their story. Neither of them had even mentioned being worried about who saw them, so I let them leave through the front.

After they left, Parker asked me if I believed them. I did. Of course, there was no proof, but I don't think they had a reason to lie. They weren't trying to get attention, or they'd have gone public with the information. They weren't melodramatic while speaking about it, so I knew they weren't embellishing the story or trying to impress us. Before she brought them over, Parker had already told me not to mention the police. They had both shown honest concern to her about not telling anyone.

"How did you find out about them?" I asked Parker once they'd left.

"They go to school with a girl who waits tables with me," she said.

"And they told her?"

"No, they've been too scared to tell anyone, but she knew they were hiding something. When she told me they'd both been fired from Bacon Me Crazy, I got curious. Then Lucas came in and asked for an application on one of my shifts. My coworker introduced us, and we got to talking. I mentioned Hunter Lowery, and he turned white in the face. He looked at me like I knew something, so I pulled him aside. He said he needed to talk to someone, so here we are."

The next day, I noticed they'd already started the demolition of the restaurant. It was leveled to the ground and cleared within two days. A follow-up article in the paper said they intended to build the new restaurant and reopen within eight weeks. The story mentioned the interior and kitchen needed to be brought up to code, which included a larger freezer with a keypad combination, and only managers would have a code to ensure the utmost food safety.

CHAPTER 35

"YOU SHOULD have invited him over," Ash said when I told him about Rose's son, Spencer.

"What? His mother was standing right there!"

"You're smart. You could have slipped him your number or something. You said he'd been playing basketball. Maybe he was doing it at that park."

"What are you saying?"

"I'm saying go find him. It's a small town. You've been following everyone else around, so it can't be that hard. You need to get laid. Relieve some of your frustrations."

"Have you been getting laid while I'm gone?" I meant this as a joke, but I secretly hoped he hadn't.

"Nope."

"Why not? You've got the place to yourself," I reminded him.

"I'm not frustrated like you."

"That's never stopped you before."

"You're right. What's Mitzi's number?" he joked.

"Ha! Very funny."

"I miss you, Toby," he said. Jokes aside. I knew he was being serious.

"I miss you too," I said.

I don't know why I did it, but I drove by the park later that afternoon. Ash had been right about Spencer playing ball there. I spotted him at one of the goals doing layups or whatever. I knew nothing about sports, but he seemed to be pretty good at it. He was alone, so I pulled into the parking lot. I rolled down my window. It didn't take long for him to see me and walk over.

"Hey, man. We met the other day. It's Stephen, right?" he said. He put his ball on the ground between his feet and bent down so we were face-to-face. He propped himself against the door of my car, practically leaning inside.

"Yeah. And you're Spencer, right?" I knew exactly who he was.

"Yep, Spin for short. You can call me that if you want. Everyone else does."

"Cool," I said, trying not to be nervous. I had no idea where this was going. I didn't have to wait to find out. Spin was happy to lead the conversation.

"Did you know that dead guy? Nate Perkins?" he asked.

"No, I never met him. Did you?"

"I'd seen him around town before. He used to date that chick from the paper."

"From the newspaper?"

"Yeah, hold on and I'll show you," he said, digging in his pocket and pulling out his phone. He tapped and scrolled for a bit and then handed it to me.

It was a picture of Nate Perkins with Celeste Lowery on Facebook. I checked the date at the bottom and it was from a few years ago. His arm was around her shoulder and their faces were pressed together while she took the selfie.

"Swipe to the next one," he said.

It was a photo of the two of them kissing. I handed him his phone back.

"I wonder why they broke up," I said aloud. I was just speculating. I didn't expect him to know. But in case he did, I was also fishing for information.

"I don't know, but they both traded up. Her husband works at the bank. His family is super rich. And that new girl Nate was with? Christine? Man, I'd hit that," he said, shaking his hand to indicate she was hot.

He picked up his ball and stood. His crotch—a large round bulge protruding from his gym shorts—was now level with my window. I turned my head to avoid staring at it. As I glanced forward, I saw a couple walking through the park and approaching us. They'd rounded the path and were now headed toward the parking lot. It was my brother and his wife.

"Umm, I should probably be going. I just thought of an appointment I have, and I'm going to be late," I said, quickly starting the car.

"You wanna come back by later? We could play H-O-R-S-E or something."

I assumed he meant a ball game of some sort and not a double entendre.

"That sounds fun, but I've got some errands to run. I really need to get going. Raincheck?" I said, rolling up my window.

"Alright. You got a hoop at your house? I could swing by sometime," he said, backing away from the car as I put it in reverse.

"I wish," I whispered. "No, sorry. I don't." I said.

But I could get one installed, I thought to myself.

"Well, I'm here at the park a lot. You can just look for me, okay?"

"I'll do that," I said, just before the window shut.

Watching me pull away, Spencer casually scratched at his crotch. I gave a nod, hoping it didn't look like I was focusing on anything below his waist. He nodded and then dribbled his ball and turned back to the hoop.

"Fuck, fuck, fuck," I whispered to myself, backing up and trying to exit the park as quickly as I could. I checked my rearview mirror. I didn't think Samuel had noticed me or recognized my car. I wasn't sure since I'd been so focused on Spencer. Up until now, I thought I'd done a pretty good job of avoiding any run-ins with my family.

As I sped away, I thought about Ash. He would have killed me. This guy had invited himself to my house, and I had turned him down. I should have lied about the basketball hoop. They couldn't be that expensive. I thought about the small plastic hoop Samuel had hanging on his bedroom door back home and the orange foam balls we tossed into it. Would one of those toy hoops suffice? I laughed to myself because it was silly, but it would have certainly gotten Spencer into the bedroom.

Back at the duplex, I immediately grabbed my phone and looked for Nate's profile on Facebook. I found the photos Spencer had shown me and sent them to Parker.

"WTF?" she texted back.

I didn't tell her what Spencer had said about them dating. I didn't want to have to explain who Spencer was to her. The photos made their relationship pretty obvious, and the fact that Nate had not deleted the photos was an indication that it might have been pretty serious. The tone of Celeste's reporting suggested something completely different. There was much more to their relationship—probably things that should remain buried—and I was pretty sure it had something to do with the Pink Poodle Club.

CHAPTER 36

THERE WAS a knock at my front door the following morning. Other than Parker and Officer Harland, no one had knocked on my door since I'd been there. The landlord had never even stopped by since the first day I met him. I wasn't expecting anyone, so I thought it might have been the mail carrier. It wasn't.

I opened my door to a woman, maybe in her late fifties, whom I'd seen walking a beagle in the neighborhood. She had short, pixie-cut hair and was short in stature herself. She was lean and wore sports bras and leggings. When the dog wasn't with her, she swayed her arms intensely like those walkers doing laps around the shopping mall.

Since I recognized her from the neighborhood, I wasn't too worried. Maybe she was here to invite me to a neighborhood watch, or perhaps she was attempting to play the old mail trick I'd intended to do over at the Perkins house back when I wanted to try to learn their names. I still wasn't getting any mail of my own at the duplex, but the box was always packed with advertisements from local businesses and stuff for the previous occupant.

"Hello," I said after opening the door.

"I have something you might want to see," she said, not introducing herself.

"I'm sorry?"

"I live next door to you. Directly across from Linda's house." She pointed to her house. "Sorry, I'm Maddie Sheffield."

"Hi, Maddie. I'm Stephen Glass," I said, offering my hand.

"Oh? Your landlord told me your name was Toby." She gave my hand a single firm shake. She knew I was lying.

She raised her other hand to show me a flash drive she was holding. I didn't acknowledge what she said about my name. Letting go of her hand, I stood back against the door, indicating she could come inside. Before shutting the door, I gave a quick look outside, expecting to see someone watching out for her, but no one was in sight.

"A few days ago, Linda knocked on my door and asked me to check my doorbell cam for her. She thought something suspicious might have been happening on her property while she was gone one evening," Maddie said.

"Oh really? What night was that?" I asked.

"You know what night it was," she said.

"Are you a cop or something?"

"No, and in case you are wondering, Linda and I are not friends. I've never liked her. She's a bitch, but you probably already know that about her. I never liked her husband either. I have a pretty good feeling you might feel the same way about her, Mr. Glass," she said.

"I don't really know her."

"You sure?"

I was silent for a bit, choosing my words carefully, but then I asked, "Did you show Linda anything from your cam?"

She handed me the flash drive. I went to my desk and opened my laptop. I turned it around so that we could both see it. I inserted the drive and waited for my laptop to recognize it.

"May I?" she said.

"Sure. Go ahead."

Maddie leaned down to navigate the viewer to the appropriate time or video. She pressed Play and then leaned back up, standing beside me with her arms crossed. I felt as if I was a student who'd been called to the principal's office or a shoplifter at a mall who'd been caught on camera.

"My cam has a really broad view. I can see the street at the end of the block where you like to walk up the hill and cut through the alley on that side. I take the same route with my dog sometimes," Maddie explained as the video began to play.

On the last night I'd gone into Linda's house to look for the logbooks, I had entered the alley from the opposite side, which was farther up the street and out of her camera's view. She knew this already. The camera played a dark and mute view of the street except for the streetlamps and porch lights. A car pulled into view. It parked along the street. I knew right away it was Linda's.

"This is Linda arriving home that night. She's just getting out of her car when your girlfriend runs out the door to talk to her," Maddie said.

I wanted to correct her and tell her Parker wasn't my girlfriend. I wanted to tell her Parker lived in the other side of the duplex, but if Maddie knew my land-lord and had talked to him, then there was no reason to lie. That would just make me look petty. I corrected her anyway.

"She isn't my girlfriend."

"I didn't think any of this was unusual, but then I noticed something. Look here," she said, ignoring me. She bent over to stop the video and start it again. She pointed to Linda's window as the video started again.

"Did you see that?" she asked.

"Someone must be home," I said, trying not to sound concerned. My heart was pounding so hard I was surprised she couldn't hear it.

"Ya think?" Maddie said with sarcasm, looking back at me.

She stopped the video again and zoomed in on Linda's window. I could see the curtain move and my silhouette when I peeked out. It just looked like a fuzzy shadow, but you could tell it was a person. She sped the video forward.

"Here you are walking out of the alley just as Linda and your friend wrap up their conversation. You stop to look at your phone. It's odd how your friend is walking back up to your door and checking her phone at the same time. But I also thought it was strange that you were out taking a walk at night while your friend is in your house."

"Did you show this to Linda?" I asked, hoping I didn't sound guilty.

She stopped the video. "No, I didn't. I told you I don't like her. Never have and never will."

"Then why are you showing this to me?"

"I have something else you might want to see," Maddie said.

She fiddled with the laptop again. When she stepped back so I could see it, the same familiar neighborhood footage was playing on the screen. Not recognizing what I should be looking at, I watched Linda's house again. A car came into view and pulled up in front of the Perkins house. I expected to see Parker running out my front door again, but this wasn't Linda's car. This wasn't the same night's footage, but I had seen it before. This was from the night Nate and Christine came home and had their argument. It was the last night Nate was seen before he disappeared.

"Is this—"

"Keep watching," Maddie interrupted.

The argument Christine and Nate had that night on their front lawn played out. He'd come back outside and sat down on the porch. You could only see his silhouette on the video, thanks to the light from the open door behind him. That was the last time I'd seen him. I remembered stepping away from the window. She let the video play for a good minute with Nate just sitting there.

"He sits there for seventeen minutes. I thought he'd fallen asleep on the porch." Maddie reached down to fast-forward the video. "Here he is finally getting up and going inside. Just before he gets up, he looks over his shoulder. I think she was calling to him from inside."

We both watched Nate go inside. Maddie paused the video. I could tell she was enjoying her presentation. She was one of those women who lived for television court dramas and late-night crime shows. She read true crime books. She played those solve-a-crime games on her computer. I wondered what she did for a living. She would have made a good lawyer or private investigator.

"Thirty minutes later, a truck shows up," she said.

"A truck?"

"It looks like a Land Rover to me. Watch this." She started the video again.

It pulled in front of the house and stopped in the middle of the street. Christine ran out the front door and down the steps to greet the driver, who stayed in the vehicle. They rolled their window down to speak to her. I could not see who was inside. Christine ran back up to the house. The Land Rover drove to the end of the block and then turned up the side street and then down the alley behind the house.

"Twenty minutes later, this happens," Maddie said, fast-forwarding the video again.

The Land Rover reappeared coming back down the street again, so they had driven the length of the alley and come out the opposite side, out of view. Just as it reached the front of the Perkins house again, Christine came out the front door and raced down the steps. She waved to the driver. Then she got into her car and pulled away as they followed her.

Maddie stopped the video.

"Anything after that?" I asked.

"Yep. That same vehicle brings Christine back to the house just after 3:00 a.m. She doesn't come back in her car."

"Let me see," I said.

Maddie started the video again and moved it forward a few hours. The Land Rover appeared, just as she said. Christine got out of the passenger side. She did not wave goodbye as she got out of the vehicle. They sped away before she'd made it up the steps to her door. The driver, or whoever else was in that vehicle, was someone Christine either didn't know or didn't like. Anyone else would have been polite and waited to make sure she got in her house okay at that hour, or they would have parked and walked her to the door. All of this seemed very strange.

"What do you think of all this?" I asked her.

"I was about to ask you the same thing. I think Nate Perkins was in that truck," she said.

"Me too."

"I don't know if he was alive or not, but he was in it."

"Do you think Christine killed him in the house and then called someone to help?" I asked.

"It's possible. Why would they have pulled around the back? Why didn't Nate and Christine just come out the front door, unless he couldn't because he was dead, or at least incapacitated?"

She'd given a lot of thought to all of this. She'd watched the video again and again and written down every angle she could think of that was possible.

"Have you showed this to the police?" I asked.

"No, they haven't asked."

"A cop came to my door the day after Nate went missing," I told her.

"What did he want?"

"He asked if I'd seen anything. He even asked if I had a doorbell camera. He said they were asking everyone on the street to check their security cameras."

"Really? No one has asked me. Do you know who the officer was?"

"Officer Tom Harland. He gave me a business card."

"Can I see it?"

It was still lying on the desk. I picked it up and handed it to her. "I think he's related to Christine," I said.

"Oh really? Why's that?"

I told her about how I had noticed the name on the business card that day. I didn't go into the details about Christine being born Chris. I said I'd known her from high school and that her maiden name was Harland. She shook her head while still looking at the business card.

"This isn't a local cop," she said when I was done.

"What do you mean?"

"I've seen most of our law enforcement's business cards. This is either from a different jurisdiction, which is unlikely, or it's a fake."

"A fake?"

"Yep." She licked her thumb. "Do you mind?"

"Go ahead," I said.

She rubbed her thumb on the law enforcement seal printed on the card. She held up her thumb to show me the blue ink now streaked across her thumb.

"This is a cheap job, probably printed on some- one's home printer. Official business cards for lawyers and police officers use thermography or a high-gloss laminate."

"Thermography?"

"Raised ink. Ever look closely at a business card, and it almost looks like foil or wax?"

I never had, but I knew what she was talking about.

"Yeah, if he were real law enforcement, I wouldn't be able to smear the ink on his card that easily. I bet whoever came to your door isn't a cop at all. Was he in a police car?"

"An unmarked vehicle with a single light on the dash."

"Anyone can get one of those," she said. "What about a uniform?"

"Nope."

"A cop at your door that quick would have been in a cop car and had on a uniform."

"Why would he knock on my door?"

"You are directly across the street from them. I bet he didn't realize some of these door cams have a pretty wide view, like mine. Since you are right in front, he checked the most obvious house."

"Do you think he knew what happened to Nate?" I asked.

"Yep. Maybe he was in on it. Maybe he knows what happened in that house that night and was just checking to see if you saw anything. Maybe he was the driver of that truck that night," she said.

I didn't think that Officer Harland, or whoever he was, drove the Land Rover that night. I had recognized it right away, but I didn't tell Maddie because that would have led to unwanted questions.

The Land Rover in the video was the same one I'd been following for days. It belonged to Hunter Lowery.

CHAPTER 37

MADDIE'S PARTNER, Tina, had been dead seven years. Breast cancer. Their first place together had been the house next door to me. They'd both grown up here and dated since high school. They worked together at the local hospital. Maddie was a nurse. Tina was an X-ray tech. They enjoyed vacationing in Florida once a year and took trips on cruise ships. They kept to themselves and had never really faced any sort of prejudice since high school. Even back then, it was just name-calling.

That had all changed when they moved in across the street from Linda Reyes.

Maddie and Tina had always had a dog, but they kept it leashed, and the dog was well-behaved. Several times, animal control had knocked on their door responding to noise complaints, even a few weeks after their dog had passed away. Maddie and Tina had served as volunteers for several local charities, but their help always got turned away if Linda was on the board. After Tina passed, Maddie formed a race team at the hospital, and their entry fees were lost the year that Linda was president of the race. Even after the hospital offered to pay, Linda still tried to block them from participating. Packages disappeared from Maddie and Tina's porch. Mail was stolen. Their car tires were occasionally flattened.

Maddie said it all started years ago, just after she and Tina moved to Maple Street. They were celebrating their anniversary at the Milieu. Tina had gone to the restroom, and Maddie was sitting at the bar waiting for their table. Linda's husband had recognized her as his new neighbor and introduced himself. She'd pushed him away when he wrapped his arm around her waist and put his hand on her buttocks.

He'd spilled his drink and started to yell at her, so she ran to get Tina, and they left the restaurant. After that incident, there was always trouble. Maddie was the temperamental one. She'd wanted to go across the street and knock on their door, but Tina wouldn't let her. She wanted to keep the peace. When Linda's husband passed away a few years later, things finally began to settle down for them. Despite Tina encouraging Maddie to look the other way, she'd still held a grudge against Linda all these years.

"Do you know about the Pink Poodle Club?" I asked her.

"Oh yeah, everyone knows about that. Every Friday night! She and her husband started the club together after they retired. If it weren't for the sex club and those damn birds, the hotel would have closed a long time ago."

"Did you know that Nate and Christine Perkins were members?"

"No, I didn't know that," she said, studying my face. "How did you know?"

"My friend that you've seen here. She works at the hotel. Your video, their argument, that was a Friday. It takes place right after they returned home from the hotel."

"So Linda knew them?"

"I'm pretty sure she did. I saw them talking to her on the day they moved in."

"Wait!" she yelled out, holding up a hand.

She knelt and rewound the video from the night of Nate's disappearance. She let it play right at the part where Nate got up and went back into the house after he'd been sitting on the porch. We both watched the screen in silence.

"Watch this," she said, after a few minutes of nothing happening. She looked at me. "Did you see that?"

"What am I looking for?"

"Linda was already home, right? And this is Nate and Christine coming home from the hotel, as you said. They argue. She goes inside. He sits outside for a bit and then goes inside. Thirty minutes later, that mysterious truck shows up," she said.

"That's right."

"Watch Linda's front window about ten minutes after Nate goes inside," she said, rewinding the video. "Her lights were on. She stays up late—always has—so I didn't think anything about it until now."

"Can you zoom in?"

"Yeah, I think so," she said, enlarging the video.

We could see a shadow move across Linda's office window, reminiscent of when I had been inside the house and looked outside. It had to be Linda getting up from her desk to leave the office. She turned out the light behind her. The same shadow passed in front of the living room window on the opposite side a few

minutes later. Another different shadow followed behind her.

"She wasn't alone," I said.

"Nope. I bet that was Christine."

Someone had knocked on the back door. Linda had
gotten up to answer it and let the person inside. Maybe
Christine had gone to Linda's for help but had chosen
to go to the back door. Anyone else would have just
gone to the front out of habit, but if it was Christine,
maybe she did not want to be seen.

"Maybe Christine killed Nate after he went inside.
She ran next door to tell Linda. Linda called whoev-
er was in that truck. I'm just speculating, of course,"
Maddie said.

"No, I was thinking the same thing."

The two shadows crossed in front of the window
again, and then the light went out. The truck arrived
in front of the house minutes later before circling the
block and pulling into the alley. I asked if Maddie had
also seen Christine's car the night Parker and I saw
someone at the house.

"Yeah, she cut her hair," Maddie said. "The girl.
Christine. She's been back to the house several times,
day and night."

"In her car?"

"Yeah."

"You are sure it's her?"

"Definitely. I walked right past her on that side of
the street one afternoon when I was walking the dog.
I don't know why she cut her hair like that. She looks
like a guy."

Once again, I ignored the topic. That meant Parker
and I had seen Christine at the park that night and later
back at the house. We just thought it was a man because

of the short hair. Neither of us had considered Christine might have cut her hair. Either she did it to disguise herself, or maybe she was living as Chris again.

"So that leaves one final question," Maddie said, looking at me.

"Yeah?"

"Was that you in Linda's house?"

I chose not to tell her about my father's affair with Linda. That didn't seem as crucial, since Maddie was also focused on Nate's murder. Instead, I explained that Parker and I had been doing our own investigating. Parker knew about the logbooks that Linda kept about the club, so I told Maddie I'd gone into Linda's house looking for those. It wasn't a lie.

"Did you find the books?"

"Yeah, I did."

I didn't see any harm in telling her that Nate and Christine had shared a room with Hunter and Celeste Lowery. She knew of the Lowery family and their footprint on Shadow Wood, but she had never met any of them. She recognized Celeste's name from the *Gazette*. She agreed with me that Celeste wasn't a very reliable reporter.

"You think they are involved in all of this?" she asked.

"Yeah, we do."

Maddie let me have the flash drive. She said it was a copy anyway. I told her I'd keep her informed if we learned anything new; she agreed to do the same. She also told me not to worry about the video. She was never going to share it with Linda. I believed her.

"Welcome to the neighborhood," she said with a smile and a tone of sarcasm.

"Thanks," I said. I saw no reason to tell her I wouldn't be staying. "Maddie, you said you've lived here a long time. Did you ever see other people coming and going from Linda's house?"

"What do you mean?"

"Other men."

"Oh yeah, before and after her husband died. Before we knew about the Pink Poodle Club, Tina and I used to joke that she was running a brothel over there."

"If I showed you a picture of a man, do you think you might recognize him?"

"Maybe. I don't know. That was years ago. It's pretty much just been her or her sons the last few years."

I went to my desk. Melaine had given me an envelope that contained copies of some of the photos we'd displayed at Dad's funeral. I tried to find one from around that time. I found one of him opening his Christmas gifts. I wasn't sure of the year it was taken, but it was in our house, so he and Mom were still married then. I handed the photo to her.

"Ha! Yeah, I know him. That's Mr. Owen," Maddie said, smiling while admiring the photo.

"You know him?"

"Yeah, Tina and I were out walking our dog once, and she slipped her leash to chase after a squirrel. Mr. Owen was just leaving Linda's house. He saw what happened and helped us chase her down."

"He was leaving Linda's house," I repeated, making sure I had heard what she'd said.

"Yeah. Nice man. I saw him a few times after that, and he always waved at us. I thought he was Linda's brother or something until I saw them kiss once on her porch. All the men coming and going after that made sense. How do you know him? Wait. Is this—"

"He's my dad."

"Oh man, I'm so sorry."

"It's okay. That was years ago. I've known for a while. I mean, I knew he had an affair. I didn't know it was with Linda until recently, just after he died."

"I'm sorry. He was a nice man," she said.

"Thanks."

"I always wondered what happened to him. He just disappeared. He stopped coming around, so I figured he and Linda broke up. Did your mom know?"

I nodded.

We were both silent for a moment, processing. I knew this silence well because I'd experienced a lot of it. I was glad that my dad had been kind and helpful to Tina and Maddie, unlike Linda. She handed the photo back to me with a stern hand, her opinion of my father swaying.

"It's okay," I said. "I'm okay."

She nodded, reluctant to believe me. I didn't believe myself either.

She patted my shoulder, the gesture of a coach of the losing team. I walked her to the door, and we stepped out onto the porch. She looked like she had something to say but kept it to herself. Maybe she knew something else, or maybe she wanted to offer some words of encouragement but knew they'd be useless. Maddie was an honest, no-bullshit kind of woman. I appreciated that.

We both stood there, looking over at Linda's house for a minute, before she said goodbye and walked home.

It was true what they say, about how you can live on a street for years and never really get to know your neighbors. I'd only lived on Maple Street for a few weeks, but I felt like I knew everything. And yet, in a way, I didn't know these people at all. I'd never spoken to Nate or Christine. I'd never spoken to Linda either. Words exchanged or not, everyone in a small town was still a stranger.

I went back inside to watch all of the videos again, hoping to find footage where Christine returned to the house after Nate's death. She came back to the house several times. She never stayed very long. She always came out with bags of clothes and small boxes, filling the car's trunk with various belongings. I was never at the duplex to see her because I was out following Linda or Hunter Lowery. Christine was indeed moving out.

During one of her trips to the house in the daylight, I zoomed in and recognized Christine right away. The hair was short. She wore a bulky sweater and jacket, concealing her breasts. It was the same person we'd seen in the park, the same Chris from high school.

Though the video from Maddie's doorbell camera painted a different picture, I still wasn't convinced Christine and Linda both were involved in Nate's murder. But there was no doubt that another person besides Christine knew what happened to Nate.

That person was Hunter Lowery.

CHAPTER 38

THE MORE I learned about Nate and Christine Perkins, the less I obsessed over my dad's affair with Linda. The mystery behind Nate's death had become a welcome distraction. I could have walked across the street at any time and knocked on Linda's door and just asked her for answers. She probably would have slammed the door in my face or called the cops. Or maybe there was another side to the story that I didn't know, and she'd invite me inside to tell me about it. Her story.

Maybe others in this town were wrong about Linda Reyes. Maybe she was just a lonely, eccentric old woman keeping up appearances. I think, in a way, I wanted her to be that. The truth was that Linda had a dark side, as did most people with any status in this town—in any small town, for that matter. Whether it was skeletons in the closet, or dirty laundry for everyone to see, we all had secrets that were hard to keep. We all had stories. I was no different except that no one knew me. No one knew Toby Kipton. No one knew Stephen Glass. It wasn't easy to be invisible in a small town unless you were nobody.

Either way, I'd been too afraid to find out the truth about my father. I wouldn't have believed her. Instead, I'd gotten wrapped up in the lives of the neighbors—Linda's neighbors and mine. I'd never intended to avoid getting the answers I wanted from her, but that's precisely what I had done. I didn't know if I cared about the affair anymore. I was beginning to realize why my family had kept it quiet. Put enough time between yourself and a problem, and sooner or later you stop worrying about it.

So I went to my dad, looking for the answers. I drove back out to the cemetery, much like he'd done all those years ago when he visited his father's grave. I parked at the church and crossed the street. A brisk wind ushered me up the tired concrete steps. I ignored the others eternally resting before me as I cut through the rows of gravestones to get to my father's grave.

With thousands of words burdening my mind, I stood there with my hands in my pockets and said nothing. I took a deep breath, savoring the country air like a long drink of cool water from the garden hose on a summer day. I searched the sky for a hawk, any piece of familiarity to focus on so this didn't feel so awkward. It was still awkward.

"What am I doing?" I asked out loud for both of us.

I couldn't make up my mind if I regretted being here or if there was other unfinished business to reflect upon. I thought I heard a radio or a car door slam. Or was it just the sounds of civilization miles away from this place still lingering in my mind? Was it the sounds of nature catching up to me? That hawk overhead or a dog howling in the distance. Or something else? I was too caught up in my own thoughts to register anything else or to look around to see if someone—

"I knew sooner or later we'd cross paths. Didn't expect it would be here," a woman spoke from behind me.

I wanted to jerk my head to the side, to jump back, the impulse of a wild animal caught off guard. I wanted to be a snake raring up and heaving itself into the corner of a barn, ready to strike, intimidated, desperately looking for a way to escape. But instead of striking, I also wanted to just slither away.

I didn't give her the satisfaction of knowing she'd caught me off guard. I exhaled and turned my head slowly. Linda Reyes was standing behind me. I looked back at my father's grave, not wanting her to witness one single tremor on my face. She didn't deserve the satisfaction of knowing she made me feel tense. I'd seen her relish in that feeling so many times with Rose and others.

"Despite whatever you think of him, Owen, your father, was a good man," she said, taking a few steps closer to stand beside me to look down at my father's gravestone.

"You don't know what I think of him," I said. It sounded defensive. Maybe it needed to sound that way.

"I have a pretty good idea. I think you want to be wrong about him. Isn't that why you moved in across the street from me, Toby?"

"How do you know my name?"

"Your father loved you. Melaine. Samuel too. He talked about all three of you all the time. Showed me pictures. You're the same age as my youngest boy, Vic."

I had more questions, but I didn't know where to start. I didn't know how to ask them without yelling at her, without turning on her now. Some part of me wanted to hit her, to spit on her, to bury her right here next to my father with my bare hands.

We all have that monster inside of us that slides up our throats sometimes, trying to get out. Yet I was almost afraid of her. Her inner monster was looming too and seemed much stronger. I just stood there and held it back and let her talk. I let her tell her story, which was all I'd wanted since the day I stood here and read her letter to Melaine. I wanted to hear her side of it.

She told me she'd been a reckless teen girl, always in love or pining over some jock or popular boy. My father had been neither of those stereotypes, so she must have broadened her taste in men as she got older.

She'd been prom queen and president of every club that only required good looks and your parents' money to get votes. She'd certainly held on to that trait later in life. She was a straight-A student and intelligent—learning came easy, and she never had to study—but that didn't stop her from sneaking out of her bedroom window at night.

She kept up appearances for the sake of her parents. Linda could ruin another girl's reputation if they gossiped about her. Boys were too afraid to talk or compare notes outside the locker room. She worked hard to keep the upper hand and threatened to devastate anyone who stood up to her.

She'd kept that reputation later in life. That power she had over others, that ability to dominate or be feared, had been useful. Her parents worried about what would become of her after she graduated, so her mom forced her to take that job at the meat plant.

I kept my head turned away from her. I didn't want her to catch me rolling my eyes. I still felt like she could sense my expressions, so I avoided any that feigned arrogance. She was proud of her accomplishments. Hearing her tell it, you would have almost thought she killed her mom just to get the secretary position at the plant. Maybe she had.

Dad had flirted with her. She flirted back. Several of the men at the plant took notice of her. This game came naturally to her by now. It seemed even more fun after she got married. She could never marry a country boy, a farmer, anyone who worked in the processing plant. Her parents would have disowned her. They'd introduced her to a doctor. They'd only been dating a few months before he proposed.

He wanted to build a house for them, but she'd chosen the house on Maple Street. She wanted a smaller house because it would be easier for her to clean and look after it if something ever happened to him or if they divorced. What kind of woman picks a house based on the possible demise of her marriage? I already knew the answer to my question.

She loved my dad. He told her that he loved her too. Her husband worked nights at the hospital, so she was home alone after work for a few hours. She invited my dad to her house so they could have more time to themselves with no risk of getting caught by someone at the plant. Then she got pregnant. She was afraid it was his, but they got lucky. It wasn't. When her first son was born, she wanted to stop.

She needed to become a responsible mother. Even though her infant son was too young to be aware of what was happening around him, she still felt guilty. My father would often arrive at her house, and they'd undress and go to her bedroom with her new baby sleeping in the next room. That guilt would creep in, and she'd ask him to leave.

Eventually her son would be old enough to know this man shouldn't be here. He might slip up and mention the man to his father. Sure, there would be day care or babysitters. She could tell them she was running late. They could get a motel room. She could make it work; she could find the time for her and my father to be together. But her husband was pressuring her. He wanted another child. Her mother passed, and Linda got promoted at the plant. Life was moving fast. She was afraid they'd slip up. Then, one day, my mother left a note at Linda's door.

"My mother came to your house?" I asked.

"I always assumed it was her."

"What did the note say?"

"It said: *Owen, this woman is going to ruin your life. Go home to your family.*"

"You didn't see who left the note?"

"No, it was in the mailbox. I never showed it to him. I found out I was pregnant again a few days later."

"And?"

"It wasn't your father's. But I was overcome with all of that angst and dread all over again, just like before. I knew I couldn't keep doing this."

She ended it with my father shortly after her second son was born. He'd begged her not to do it. He said he'd leave my mom for her, but Linda knew she couldn't leave her husband. Her kids. She thought of his kids—Samuel, Melaine, and me. Their affair had always been a game to her, nothing serious, just something to help her cling to her brassy youth. She didn't want to be responsible for ruining another family, much less her own. They had to stop seeing each other.

"But he refused to end it, so you got him fired from the plant?" I asked.

"No! What made you think that?"

"He told us he retired, but he didn't go to the company's retirement party. There was no plaque. We thought maybe you did it out of spite or to end it."

"No, it wasn't me. I promise," she said, shaking her head, embarrassed by the false blame. "It was your father trying to spite me."

Dad had started another relationship with a young girl at the plant. It only lasted a few months. They were sloppy, kind of the way Linda and Dad had been in the beginning, sneaking time together at lunch in their cars or in a bathroom stall in the back of the plant. They got caught. The girl got fired. Dad got let go too, but because he'd put in so many years, he was still entitled to his pension.

I was more like my father than I expected. The only difference was there was no one at home, no one who loved me, to be hurt by my illicit behavior. Or maybe there was, and I just didn't know it. Had my actions hurt Ash?

"I did love him," she said as if somehow that might offer some healing or fix whatever was broken.

She didn't know it, but she'd already fixed a lot of what was busted inside me just by telling me all of this. She'd given me the information, the answers I'd been seeking all this time. I felt like I had more questions to ask, but it was just me wanting to fill the space. I couldn't think of any questions—any words—to say to her. She could have been lying, but I didn't care. I realized now I'd never know the difference. This was their past. Not mine.

"So, is it just a coincidence that you rented the house across the street from me?" she asked. "Or is there anything else you need to know?"

"How did you recognize me?" I asked.

"I saw you at the funeral and knew you must be Toby. I asked your cousin just to be sure."

"You know Jenny?"

"No. I was sitting in my car that day, and she was parked next to me. I rolled down my window and asked her. Don't you remember? I'm pretty sure you saw us."

So many pieces of the puzzle had fallen into place without any effort.

There was still the mystery of Nate Perkins. I had not even mentioned the Pink Poodle Club. I'd let her own the conversation, to tell her part in all of this. I had a feeling she'd been honest with me. Otherwise I don't think she would have accepted the blame. She could have easily lied and blamed all of it on my father. I knew she was relieving a burden that both of us had been carrying.

Despite their lengthy affair, I now knew my father had not left my mom for Linda. I think my family had always thought it was her. It was easier to accept a tragic event in your life when you had someone to blame, someone you didn't know or didn't love. Dad had let Linda carry that because she'd broken his heart. I had no sympathy for him for that.

Maybe it was his guilt. Maybe it was his love for another woman he couldn't be with. Maybe it was the enticement of finding someone else who could be with him. I could ask him, but he couldn't tell me, so none of that mattered now.

Linda turned away, indicating she was ready to leave.

"Was my father involved in the Pink Poodle Club?" I called out.

She turned back to look at me. I couldn't tell if it was fear or anger in her eyes. Or was this where she would start lying to me?

"You know about that?" she asked, looking me straight in the eyes.

"Was he?"

"No. That all started after your father. How much do you know?"

"I just know what everyone else in this town knows."

"It saved that damn hotel, ya know," she said with a hint of irritation. I could tell she was accustomed to having to defend her actions. She was good at it.

I held up my hand and shook my head to let her know I wasn't judging her. I'd done plenty of that already. She turned back around and started to walk toward the steps. I followed her, ready to leave this place myself.

"What do you know about the death of our neighbor?" I asked, figuring it was safe to do that since her back was to me. It was time to ask the questions that didn't involve my father. I doubted she would answer them.

"Nate?" she said, freezing in her steps.

"Yeah."

"He and his *wife* should have been a bit more honest," she said.

"About Christine being transgender?"

"About a lot of things," she yelled over her shoulder. She picked up the pace and beat me across the street to the parking lot.

She kept her back turned to me as she got into her car. I stood there, expecting her not to even look at me as she drove away. Instead, she rolled down her window to say one last thing.

"You took something from my house. I want them back," she said.

I started to speak—to defend myself—but she cut me off and raised a hand for me to stop.

"You can return them to me by putting them on my back sun porch. You're well acquainted with my backyard, right?"

I nodded.

"No questions asked. You can do it on Thursday while I'm out. In case you are wondering, I moved my house key. Oh, and one more thing. Stop following me around town. You should know me well enough by now to know that you don't want any trouble."

And then she drove away.

CHAPTER 39

LEAVING THE cemetery, I felt like I could just leave Shadow Wood right now. I was done. All of this was done. I knew everything I had wanted to find out. About my dad. About Linda. Nothing else mattered at this point. I could call my landlord and tell him I'd had to leave town. He could keep the furniture. Then I would text Parker and tell her I'd gone back to the city. It would be easier if I didn't have to face her.

But something wouldn't let me do that. Not yet. I knew what it was too. It was the whole mess with Nate and Christine Perkins. Driving back to the duplex, I called Ash to tell him about my conversation with Linda.

"Do you think she followed you to the cemetery?" Ash asked.

"I don't think so. I do think Linda loved him. I think she regrets they couldn't be together."

"Well, you have some answers now."

Some answers, I thought.

"Yeah. Yeah, I do."

"I can't believe you didn't ask her more about Nate Perkins."

"I didn't know what to say. I was also afraid of how she might answer. She's a very domineering woman. You should have seen how the look on her face changed just when I asked her about the swingers' club. She jumped in her car and left before I had a chance to mention anything else."

"So when are you coming back? I'll throw a party," Ash asked, dismissing all of it. He was ready for this to be done. So was I.

"No party, please. I've only been gone a few weeks."

"A few? It's been two months."

"Really? That long? Well, that's eight weeks."

"Which is more than a few."

"It's still no reason to celebrate. I'd enjoy some time with just the two of us."

"Drinks, then! Dinner! There's a new restaurant in Midtown that just opened. I've been dying to go, but I can wait," he said.

He had not given me saying *just the two of us* a second thought. Why would he? It had always been just the two of us. I was never good at expressing my emotions. Maybe I should have said more, but I decided to wait.

He was disappointed that I wasn't coming back right away. So was I. But I felt like I had a few more loose ends to take care of in regards to Nate and Christine. I doubted I could do anything to help the police solve Nate's murder—if they were even trying—but it was worth a shot because of the video Maddie had shown me.

I had one last thing I wanted to try before I went back to the city. I was already in this deeper than I had imagined or ever wanted to be, so why stop now? I also felt like I owed it to Parker. She was a good friend, and I could use one of those in this town.

I beat Linda back to Maple Street. Maybe she'd had errands to run. I could have checked my notebook and probably guessed where she was going next. I parked and walked next door to see if Maddie was home.

"Hi, Toby," she said, opening the door and holding back her curious beagle. "Sorry, I can put her up if you don't like dogs."

"No, it's okay."

"Come inside," she said, pulling the happy pup away from the door by its collar. "This is Lily."

I knelt and let Lily sniff my hand. She immediately rolled over, wanting her belly to be rubbed. Her tail flapped against the floor with excitement as I petted her. I found a sweet spot under her ears that calmed her.

"She loves that," Maddie said, smiling down at us.

"I stopped by because I wanted to ask you something," I said.

"Sure. Want a drink?" she said.

"Yeah, that would be nice."

"Beer okay?"

"Of course. Thanks."

I followed her to the kitchen. I wasn't much of a beer drinker, so I was relieved when it was two bottles of Corona she pulled from the fridge.

"This okay?" she said, already twisting off the caps with her hand and not waiting for my response. "I can cut up a lemon or lime if you want."

"Nah, this is perfect," I said, taking the bottle.

"What did you want to ask me?"

"This is going to sound strange, but did you leave a note in Linda's mailbox once? For Owen? For my dad?"

Her eyes felt heavy on me. She was studying me, trying to decipher how I'd found out. She was a guilty child trying to conjure up a fib. I smiled at her to let her know I was okay with it if she had done it.

"Yeah. I did. How did you know?" she asked.

"My sister found it in my dad's things." I was a child telling a lie now. "We knew it wasn't my mother's handwriting, so…."

"I can explain," she said.

She'd noticed my dad's wedding band and had written the note for Linda to find. She wanted to frighten her more than anything. It was a nerveless attempt at getting back at her neighbor. I wanted to tell her that it had probably saved my parents' marriage at the time, but who knew if that was true?

"I'm sorry I didn't tell you earlier," she said.

"Oh, don't be sorry. I'm not mad about it. I kind of like the idea of my dad being caught off guard back then. I love him, but he deserved that."

"I had actually written it for Linda's husband to find. I guess that didn't happen."

"Is this Tina?" I asked, noticing a framed photo of Maddie with a woman on her mantel.

"Yes, it is. That was taken on one of our cruise ship vacations."

"You two were a cute couple."

"She was the love of my life."

We stood there in silence, looking at the photo and sipping our drinks. She was thinking of a memory of her and Tina, maybe from the cruise ship or just of their life together in general. I was thinking of how much I wanted that and how much I missed Ash.

"Do you have someone?" she asked me.

"No," I said, turning away from the photo to look at her. "But there is always the hope of someone."

"Stop hoping," she said. "I had thirty years with Tina. I'd take thirty more if I could have them."

"That good, huh?"

"Oh, it wasn't always perfect. We had our ups and downs. Relationships take work. Sure, there were days we probably hated each other. We argued a lot. But our love for each other outweighed everything else. It was hard, but we always attempted to never go to bed mad at each other. We always made up before we went to sleep."

"Why's that?"

"Tina said her dad once told her that you should never go to sleep being mad at someone because we aren't promised tomorrow."

"That's good advice."

I admired her. I couldn't imagine spending thirty years with anyone, but I knew it would be with Ash if I had the chance. We'd already said we'd be old maids together if we didn't have boyfriends by the time we were fifty. Why couldn't we be each other's boyfriends now and stop waiting? Stop hoping, as Tina had said.

"Can I ask you something else?"

"Sure," she said.

"Why did you stay in Shadow Wood?"

She smiled and nodded and then took a huge swig from her Corona bottle. "Tina wanted us to leave after high school, but I didn't want to go. I don't know. Small-town girl, I suppose. I always felt safe here. We bought this house and just settled in."

"She stayed here because of you?" I asked.

"She stayed here because of us."

"Do you feel like you held her back?"

"Nah, she could have gone if she wanted. Now that I think back on it, had she chosen to leave, I probably would have gone after her. I wouldn't have let her get away that easy. I loved her."

Maddie had so much life experience, completely different from anything I'd experienced, even though we shared a common bond. We were both gay. We'd both grown up here. Yet she'd felt a connection to Shadow Wood and chose to live her life here. It made me wonder what my life might have been like had I stayed here. I didn't regret the path I'd chosen. There was no reason to look back in life, but it is okay sometimes to ponder the what-ifs.

Maddie was right. I should stop hoping. Instead, I should do something about it.

CHAPTER 40

MADDIE'S WORDS motivated me to finish up in Shadow Wood, even though it still felt like I had no idea what I was doing. Until now, events had happened mostly without me getting involved. Breaking into Linda's house had been an attempt to learn more about her affair with my father. It had only revealed Linda's extracurricular activities. I'd followed her to the hotel and learned about the swingers' club. Then Nate's murder had happened. Through all of it, I discovered that Shadow Wood was an immoral small town full of secrets, which I'd known since I was a kid growing up here.

Sometimes, children were completely unaware of such stresses in their community. They had no life experience to expose them to the filth and gossip that tainted the town they grew up in. They were innocent lambs carefully guided and protected by their sheepdog parents, taught to ignore what might be happening to other sheep just across the fence. But the lambs grew up. They became those sheep. They ignored their protectors' warnings. They strayed into other fields, where they did not belong. That was me now, anxious to get back to familiar pastures even though I was right where all of my questions had led me.

Maddie leaving the note for my father gave me an idea. I took her flash drive and went to Sacred Grounds, Shadow Wood's only local coffee shop. Despite everyone having their own laptops, tablets, or cell phones these days, Sacred Grounds still had a few public Wi-Fi computers available for their customers to use. There, I used one of the computers to create an anonymous email address.

After looking up the *Shadow Wood Gazette* website and locating Celeste Lowery's contact information, I used my new email address to send her a copy of the video from the night of Nate's disappearance. For a message, I typed, *ISN'T THIS YOUR HUSBAND'S LAND ROVER?* I hit Send and left the coffee shop.

I texted Parker and asked her if she wanted to stop by later that night after work. I didn't tell her about my unexpected meeting with Linda. She would have been upset with me for not asking Linda more questions about Nate. I also didn't tell her about sending the video to Celeste.

Parker texted back and asked if I could pick her up from the hotel instead. I didn't question why; I just texted back that I'd be there. When I got to the hotel, I pulled up beside the front of the building. She was already waiting for me by the entrance.

"What's up?" I asked as she opened the passenger's door and got inside.

"Want to go back to high school?" she asked with the giant grin I was accustomed to seeing when she was excited about something.

"Not really. Why?"

"Lucas started working as a busboy this week. He's friends with Eric Harland," she said.

"Who's that?"

"Christine's brother."

Lucas and Eric ran track together. When I met him, Lucas didn't strike me as the athletic type. He looked more like a pothead to me. I guess I was a lousy judge of character when it came to teenagers. That was predictable. They were still trying to figure out themselves. No one else could do it for them.

Eric didn't like to talk about anything going on with Christine, but he'd mentioned to Lucas that his older brother had recently moved back in with him and his mom. Curious, Parker asked Lucas how many siblings Eric had. He said only one. That meant his brother was Chris Harland. He might have just called Christine his brother by accident, but Parker was already thinking what I knew to be true from Maddie's security cam footage. Christine was now living as Chris again.

Parker asked Lucas to get Chris's phone number from Eric. She explained that she'd gone to high school with Chris and just wanted to get in contact with him to say hello and catch up. It seemed too easy, but it worked. Lucas had the number just a few minutes later. Eric might have been too naïve, but Parker hadn't lied. She did want to talk to Chris.

"So you just called her?"

"Sure did! She was hesitant at first, but she agreed to meet us."

"Did she ask how you got her number?"

"Nope, and I didn't tell her. I don't want to get Lucas in trouble."

"At the high school?"

"I suggested it. She didn't want to come into the city, and her parents live out near the meat-processing plant."

Shadow Wood High School's main building was shaped like a giant E, with three main halls for classrooms extending off the lobby and front offices. Those spaces between the halls were commons areas with picnic tables. They were decent outdoor spaces for students on their lunch breaks, and since there were no outdoor windows where teachers could monitor you, they were also a hangout for smokers or students skipping class. Behind the main building was the student parking lot. Parker told Christine we'd meet her in between the first and second halls.

"She's already here," Parker said, spotting Christine's car as I pulled in. I parked next to it. The car was empty. I looked at the back window and noticed the pink poodle sticker had been torn off.

At one time, the spaces had been well-lit with outdoor security lights. Over the years, vandals had knocked out the lights so the areas could be used for extracurricular activities at night. Most students didn't like to eat outside in the spaces because of the litter, used condoms, and beer cans accumulated from the weekend.

Replacing the lights had gotten expensive, so the school had stopped trying. A heavy chain extended between two poles with a sign that warned trespassers to stay out of the area after school hours was the school-board's inept solution. The spaces were so dark that stepping over the chain felt as if I was about to traverse into a dark cave on the side of a mountain.

"Over here," a voice called out from inside the commons.

A faint glimmer of moonlight fell upon the picnic tables between the two halls. As my eyes adjusted, I could make out a dark, hooded figure sitting at one of them. Was this Christine or someone else? They reminded me of the figure who was in the park and at Christine's house that same night.

As we sat down across from them, they pushed the hood of their jacket back and revealed it was indeed the person we'd seen that night.

CHAPTER 41

"HI, CHRISTINE," Parker said.

"It's Chris now," she said, sounding exhausted. "I'm Chris. Again. For now."

She pulled her jacket away from her chest, an attempt to hide her breasts. I felt sorry for her. She'd spent so much time and energy trying to find out who she was, and it was evident from the Christine I'd seen from the first day they'd move in, she was finally succeeding at that. Now, for some reason unknown to us, she was turning back into the version of herself she'd always hated.

"Hi, Chris. I'm Toby," I said, looking into her eyes. They were sad eyes. I could tell there was someone else in those eyes, and they were growing tired of hiding behind them.

"Yeah, Parker told me over the phone. You lived across the street from us, right? On Maple?"

"Yeah, that's right."

"Were you spying on us?"

"Not intentionally."

"Toby's dad had an affair with Linda Reyes," Parker offered.

"Oh, that explains a lot," she said with a sneer.

Her look was toward Linda, not me. I wasn't sure it explained why I was living on Maple Street, but I left it alone.

"It was a long time ago," I added.

"Parker said you saw us that night?"

I looked at Parker. She nodded. So I began to tell what I saw.

"You and Nate were arguing that night. I couldn't hear anything. Then you went inside. Nate came back out and sat outside on the porch. I looked back out the window before I went to bed, and he was gone, and so was your car. Then I saw you with a cop next morning."

Christine shook her head as if she was annoyed with someone. She blinked and pursed her lips. She was quiet for a beat, looking down at her lap or the ground. Parker started to speak up, but I put my hand on her arm and nodded for her to let Christine take her time.

"That wasn't a cop," Christine finally said, looking up at us.

"Who was it?"

"They call him Vey. I think it's short for Harvey or something. He's one of Hunter Lowery's men. He's the manager at Jake's too. Does odd jobs for Hunter. He's basically a hit man."

"A hit man? Has he—killed people?" Parker asked.

"Oh yeah," Christine said. "You don't want to fuck with him. Or with the Lowerys."

"He came back to my door the next day," I said.

"What for? What did he say?" Christine asked with a bit of worry.

"He wanted to know if I saw anything. He asked if I had a security camera."

"What did you tell him?"

"I told him I didn't hear anything and that I didn't have a camera. That was the truth. I don't."

"Be glad. If you did, you'd be dead now."

"I thought he was your father," I said.

"Why did you think that?"

"He said he was Officer Harland. He even had a business card. I showed it to a friend, though, and she said it was a fake. I would never have linked it to you until Parker told me you were Chris Harland from high school."

"Um, yeah. It was definitely fake. My dad was a cop. He was retired. Left the department years ago. He died last year. I can't believe that asshole used my father's fucking name!" Christine said.

"How did your father die?" Parker asked.

"They said it was a hit-and-run, that a drunk driver ran him off the road and left the scene, but I didn't believe that. I was working at Jake's and deep into trouble with Hunter by then. I can't prove it, but Hunter probably had him taken out."

"Were you and Hunter seeing each other?" I asked.

"Are you kidding me? No! What made you think that?"

"One of the girls working at Jake's told us some stuff," Parker said.

"Those whores? And you believed her?" Christine yelled, standing up. I thought she was going to walk away, but she was only trying to make a point. She sat back down.

"No, we didn't believe anyone. We're just trying to figure everything out," I said, hoping to calm her down.

"Look, you want to know what really happened to Nate?" Christine asked, showing impatience.

We both nodded.

Christine started by telling us that any rumors about her and Hunter were not true. Once Vey found out she was going to have surgery, he told Hunter. Christine had wanted to work up front with the other girls, but Hunter refused. So Vey fired Christine.

Nate and Christine had met at Jake's, but Nate would have never gone there had he known that Hunter Lowery owned the place. Nate went to the same private school as Celeste, and they'd been high school sweethearts. They continued to date while she was away at college until she cheated on him with Hunter. Celeste's affair with Hunter, coupled with Nate now dating one of Hunter's employees, was the main reason for the ongoing hatred between them.

"What about the Pink Poodle Club?" I asked.

"It was a complete accident that we ended up coupled together that first time. It's a random draw, and you never know who you are sharing a room with until they show up. I got to the room first. I peeked in and saw Hunter and Celeste already in the room. Nate was still in the bar, so I went and got him, and we left. I told him I was nervous and couldn't do it, which was the truth. I wanted to quit the club, but I didn't know how to tell Nate."

"And what about the second time?"

"It was either just coincidence, or Linda did that on purpose since we didn't go to the room the first time. Unfortunately, Nate got to the room before me that night. He and Hunter got into an argument. Hunter told Nate that I owed him money. I'd never told Nate about that, so that's why we were arguing when you saw us in front of the house."

Most of the money she'd earned from working in the Romeo Room at Jake's had paid for her breast and cheek implants, but she had asked Vey for a loan to cover the rest. She'd never told him what the money was for, but he gave it to her. She never paid it back after she got fired.

"What happened inside your house that night?" I asked.

Christine took a deep breath and hung her head again. Parker reached over to take her hand to offer support. Christine pulled her hand away at first. She seemed frightened or unsure of Parker's comforting gesture, but then she gave in and let Parker hold her hand.

"I think Vey had been watching our house after Hunter learned we'd joined the Pink Poodle Club," Christine said.

"Do you think Linda told him where you lived?" I asked.

"It doesn't matter. Most mortgages in this town are backed by Hunter's bank anyway. He wouldn't need Linda to find out where we lived. Vey was parked in the alley that night waiting for us to come home. He probably thought we parked in the garage and planned to confront us in the alley.

"He heard us arguing, so he knew we'd just gotten home. He knocked on the back door while I was inside. I didn't know Nate was sitting outside on the porch and that the front door was open. I thought it was Nate at the back door. I thought he had locked himself out or something, so I opened the back door. Vey forced his way in. I yelled for Nate. He heard me from the porch and came inside."

"Did Vey...?" Parker asked.

"No, not then. Not in the house. They were arguing. Nate tried to hit him, but he was too drunk to do anything. I got Vey to back down. Vey called Hunter and told him our address. Hunter came to the house, and they wanted Nate to leave with them. He said they just wanted to talk, but I knew better.

"Nate said he'd go with them. Hunter told me to follow them in our car. They took him to that vacant parking lot behind the Bacon Me Crazy restaurant. I knew they were going to beat him up or something worse. Nate was afraid they'd hurt me too, and he wanted me to go. He told Hunter to take me home. I should have stayed, but Hunter told me to leave the car for Nate to get back home. He said Nate would be okay. Nate begged me to leave. So I let Hunter give me a ride back to the house. Nate never came home."

"Did you call the police?" I asked.

"Of course, and Vey showed up at my door. He's an ex-cop. In case you don't know by now, Hunter Lowery and his family have the cops in the palms of their hands, and the sheriff is mixed up with the Poodle Club. So when I called the police, someone there tipped off Hunter. He sent Vey to warn me not to talk to anyone, or they'd kill me. Just like they did Nate."

"Someone said Nate had been poisoned," I said.

"Yeah, and Celeste Lowery wrote in the paper that he drowned in the park. I've heard it all. Look, I don't know what they did to him. Doesn't matter. The damn autopsy report said he died of exposure. It's not even winter!"

If the body had been stored in the basement freezer at Bacon Me Crazy, that would explain it showing signs of exposure to freezing temperatures. I wasn't going to share what Ali and Lucas had told us. I was glad Parker didn't either.

Everything I'd seen on Maddie's security camera footage corroborated what Christine had said happened that night. There was just one detail left unexplained.

"Did you go next door to Linda's house that night?" I asked Christine.

"No. Why?"

"Someone else was in her house that night right before Hunter showed up at your house. I saw two shadows through her front window. Linda wasn't alone," I said.

"How do you know all this? I thought you said you'd gone to bed sometime after Nate had gone inside," she asked.

"I did. I don't have a door cam or anything, but my neighbor does. A few days ago she showed me the footage from that night. I saw Hunter's Land Rover come to your house and pull around to the back. I saw you leave in the car, and it shows Hunter bring you back to the house."

"What did she do with the video?"

"Nothing, but I may have messed up," I said.

I explained that she'd given me a copy, and I'd anonymously emailed part of the video to Celeste Lowery, asking if that was her husband's vehicle in the video.

"When did you do this?" Chris asked.

"Earlier today."

"Did you tell your neighbor what you were doing?"

"No, I didn't."

"Do you have her phone number? Can you call her right now?" Christine said with sudden concern in her voice.

"No, I don't have it. Why?" I asked.

"Your friend could be in danger."

CHAPTER 42

"I CAN'T believe you sent that video to Celeste. Did she reply?" Parker said in the car.

"I don't know yet. I sent it from a made-up email address from the coffee shop," I said.

Parker and I had left Christine at the high school. We sped back through town, but there was a cop car blocking the entrance when we got to Maple. Its lights were flashing. A cop was standing next to the car and directing traffic. I rolled down my window to ask him what had happened. He ignored me, waving me on. I told him I lived on Maple Street. He motioned for me to pull over so I wouldn't hold up traffic.

"There's been a shooting," the policeman said. "I'm afraid you'll have to wait. I don't know how long. They aren't letting anyone in or out. You might want to stay with a friend or at a hotel tonight."

"Has anyone been hurt?" Parker asked, leaning over in the car to look at the officer.

"I honestly don't know, ma'am, but even if I did, I couldn't tell you that right now," he said.

"Was it at the Reyes residence? Linda Reyes is my mother," I said, trying to think of something to get the officer to reveal what he might know.

"Let me check. What's the address? Here, write it down for me."

He pulled a small notepad and an ink pen from his shirt pocket and handed it to me. I wrote the address down and handed the pad back.

"Stay here," he said.

He walked back over to his car and got inside. I could see him through the window talking on his car radio.

"Smart of you to say you were Linda's son," Parker said, looking at me. She spoke in a soft, worried voice as if we were teenagers who'd been pulled over and were waiting while the cop checked out our licenses. I hoped for our sake that he didn't.

"Thanks," I whispered back.

We waited several minutes. Finally the cop got out of his car and walked back across the street to us.

"I'm relieved to tell you it wasn't your mom. She's fine. It's something going on across the street from her house. That's all I can tell you," he said.

"Thanks, Officer," I said. I rolled up my window and pulled the car back onto the highway.

I circled the neighborhood to reach the other end of Maple Street across from the park, but a cop car had that end blocked too. I pulled the car into the parking lot at the park. I didn't know what to do or where to go next. I didn't have Maddie's phone number, so I had no way to reach her.

"What do we do now?" Parker asked.

"I have no idea. I don't know how to get in touch with Maddie."

"Didn't you say she had a dog?" Parker asked.

"Yeah. Why?"

"Is that it?"

Parker pointed across the park. A short beagle was walking around, sniffing at the playground equipment. It was not on a leash, and I didn't see anyone with it.

"Yes, I think that's Lily!"

We both got out of the car and started calling out Lily's name. The dog looked in our direction, raised her ears, and then began to run toward us. She must have remembered me. She started jumping up on my knee and nipping playfully at my hand. I picked Lily up and told Parker to check her collar for an ID tag.

"Yep, Maddie's name and number are on a plate on the inside of her collar," Parker said, trying to hold Lily's head still. Lily fought back, determined to lick Parker's hand.

"Call her!"

Parker dialed Maddie's number and handed me her phone. I put Lily in the back seat of my car.

"Hello! Who is this?" a voice said on the other end.

I could sense that she was upset. I could hear people talking in the background and what sounded like a police radio.

"Maddie, is that you?" I yelled.

"I said who is this?"

"Maddie, it's me. It's Toby. From next door. Are you okay?"

"Toby, where are you? Why are you calling? I'm sorry. I'm outside. I can't hear you very well. A lot is going on here. I'm trying to find Lily."

"I have her. I've got Lily. Maddie, I'm at the end of the street. I'm at the park. The cops have the street blocked off. What's going on?"

"Did you say you have Lily?" she asked.

"Yes, she was in the park. She's safe."

"Oh, thank God!"

"The cops won't let us onto the street. Maddie, what happened?"

Maddie told me to stay there. She wouldn't be able to walk down to the park, but she would try to get someone to let us onto the street. She'd either call me back or send someone to the park to meet us. I hung up the phone.

"What happened? What did she say?" Parker asked.

I could feel my face going numb and cold as I broke out in a light sweat. I felt light-headed. I was holding my breath. I quickly exhaled, wiping my forehead and leaning against the side of my car.

"Damn it, Toby! Are you okay? What did Maddie say? Tell me what happened," Parker said, putting her hand on my shoulder.

I looked at Parker and repeated what Maddie had told me.

"She shot someone."

CHAPTER 43

MADDIE CALLED back a few minutes later and asked that we wait at the park. It wouldn't be much longer before cops allowed people back onto the street. She'd call again if there were any changes or delays. We sat in my car with an anxious Lily. She peered out the window, looking at the empty park and wagging her tail. We waited at least an hour before the cop car moved and Maple Street was open again.

As we drove up Maple Street to find a place to park, I saw Hunter Lowery's Land Rover parked in front of the Perkins house. Up and down the sidewalk on both sides of the street, neighbors had gathered to watch the commotion taking place right where they lived. Several police cars were still parked in front of Maddie's house and the duplex, blocking the road. Their spinning lights painted the surrounding homes with beams of red and blue. Police officers and investigators were standing around everywhere. It was an eerie image I'd seen before, the night Nate Perkins's body had been found in the park.

I had to park a few blocks away, and Parker and I walked the rest of the way with Lily tucked under my arm. When we got closer, we could see yellow police tape extended from the mirrors of the cars and around Maddie's front porch. Maddie was watching for us from the front yard. When she saw us appear on the sidewalk, she raced across her yard and under the yellow tape. She took Lily from me and hugged her.

"Thank you so much, Toby. I was so worried about her," Maddie said, kissing Lily's face. Lily's tail thumped against Maddie's hip as she looked around at all of the activity and people.

"What happened?" Parker asked.

"Some guy showed up at my door and wanted to come inside and talk. He said he wanted all copies of my security-camera footage from the night Nate Perkins disappeared. He said his name was Officer Harland, and he gave me that same business card you showed me. I remembered it was a fake.

"The app on my cell phone chimes when there's movement out front. I was already watching him as he got out of his vehicle and approached my door. I recognized that Land Rover from that night, so I ran to the bedroom and got my revolver."

"And you shot him?" I asked.

"I refused to let him in. I tried to shut the door, and he stuck his foot in the way. He forced his way in. I backed up a bit, letting him just make his way inside the door. I was ready for him. He came for me, and that's when I shot him. The noise scared Lily, and she ran out the door."

An investigator walked up to us. He tapped Maddie on the shoulder.

"Excuse me, ma'am. Oh, your dog came back," an investigator said, patting Lily on the head.

"My neighbor found her in the park and brought her home," Maddie said.

"Here's the ID the perpetrator had on him. Do you recognize this man?" the investigator said, holding it up with a gloved hand. He shone a flashlight on it for her to see it better.

"Harvey Reyes," Maddie said, reading the name out loud. She turned her head and looked at me, wide-eyed.

Parker looked at me and whispered, "It's Vey." Chris had thought his real name was Harvey.

"Did you say Reyes?" I asked, looking back at Maddie.

"He's related to Linda Reyes," Maddie said.

"Who?" the investigator asked.

"Linda Reyes is my neighbor, over there across the street," she said, pointing to the house.

"Can I have a look at that?" I asked.

The investigator turned the ID so that I could see it. It was an older photo of him, but it was the same man who'd come to my door that day claiming to be Officer Harland. I'd know those eyes anywhere. Before, I thought I had known him from somewhere else but couldn't figure it out. I didn't say it out loud now, but I was pretty sure I'd seen photos of this man on the walls and in the photo albums inside Linda's house. Harvey was indeed one of Linda's sons.

The investigator walked across the street to knock on Linda's door, but she was not home.

Parker and I sat on my porch and watched as the crowd of neighbors and cops dissipated late into the night. Maddie, making herself available for questioning, stood in her front yard holding Lily. Lily and Maddie both seemed excited about all of the activity that surrounded them. A coroner and several medical examiners crowded the front of Maddie's house, and Harvey's body was taken out in a black body bag several hours later.

"I guess this is over," Parker said to me.

"I certainly hope so," I said.

"Hey! I've been meaning to ask you something. Did you ever learn more about your dad and Linda?"

"Yeah, I learned all I need to know," I said. "Look over there."

I pointed toward Christine and Nate's house. The sheer curtains in the picture window had remained drawn since that last night Nate was there. Other than the few times we'd seen Christine collecting belongings and clothes, the house had remained dark and still. A faint light now glowed behind those curtains, maybe from a flashlight or a dim lamp inside the house. A slender, hooded figure stood at the curtains, peeking out.

CHAPTER 44

MAPLE STREET was quiet the following day. I got up before the sun and dressed for a walk. It would be the last time I kept up appearances to appease those watching their doorbell cams or the elusive neighbors hiding behind their curtains and blinds. They didn't matter now, but I still felt the need to blend in.

I walked across Maple and to the end of the block. I took the side street up to the alley. I did not hide under the willow tree or crawl across the lawn. I did not worry about any neighbors who might be outside and who could see me. I walked straight to the sun porch and placed the logbooks on a plastic lawn chair sitting by the back door.

I knew Linda was not out of bed yet. If she obeyed her usual schedule, it would be hours before she came outside to trim the hedges. With the death of her son, today's routine might be different. I did not knock on the door. I turned and walked right back to the alley and down the side street again, and back to my side of Maple Street.

I knocked on Maddie's door. I was greeted by Lily's bark. I waved to Maddie through the doorbell cam. Lily was quickly hushed by Maddie.

"Don't worry. No gun," Maddie joked as she opened the door and invited me in.

"I just wanted to let you know I'll be leaving soon," I said.

"Moving already?"

"I'd never planned to stay this long."

"Well, I hate to see you go. You've been a good neighbor."

"I wouldn't call me that. I also wanted to apologize. It's probably my fault that Harvey Reyes showed up at your door last night."

"You saved Lily. That's more important to me than anything."

I told Maddie how Parker and I had met with Christine earlier that evening and she had alerted us that Maddie might be in trouble. Maddie was capable of taking care of herself and reminded me that had we not rushed back, Lily could have been picked up by someone else or hit by a car. She wasn't too enthralled with all the details, especially if Linda was involved, but in a way, she'd helped Christine. She could have some closure now and possibly go back to living as her true self with no need to hide.

I left Maddie's house and drove back out to the cemetery. This was not a wonted visit. There had been enough of those already since the funeral. The patch of dirt where Melaine and I had buried the letter from Linda was still visible. The soil was soft, and I pressed two fingers into it and found the folded paper with ease, just a few inches beneath the surface. It was damp with moisture from the earth but still intact. The ink on the envelope was still legible. I pulled it from the dirt, ripped it into several pieces, and stuffed them into my coat pocket.

My father deserved peace. He'd had all of this blame hovering over him for years while he was living. They were his mistakes. It was his past, not mine. But there was no reason to let it linger over him while he was dead.

"I'm sorry, Dad," I said as I turned and walked away.

Back at the duplex the following day, I packed my car with what few belongings I needed. Parker drove up just as I was finishing.

"You weren't going to leave without saying good-bye, were you?" she asked.

"Not at all. I thought you might be working, and I was going to swing by the restaurant. Do you want to grab lunch somewhere?"

"Sure. Where would you like to go?"

"Anywhere except Bacon Me Crazy!"

I took her to the old diner downtown on the court square where Dad had always liked to eat. Charlene was our waitress. She did not recognize me from the last time I'd been in with Samuel and Melaine on the day we'd had to plan Dad's funeral. I told Parker about how the diner had been my father's favorite place to eat.

We realized there were so many things that we didn't know about each other. We'd become such immediate friends, drawn together over the turmoil and dark secrets that plagued our hometown, the kinds of enigmas that often bring people together when they need support or an alliance. You could find friendships anywhere and in anyone. You could foster them for years or only know someone for a few days. No matter how long that friendship lasted, you might still never feel like you really got to know someone. I suppose the same was true with relatives. So, over an order of greasy burgers and fries, she told me about her life and her family, and I told her about mine.

After saying goodbye to Parker, I finished up at the duplex. My landlord told me to leave the key under the rock out front. I'd given him Parker's name as a possible new tenant. I told Parker she could have my furniture. I called Ash to let him know I would be back in the city by late afternoon.

"Well, damn, I was just about to have some guys over. I'm starting a swingers' club," he teased.

"And what do you plan to call it?"

"Purple Papillons?"

"I like Houndstooth Hound Dogs," I said with a laugh.

"How about Chartreuse Chihuahuas?"

"Just don't let any dogs in my bedroom."

"It's been so long I was beginning to think I needed to find a new roommate to fill your bedroom."

"It's only been a few weeks."

"You know that's a long time in gay years," he quipped.

"Yes it is, but I swear I'm on my way back now!"

"I can't wait to see you. We should celebrate."

"Hey, Ash, do you remember how we said that if we didn't have boyfriends by the time we were fifty, we'd just stay together and be old-maid spinsters?"

"Ha! Yeah. We're pretty much already there, aren't we?"

"I was thinking we could be boyfriends. If… you… are… willing… to give it a try," I said. I was nervous but trying to say everything I wanted to say.

"You and me?"

"Yeah. If you aren't—I mean—if you don't think it's a good idea, I don't want this to be awkward between us. We can pretend this conversation never happened."

"Toby, it's not awkward. I admit I kind of had a little crush on you when we first met."

"Really? Why didn't you ever say anything?"

"I didn't know how you felt. For once, I was too afraid of rejection."

"I think I've always had a crush on you too. I just didn't know it until now. All this time I've spent away from you made me realize I want to be with you. I was so afraid you might meet someone while I was gone. It made me feel so jealous. "

"You were jealous? Why? You know my relationships never last longer than a few months. Do I even have the right to call them relationships?"

"Ours has lasted."

"Yeah, you are right. It has lasted. Hasn't it?"

"So why now, all of a sudden?"

"While I was here, I met a woman who had been in a thirty-year relationship, and she lost her partner to cancer. She helped me to see that I shouldn't wait and hope I meet someone or just stand by and watch you meet someone else."

"I'm not going anywhere. Well, your bedroom is bigger, so when we hang up, I am going to start moving some of my things into your room."

"So, that means yes? You want to give us a try?"

"Yes, Toby, I do. I thought you'd never ask."

"Me? Why were you waiting for me to ask? Why didn't you ask?"

"I told you. Afraid of rejection, I guess. Does that answer your questions?"

"Yeah. Yeah, it does. And if this doesn't work out?"

"Don't worry about that right now. But if it doesn't, I get to keep the bigger bedroom, and you can move across the hall."

Heading back to the city, as I pulled away from the duplex and neared the end of the street, it felt like I was leaving home again for the first time even though I'd only lived on Maple Street for a few months. Only this wasn't home for me. It had always been temporary. I glanced over at the park and saw two children playing on the swing set. Their mother sat nearby on a park bench, watching them. This was a safe place for them.

There were other safe places and other people in my life that had lasted longer and that I needed to feel more permanent. Both were waiting down the road for me.

I would always be a part of this town. It would always be a part of me.

CHAPTER 45

IT HAD been four months. With the events of Shadow Wood behind me, I focused on finding a new job. I wasn't too motivated about getting back into a cubicle anytime soon, but the office interviews soon lined up. I felt good about having so many options. I did not feel good about any of the work. I had started a new chapter in my life, and I needed new work to keep me inspired and motivated, not something that would just remind me of the past.

The pet salon where Ash worked as a groomer joined with a new local vet office and pet boarding facility. With the expansion, there were new office jobs available. Ash suggested I apply. I interviewed for a receptionist position, but the manager asked if I'd be interested in being their marketing coordinator instead. I'd be in charge of their social media platforms, print advertising, eblasts, and more. She took me out to lunch for the interview. We got along well, and she loved Ash, so she hired me on the spot.

Mom's birthday was approaching, and Melaine called to ask if I was planning on driving up to celebrate with them. It would be the first time I'd been back to Mom's house since Dad's funeral. I asked Ash to go with me so he could finally meet my family.

"What dress should I wear to your mom's birthday?" he asked.

"I didn't say Helen Heels was invited."

"Helen goes wherever I go," he joked.

I was nervous, as anyone is when they bring their boyfriend or girlfriend home to meet the family for the first time. Ash wasn't nervous at all. He fit right in, and that put me at ease. Mom loved Ash and wondered why I'd never told her we were dating. I tried to explain that we had not been dating—we'd just been roommates— but he shook his head at me when Mom wasn't looking, and he mouthed that it was okay.

After her birthday dinner at her favorite restaurant, Mom and Ash sat down in front of the television with a photo album. She enjoyed torturing me by showing Ash every childhood photo of me. I knew that Ash missed having a family of his own, so I let him and my mother chide me over my cowlicked hair and pudgy grade-school face. I thought about the photo albums Linda had sitting on her coffee table, waiting there for her to show someone her family's story.

Mom and Ash gave the photos a break and settled onto the couch for a Hallmark movie when I snuck outside to call Parker. She'd moved into my duplex and signed a year-long lease just a few weeks later. She'd always loved my furniture, so I let her keep everything.

She had not heard from Christine since the night we left her at the high school. She'd called her cell number, but it had been disconnected. She had not been able to follow up with Lucas because he'd only worked at the restaurant for a few weeks before quitting to take the job at the movie theater.

"I saw Rose the Realtor a few days ago. She's the agent representing Linda's house," Parker said.

"What happened to Linda?" I asked.

"I think she moved to St. Louis. A lot of her club members were from Missouri, so it makes sense. I can't imagine living next door to the woman who killed your son, and Maddie's not going anywhere."

"How are things at the hotel?"

"The hotel is gone."

"What?"

"I'm surprised you haven't read about it in the paper."

"I've been purposely avoiding the newspaper lately. What happened?"

"The Loony Bin has officially folded. The restaurant too."

"When?"

"Maybe a month after everything went down. They are redeveloping that lot now. We're getting a Wal-Mart Super Center!"

"But where will the loons stay?" I joked.

"Are you talking about the birds or the people?"

"The people, of course."

"Hopefully in another town!"

Text messages on Harvey's cell phone had linked him to the Lowerys. Celeste had thought Maddie emailed the video to her. She told Hunter, and he sent Harvey to Maddie's house to collect the video and "take care of her." Maddie had taken care of Vey instead.

Celeste and Hunter were arrested. An outside investigator had been keeping a close watch on them due to some money laundering at the bank and was just waiting for the right time to move in. The Lowerys posted their half-million-dollar bail and then attempted to skip town. News reports said they were both killed by a trucker who'd fallen asleep at the wheel on the freeway. Neither Parker nor I believed they were dead.

"What are you doing now that the restaurant is gone?" I asked.

"You are speaking to the new head reporter for the *Shadow Wood Tribune*," she said with pride.

"What happened to the *Gazette*?"

"I guess you could say it folded too. Celeste's parents sold the *Gazette* to a new firm, and they changed the name. And after all of our sleuthing around town, I decided to give journalism a try."

"That's awesome. I'm proud of you. What about Bacon Me Crazy?"

"Still yummy! I don't care what they store in the freezer. Sorry, that sounds gross. My first story for the paper was the grand reopening of the flagship location. I told Mr. Lowery, Hunter's father, that I was sorry to hear about the loss of his son and daughter-in-law, and he looked at me like I was—well, crazy."

"You better be careful. You don't want to end up in the new freezer."

"Mr. Lowery gave us a tour of it! It's quite roomy. I wouldn't mind *living* in there during the summer. You know July in Shadow Wood is unbearable. I'll send you a photo of it that we ran in the paper. Oh, I can tell you some news we didn't run in the paper."

"What's that?"

"Jake's is now called The Gentlemen's County Club and Steakhouse."

"Sounds fancy."

"It is! I haven't seen it, but Mitzi said they got rid of the porn shop and the arcade. They put in private dining booths and lots more stripper poles. The Romeo Room is also gone."

"Wow, who would have thought the strip clubs would remodel? Things are looking up in Shadow Wood. What's next? One of those payday loan places?"

"Ha! We already have two of those now."

"Where did you see Mitzi?"

"Ran into her at the dollar store. She said to tell you hello. She's the Mother Hen now."

"Good for her. Well, it sounds like things in Shadow Wood are improving for everyone."

"Speaking of improvements, how's life with you and Ash?"

"It's great, actually. I'm working again. I love my job. We're doing great."

"I can't wait to meet him tomorrow. Maddie's going to join us for lunch. I hope that's okay."

"Yes, that's sounds great. I can't wait to catch up."

Catching up sounded odd. Parker and I had just done all of that on the phone. A lot had happened in four months, but what else could there be to catch up on? Maddie and Parker would get to meet Ash, at least, and he'd get to meet and learn about them. These two parts of my life, my small town and big city, were aligning. The miles between all of us—my friends and my loved ones—had subsided and grown narrow.

CHAPTER 46

"TOBY, CAN I speak to you for a moment?" Mom said, smiling at Ash. "I wanted to ask you something."

It was the last day of our visit. Ash and I would be leaving soon to head back to the city.

"I'll put our bags in the car and give you two some time alone," Ash said, taking the hint.

"Thanks, Ash."

Mom and I sat down at the kitchen table. She exhaled and smiled at me, body language I was accustomed to at this point in my life. She had something to say.

"I just wanted to ask how you are doing," she started.

"I'm doing great. Why?"

"Well, I guess a lot has happened since the last time you were here."

"You mean with Dad or something?"

"No, I mean with Linda Reyes."

"Who?" I asked, trying not to sound coy. This was my mother, so I knew it wasn't working.

"Your sister told me about the letter she showed you."

"What letter?"

"You know what letter I'm talking about. She also told me she thought she recognized your car parked at the grocery store one day. I suppose it could have been a mistake. Lots of people drive the same type of cars, right? But then your brother thought he saw you at that park where they found that man's body. You were talking to a basketball player. Do you remember that?"

"Nope." I knew my lying was useless.

"Oh, I guess not. Samuel asked the man playing ball who it was. He told your brother it was a man named Stephen Glass who lived on Maple Street."

"Mom, what are you—"

"Let me finish," she said. She held up her hand for me to be quiet.

"Sorry. Go ahead."

"I probably wouldn't have given any thought to that either, but after your sister said she'd seen your car at the grocery store, and after she told me about the letter, it got me to thinking. Oh, and there were all those questions you were asking right after your dad's funeral too. So, I decided to check it out."

"Check what out? Why does all of this matter?" I was trying not to yell, but her charade seemed odd.

"Well, it seems you aren't the only one around here with questions, dear."

"Mom, I can explain—"

"Did you know that Linda Reyes lived on Maple Street too?"

I paused, considering my answer. "Yes. Yes, I knew that. Melaine told me after she showed me the letter."

"It turns out Stephen Glass, that man with the car that looks just like yours, he lived right across the street from her, but I found out he recently moved out."

She stopped. I look at her, waiting for her to go on. She held her hands tightly between her knees and just looked up at the ceiling. She was either thinking of what to say next or she was trying to avoid making eye contact with me. Was she mad at me?

"How do you know all of this?"

"My hairdresser's husband—his name is Mike—owns a duplex on Maple Street. I thought it might be the one that Stephen lived in. I wasn't sure. I saw more than one duplex while I was driving down the street looking for Stephen's car, so I thought I'd ask."

"And?" I said.

"Mike stopped in the salon one day and we got to talking about you, so I asked him about his renter and it was indeed a man named Stephen Glass. I showed Mike a photo of you I had in my wallet. It turns out Stephen and you look quite a bit alike. You even drive the same type of car. Isn't that funny?"

"Funny? Why are you even telling me this?"

"No reason, Toby. I was just curious if you knew him. That's all."

"That's all?"

"Yep."

"I don't think I know him."

"Really? I looked through a copy of one of your high school year books and it turns out you went to school with Stephen Glass. He looks nothing like you—."

"Mom, why is all of this so important to you?" I asked, cutting her off. I'd heard enough.

"Like I said, I just want to make sure you are okay now," she said.

"I'm okay, Mom," I said. "I'm okay."

"Good. That's all that matters."

"Did you have any other questions, Mom?"

"No, dear," she said, standing up and rubbing my shoulder. " You and Ash have a safe trip home, okay?"

Ash was waiting by the car. We hugged Mom and said our goodbyes. As we slowly began to drive away, I rolled my window down to tell her that I loved her.

"Oh! Toby, I forgot to tell you one thing," she called out.

"What's that?" I asked, abruptly stopping the car.

"Mike said to tell you he loved what you did with the place."

CHAPTER 47

IT WAS a Thursday, and Ash and I were celebrating our one-year anniversary. We'd had a nice dinner out, and we were wrapping up the evening with drinks at Backstreet. We sat at the bar, and Jimmie gave us a free round. I was eager to get home, but Ash had insisted we stop in for a nightcap first. When he saw how dead the place was, he was ready to go, but I had already put a dollar in the jukebox. I told him he'd just have to wait until all four of my songs had played. Ash pulled out his cell phone, but I took it from him and sat it on the bar. I stepped between his legs and wrapped my arms around his waist, forcing his attention on me.

"Happy anniversary," I said.

"Same to you. Can you believe it's been a year already?" he said.

Maddie had been right about not waiting and not hoping. I couldn't think of a happier time in my life than the past year with Ash. He was my best friend. He was an excellent lover. He was the stability I had needed and craved in my life for so long.

I looked around the bar, recalling the last time I'd been in here on a weeknight. It looked much the same as it had back on that restless night when I came in for a drink and some distraction. There were a couple of older gentlemen playing a game of pool. A young kid was in the back entertaining himself with one of the arcade games. It was a familiar setting, but far from that night I'd come here alone searching for a distraction I didn't need.

A young couple sat next to us at the bar—an attractive young man and a girl. She was turned away from me, and she had leaned into him and put her head on his shoulder. He spoke softly to her, and I thought she might have been falling asleep until one of my songs came on. It was an infamous Tina Turner ballad.

The girl raised her head and said something to the man. He laughed and shook his head as if he were embarrassed. She got up from her barstool and started to pull him up by his hand. She wanted to dance.

"C'mon! Please," she pleaded.

You could hear the excitement in her voice. He just smiled and gave a nervous laugh. He looked around to see if anyone was watching. Ash turned to see what was happening behind him. I smiled at the man to let him know we weren't judging him.

"I think she wants him to dance with her," I whispered to Ash.

"Maybe if we danced, he wouldn't be so shy," Ash suggested.

"Okay," I said.

I turned to walk toward the small dance floor in the middle of the bar, but Ash grabbed my hand and pulled me back.

"Rude! Aren't you going to ask me to dance?"

"Sorry. May I have this dance, sir?" I said with a bow.

"Yes, you may."

There was a receiver behind the bar for the speakers. Jimmie turned up the volume a bit for us. I took Ash's hand and led him to the floor. The couple followed close behind. She'd talked him into joining us on the floor now that they wouldn't be the only ones dancing.

With my head on Ash's shoulder, we embraced during the song and did a slow step. The couple mirrored us with her head on his shoulder. As we turned, my eyes met hers. I'd seen those eyes before, but they were different then. They were eyes longing to be someone else, to be somewhere else.

But not tonight.

Catching her glance, I raised my head and winked at her. She raised her head as if she had a question, but she didn't want to interrupt this moment or the music. She just smiled and winked back. She put her head back on her lover's shoulder, and so did I. There was nothing to say, nothing to ask.

All of our questions had been answered.

Keep reading for an excerpt from
Dark Tide
by J.S. Cook

Prologue

IT WAS very early in the morning, nearing sunrise, with the gulls screaming their usual noise off Belbin's Rock and a thick fog hanging low about the village. He parked the car a little distance past the government wharf, hidden behind Jack Strickland's fishing stage and far enough under the disused flakes that it couldn't be seen from the road. Not that anyone was about, not at this hour, twelve minutes after four on an ordinary June morning. There was a time when men in boats would have long since steamed out of the harbor, heading for the richest fishing grounds in the world, but the cod moratorium had put paid to that. Now every man and his brother was a hangashore.

He popped open the trunk and extracted the bundle, grunting a little as he heaved it over one shoulder. For a lesser man this would have been an impossible task, but he was more than up to it. No one in the village could best him at the arm wrestling or heave a dory far inshore like he could. He'd won a medal once, for swimming out to save a drowning man and his little son whose open boat was taking on water and sinking, and that was in March month and the harbor choked with sea ice. All the old fellas waiting onshore for him, smoking their pipes and nodding to each other, knowing if anyone could do it, he could. *Sure he'll get the two of them no bother about it. He's the strongest one around, he is so. Like the bull, my son. Like the bull.*

Balancing his burden carefully, he started across the road and up the hill. It was a pleasant morning, perfect for this kind of work, not too hot, and the fog provided a convenient cover. He knew the perfect place: an old abandoned well empty of water, dug more than a century ago by the original settlers to the area. It was wide enough and deep enough, and with a few fir branches scattered about, you'd never even know anyone had been there. It was important to plan things so you didn't get caught out and get yourself in trouble.

At the top of the hill, there was an open space, a meadow once used as grazing land for sheep. In times past there had also been houses here, wood-frame dwellings and outbuildings, a root cellar dug into the side of a grassy bank, but that was all gone now. The root cellar had fallen into disrepair, nothing left of it besides a heap of broken stone, some rotted wooden beams, and the forlorn sod that had once made up the roof and walls. Of the houses nothing remained, not even a foundation, but the old well's concrete walls were remarkably intact, and it was here that he laid his burden down.

He'd wrapped the dead man in a patchwork quilt, and he unrolled it now, freeing the corpse and tossing the blanket to one side. "Time to go, my son," he murmured as he caught hold of the booted feet, levering the body over the side, the head hanging down into the fathomless darkness of the old well. "Over she goes." He released his grip and the corpse hesitated, hanging there, caught on some invisible obstacle, as if reluctant to take its leave. "Go on, for fuck's sake!" he hissed, and he shoved it until whatever had been holding it released and the body tumbled down into darkness.

He stood back, inspecting his work, rolling the quilt into a tidy bundle that he tucked under his arm. A job well done, that's what it was. He set off down the hill as the heavy drizzle thickened into rain.

A LITTLE farther north, the rain drummed hard on the surface of the sea, patterning each gentle wave as it rose and fell in a predictable, ancient rhythm. The dead thing rode the cold Labrador Current, bringing with it the icy denseness of the Greenland Sea and the dark, volcano-flavoured water of Iceland, distilled into the North Atlantic. Some fishermen, passing by in a vast pelagic trawler, mistook it for the carcass of a dead right whale, dismissed it. The sea buoyed up the dead thing floating in it and carried it down the coast past long-abandoned fishing huts and wooden boats rotting, forgotten, on a great many ragged shingle beaches. At the mouth of a small cove it hesitated, spun a little by the current where it met the colder northern air and condensed, casting a pall of dense gray fog over the land, and then, carried on the breast of a wave, it slid to rest on a pebble beach over which a flock of kittiwakes wheeled and screamed.

Chapter One

Monday, June 22,
6:00 a.m.

IT WAS barely six in the morning when his mobile phone's insistent jangling yanked Royal Newfoundland Constabulary Inspector Deiniol Quirke out of unconsciousness. He'd been lying asleep next to his partner, Tadhg Heaney, dreaming of blue skies and warmer climes when the violent clanging noise shattered his dreams. Blame Tadhg's irrepressible fifteen-year-old daughter, Lily, for changing his ringtone. Originally his phone had made a respectable jingling sound—pleasant, not overly loud, but sufficient to capture his attention. That wasn't disruptive enough for Lily, who imagined everyone else lived in the same manic whirl as she did. "Imagine if I'm trying to call you in the middle of the night and you can't hear me? That'd be tragic, Danny."

The caller was Sergeant Cillian Riley, who apologized a bit brusquely for waking him. "A local man found a body in an old well. You'd best come at once." Riley's Newcastle burr sounded more insistent than usual. "A youngish man, looks like, but I couldn't see much. Definitely a violent death."

Danny pulled on his clothes reluctantly, shivering in the chilly damp of a typical June morning, when the entire island awaited the arrival of millions of tiny fish, the annual "capelin scull" so necessary for the local ecosystem.

"What's going on?" Tadhg muttered, raising an inquisitive eyebrow in Danny's direction. "Something happening?"

Danny pulled back the duvet and leaned down to kiss him. "I've got to go, love. Riley found a body."

"Friggin' Riley," Tadhg said and lowered his eyebrow. "Ye're letting the cold air in," he added. Danny dropped the duvet back into place and went downstairs. He threw a reluctant glance at the coffee maker and decided it would have to wait. Maybe there'd be time for a brew at the office, after this was taken care of. In the meantime, he'd just have to suffer. He went out to where his car was parked in front of his rented house and climbed inside. Someone—probably Tadhg—had left the passenger side window down, and the interior of the car was damp, the upholstery and steering wheel clammy with moisture. Danny loved Tadhg with every fibre of his being, but at times like this he could cheerfully kill him and not bat an eyelash. He started the car and closed the window, turning the heater on full and hoping it kicked in before he froze to death. Nobody came to this island for the weather, it was said. People stayed in spite of it.

He parked at the bottom of the hill Riley had indicated and walked up, his knees and hips protesting bitterly. These early morning calls were murder, the exertion more suitable for a younger man, not someone with more than fifty years under his belt. He and Tadhg had shared a bottle of Shiraz with dinner the night before, and that was a mistake as well. Danny couldn't drink and get away with it, not easily, not anymore. Where once he could toss back half a dozen drinks in a night and get to bed just as the moon was setting, he now found himself feeling strung out and hobbled after even a minor indulgence. This getting older business was a proper pain in the arse.

Sergeant Cillian Riley was standing inside a fluttering line of police tape someone had erected around Simeon Durdle's old well. He saw Danny and waved. "Morning, sir," he greeted him when Danny got close enough. "The weather's shite. Sorry I had to get you up." Riley's dark curls glistened with moisture, and tiny drops had collected in the hairs of his close-trimmed beard. "It's over here."

"The beard's new," Danny observed, grinning.

Riley rubbed a hand self-consciously over his jaw. "Trying something different, sir. You know how it is." He lifted the tape so Danny could step under it. "Dog walker found him this morning." He nodded at an elderly man standing nearby, an attentive border collie prancing by his side. "Told him to stay put until we can get a preliminary statement." Danny nodded at the man, who raised a hand in acknowledgment. "I don't think he's anything to do with it. Just happenstance." He directed Danny to the well, where a pair of large black shoes protruded. "Shoved him in headfirst."

"You know it's a man?" Danny asked.

Riley sputtered for a moment. "Sir, have you ever seen a woman with feet that big?"

Danny walked a slow circle around the well, glancing at the ground, looking for footprints or the evidence that an unwary step had dislodged a rock or clump of moss. He leaned close to the rough cement and examined it, touched it lightly with his fingertips. "There's no blood. He wasn't killed here. This was just the body dump." He checked the soles of the dead man's shoes, then crouched to examine the toes. "He didn't walk here. The grass is wet and there's a fair bit of mud, but nothing on the soles. Whoever did this wanted him to be found. Otherwise he'd have gone to more trouble to conceal the body, but instead he left it out here in the open. The well is an interesting choice."

"Why?" Riley asked.

"It's a disposal site," Danny replied. "Almost like throwing someone down the toilet. The well isn't used anymore, but there are several local walking trails that run right past here. He has no fear of being caught. I'd say he wants to get caught. On some level he's proud of what he's done."

"Inspector Quirke!" Danny turned at the shout to see forensics officer Bobbi Lambert with two technicians in tow. "Tell me you didn't touch anything," she said.

"No," Danny reassured her. "We were waiting for you."

Bobbi nodded at Riley. "Morning, Sergeant. Nice beard. Now, let's see what we've got here." She walked around the well, peering down into it. "Jesus," she commented, "he's shoved in there good and tight." Danny and Riley waited while the two technicians, a man and an older woman, took photos of the scene and combed the surroundings for trace evidence, now and then crouching to collect something with tweezers and deposit it into plastic bags. When they were done, Bobbi directed Riley and Danny to help her extract the corpse. "Ye two big hairy-arsed men help me get him out." He and Riley donned nitrile gloves and, taking hold of the dead man, pulled him out of the well, and laid the corpse on the ground. He was absolutely massive, at least six feet six inches tall and weighing perhaps three hundred and fifty pounds.

"Holy shit," Riley said, "he's a big bastard." He leaned down to look at the man. "Someone's cut his face to bits." He stepped back as Bobbi, a nurse practitioner by trade, moved in to take a temperature reading. "Looks like a razor blade, broken glass maybe."

Bobbi lifted the dead man's shirt and made a small nick in the upper right abdomen before plunging her thermometer into the liver. She waited, then withdrew it, holding it up to the light to peer at it. "He's been dead about four hours, according to his temp, and rigor's barely begun. I don't think he was killed here. The cuts are post-mortem, I'd say."

"Post-mortem," Danny mused. He was glad Bobbi had been seconded to the medical examiner's office, since she could do a preliminary assessment of a corpse in situ as well as handle the forensics. "He reminds me of—" Suddenly the ravaged face of the dead man seemed very familiar.

She glanced at Danny. "Sir?"

"His name's Johnny. Johnny Locke. I… figured he was dead." Despite having returned to Kildevil Cove only a little more than a year ago, Danny would know Johnny Locke anywhere. His misshapen, lopsided face, one eye larger and lower than the other, was immediately recognisable despite the myriad deep cuts.

"You know him." Riley reached out to touch Danny's arm briefly, but Danny barely registered it. He was aware of Riley standing nearby but saw him only in his peripheral vision. John Locke, probably not named after the philosopher as far as anyone knew, born of parents who both dropped out of school in grade eight to get married because she was pregnant and that was what you did back then. Johnny was born with a small skull and eyes in strange opposition to each other, a face that seemed unable to reconcile its own shape. He was regarded by most people in Kildevil Cove as a holy fool, a shambling character of massive size with the mind of a child. He'd made a name for himself in recent years after he drove a friend's 1980 Chevette off a 400-foot cliff on a dare, in exchange for a bucket of fried chicken. Against all odds, he'd survived. "Whoever cut him up like that must have really hated him," Riley observed.

Silently Danny agreed, but he'd be hard pressed to think of anyone in Kildevil Cove who hated Johnny that much. Most people made a sort of pet of him.

"I've got everything I need here," Bobbi said as she and her technicians readied themselves to leave. "I'll send someone out to search for trace evidence at Johnny's house, and Dr. Lampe will need to collect anything on the body at the post-mortem."

"I'm sure she'll love that," Riley remarked. Like everyone on the Kildevil Cove force, he'd had his run-ins with the prickly medical examiner. "Hearse?"

"On its way," Bobbi confirmed. She pulled the hood of her white Tyvek suit farther up on her head. "This weather is bullshit," she observed. "Aren't them fucking little fish in yet?"

Danny laughed. "They don't give a Jesus about us, Bobbi. You knows that yourself. They'll roll when they're ready." He looked past her as two burly young men appeared, bearing a stretcher between them. He and Riley watched in silence as they loaded Johnny's body aboard and carried him down the hill to the waiting vehicle. "Someone has to tell his mother," Danny observed.

"She still alive?" Riley seemed incredulous. "He's what? Forty years old if he's a day."

"He was born when she was fourteen," Danny replied. "His mother's about my age." He glanced around the site, readying himself to leave. "Get a statement from the dog walker, and then he can go home. I'll send a couple constables to have a scrape around the undergrowth, just in case whoever made these cuts hove the blade away. I don't think he did, but it doesn't hurt to look."

"You said 'he.'" Riley reached for his notebook. "You think a man did this?"

"Force of habit," Danny said. "Could just as easily be a woman. Get the dog walker's name and phone number. Oh, and tell the nice gentleman to keep his trap shut, will you? The last thing we need is this place flooded with reporters from St. John's. It's all bad enough."

He zipped his waterproof and pulled up the hood as the wind picked up, blowing the rain into his face.

It was just past seven when Danny knocked at the front door of Ursula Locke's huge Nordic-style house. The massive cantilevered structure sat on an exposed point jutting out into the sea, a flat space of ancient volcanic rock surrounded on three sides by water. Its longest side was held up by a seemingly random scattering of wooden poles, reminiscent of the traditional "flakes" islanders had used to dry their salted codfish on; this narrowed to an imaginary vanishing point at the back, the illusion enabled by two columns of tiny square windows set deep into the wall. The house was glass all around, a series of openings designed to give the inhabitants a year-round view of the North Atlantic Ocean as it roared and foamed ashore. To reach the front door, Danny had to drive down a narrow avenue of hand-laid cobblestones crafted from local slate. It was a bit much when most people in the village made do with a walkway of crushed seashells, but to each his own. His knock was answered almost instantly by Ursula herself. He showed his badge and asked if she had a moment to talk.

"Why, Deiniol Quirke, as I live and breathe!" She had shed her native accent in favor of a mid-Atlantic drawl, what Tadhg called Long Island Lockjaw, and she was beautifully dressed and perfectly made-up, no mean feat for such an early hour. She wore well-tailored black slacks and a black sweater with a white blouse underneath. Her fingernails were shaped and painted dark red to match the shade of lipstick on her rather thin lips. He was reasonably certain her lustrous, thick lashes were fake, and she'd had Botox or something similar injected into her forehead, drawing up her eyebrows and giving her a falsely surprised expression. She behaved almost as if she'd been expecting him. "Imagine seeing you after all these years," she continued, standing to one side and ushering him in. "Come inside. I've just made some coffee. Will you have a cup? I'm going to have one."

To say she wasn't the Ursula Locke he once knew was an understatement. He'd heard rumours she'd met and married a rich American, many years her senior. This husband, whoever he was, obviously had money.

The Ursula Locke Danny knew was a shy, mousy girl with thick glasses and a permanent underbite who'd fallen pregnant for Bernard Locke in eighth grade. The fact that both their birth surnames were Locke led to much unpleasant speculation, but in a town the size of Kildevil Cove, everyone was related to everybody else if you went back far enough. In some cases, you didn't have to go back too far. "Thank you, Mrs. Locke," he said. "I can't stay."

"It's Mrs. Heffernan," she told him. Her immaculately smooth brow creased a little in annoyance. "I remarried after Bernard and I divorced. Sorry David isn't here. He's out of town on business."

"I see," Danny replied. "I've been away myself. Only came back to Kildevil Cove last year."

"Come into the front room," she said. "I'll bring coffee and we can talk. Surely you can have one cup?" She led him into an echoing white space with ceilings that seemed to stretch away into infinity. Everything in the room was white, except for the three-piece sofa set, two of which were a brilliant turquoise, the other an off-white. The pale walls were crammed full of abstract paintings, some mere slashes of color or simple shapes, and there were built-in niches for modern sculpture and other objets d'art. But nothing in the room appeared to exist harmoniously with anything else, just a lot of different expensive things silently at war with each other. He recognised a Finn Juhl "pelican chair" Tadhg had once shown him in a design magazine and a rag rug in a gorgeous shade of blue that probably cost the earth. It was all a bit highbrow for a small Newfoundland fishing village. Danny wondered who she was trying to impress. "Sit down," Ursula said, gesturing towards the squashy off-white sofa so heavily laden with white throw pillows that it resembled a calving iceberg. "I'll be right back."

He sank into the sofa, which swallowed him up like springtime snow, and tried not to touch anything. The rain beat against the windows, driven by the sudden wind that had sprung up earlier. After a moment Ursula reappeared with a tray bearing a bright yellow pitcher and a plate of raisin buns. "Forgive me! I apologize for the state of the place. The girl is due to come this afternoon to do the cleaning." Ursula Locke—Heffernan—had come up in the world if she could afford a "girl" to come in and clean her house for her. Employing outside staff was something nobody in Kildevil Cove ever did, except for the crab plant workers, and most of them were married women who picked up a few shifts working at Heaney's in the summertime. They would hire a local girl for a few hours a day to keep an eye on the youngsters, give them their dinner at noon, and make sure they didn't kill themselves or each other while Mam was gone to work.

She noticed Danny looking at the yellow jug and smiled. "It's Kockums. Swedish. Do you like it?" It looked like something Lily would have used when she was a little girl, but Danny didn't say this, instead muttering something about how it was very nice. "David goes simply everywhere on business, and he always brings me back a little treat or two. Have a raisin bun. I've been doing a bit of baking lately, trying new things. These are made with einkorn wheat. It's one of the most ancient grains there is. I have to get it brought in from away, but it's worth it." She filled two cups with coffee, offered cream and sugar. Despite himself Danny was grateful for the hot drink. The cold damp had gotten into his bones. "It's so nice to see you again.

Now, what can I do for you, or did you just pop in to catch up on old times?"

Danny stared at her, gobsmacked. "Mrs. Heffernan, this isn't a social call." He laid his coffee cup down on the immaculate white table in front of him and took out his notebook. "When did you last see Johnny?" he asked, flipping through to a clean page.

She busied herself adding cream to her coffee and didn't look up. "Who?"

Danny felt his eyebrows climb into his hairline. "Your *son.*"

"Oh, him." She sat down in the turquoise pelican chair opposite him. "You know, Danny… I can call you Danny, can't I? We always used names, you and I."

"When did you last see him?"

"I don't remember," she replied, deliberately vague. "David and I just got back from a holiday in Mexico. I've been pestering him for ages to take me to Oaxaca to buy some pottery." She gestured at some small pottery pieces arranged on the fireplace hearth, animals painted in bright, vivid colors that clashed with the room's overall simplicity. "David owns a number of hotels, and we travel quite a bit, usually having to do with business. You know, a working holiday." She blinked at him. "What was it you asked me?"

"We were talking about your son, Johnny."

"Oh, I haven't seen Johnny for ages. He was unwell off and on for so many years. We took him to the doctor but…."

"But what?"

"They couldn't do anything for him. Wouldn't take his medication. Claimed it used to 'give him ideas.'" She refused to look him in the eye while she said this, fussing with the things on the tray, adjusting the lid of the coffee pot, spooning sugar into her coffee. Twice she picked up and replaced a sheaf of turquoise paper napkins before offering one to Danny.

"No, thank you," he said, "I won't have anything." He tried again to get her to focus on his question: "What sorts of ideas?"

"Oh, you know." She flapped a hand in front of her. "All sorts of things." She was acting much more distracted than she was. Danny suspected this show was being put on for his benefit, that she really knew more than she was making out and was trying to throw him off the scent.

"Ursula, I've known you all my life," Danny said sharply. "I remember when your name was Eunice and not Ursula. I remember when you first fell pregnant with the boy. We went through school together. You were never a good liar. I could always tell. And you're lying now."

She laid her cup back in its saucer with an audible click and stood up, smoothing her palms down the front of her impeccable black slacks. "I think you should go now, Danny. I'm not feeling well."

Danny stood up. "Your son, Johnny, was found early this morning by a man walking his dog in the Doyle's Road area of Kildevil Cove." He waited, but she didn't bat an eyelash. "He's dead."

Again her hands slid along her thighs, then rose to chest height and clasped themselves together, the red-painted nails showing dark against pale skin. "I think you should leave. I'll show you to the door." She turned and headed towards the front hall, Danny following in her wake. When she pulled open the door, he made no move to leave but passed her one of his business cards. "It's very important that you call me if you think you know something." He watched her face, but the carefully painted features gave nothing away. "Ursula, do you understand what I'm telling you? Your son Johnny was murdered."

"So you told me." She offered him a feeble smile. Peely-wally, his Scottish grandmother would have called it: weak and not worth very much. "I really must say my goodbyes now. I'm not feeling well."

"When did you last speak to Bernard?" Danny asked. "Does he still live around here? I'd like to deliver the news myself." He stepped out onto the cobblestones of the driveway. "Unless you think he'd prefer to hear it from you?"

"Goodbye, Danny." The door swung to, shutting him outside. He shook his head, dismayed by her astonishingly callous attitude. So much for the maternal instinct, he thought, remembering that some animals ate their young. Maybe that was what had happened to Johnny after all. Her hurry to get him out of the house warranted further investigation.

He had just turned onto the main road from Ursula's house when he noticed a figure standing by the post office, dressed in dark clothing, a utility coverall that buttoned up the front. He was muscular, not particularly tall, and held his body in the aggressive posture of a professional boxer. He watched Danny but made no move or gesture of recognition, only following Danny's car with his eyes, his gaze relentless. At the corner, near the government wharf, Danny paused for a stop sign and glanced in his rearview mirror; the man was still watching him. What did he want? Was he someone Danny knew? And why was he standing across the road from Ursula Heffernan's house?

People in Kildevil Cove didn't make a habit of peering openly at their neighbours without offering a greeting, verbal or otherwise. Someone standing about by the side of the road for no real reason would be viewed with suspicion, dismissed as a "queer hand," someone to steer clear of. The locals all waved to Danny whenever he drove by and greeted him by name whenever he met them. Perhaps the staring man meant nothing by it, but in a place like this, it was passing strange.

Passing strange indeed.

His mobile phone jangled, and he reached to tap the Bluetooth in his ear. "Quirke."

"Sir." It was Constable Kevin Carbage. "There's a body washed up on the beach by Single's Bridge."

"Single's Bridge? Where the youngsters goes swimming?"

"Yes, sir. She… must have come ashore during the night, after the youngsters went home."

SHANNON YARBROUGH knew he wanted to be a writer ever since his grade school passed out free black-and-white journals each year and made classrooms devote one hour a day to creative writing. His school even hosted a Young Author's Day Festival. To attend, each student had to write and publish their very own book. Shannon wrote and created a pop-up book of poetry out of cardboard and contact paper. He's been writing short stories and novels ever since.

Born in the South, Shannon fell in love with Southern literature in college and often pays homage to his Southern roots in his story settings and in the characters he creates. From an obsessive-compulsive coffee barista searching for love in a romantic comedy to a Christmas dinner gone awry in a family psychodrama, Shannon constantly challenges his storytelling ability by rarely sticking to one genre. He even wrote a mash-up of the life of poet Emily Dickinson with the story of Frankenstein.

Shannon has called St. Louis, Missouri home for the last two decades, where he lives with his partner of eighteen years, their two dogs, and two cats. Besides writing, Shannon enjoys gardening, cooking, and reading. You can visit Shannon online at www.shannonyarbrough.com or follow him on Twitter at @slyarbrough76.

More from
DSP Publications

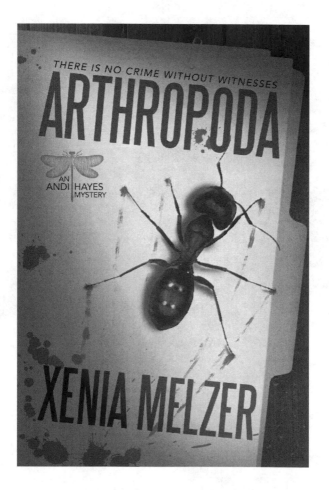

More from
DSP Publications

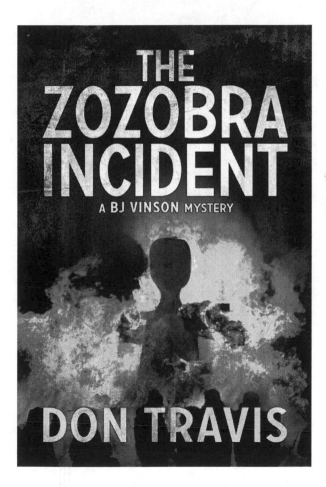

ALL THE
RULES OF
HEAVEN

AMY LANE

More from
DSP Publications

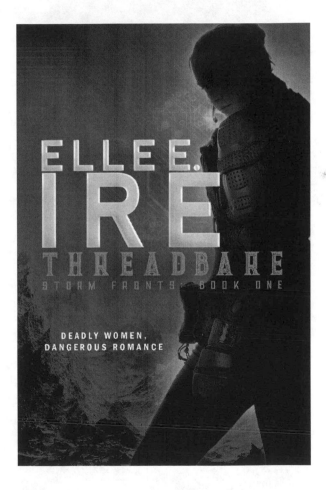

ELLE E. IRE

THREADBARE

STORM FRONTS: BOOK ONE

DEADLY WOMEN,
DANGEROUS ROMANCE

For more
great fiction
from

DSP PUBLICATIONS

visit us online.
WWW.DSPPUBLICATIONS.COM